Mayne Reid

The PlantHunters

Or Adventures Among the Himalaya Mountains

Mayne Reid

The PlantHunters
Or Adventures Among the Himalaya Mountains

ISBN/EAN: 9783743383739

Manufactured in Europe, USA, Canada, Australia, Japa

Cover: Foto ©Andreas Hilbeck / pixelio.de

Manufactured and distributed by brebook publishing software (www.brebook.com)

Mayne Reid

The PlantHunters

THE

PLANT HUNTERS

OR

ADVENTURES AMONG THE HIMALAYA MOUNTAINS.

BY

CAPTAIN MAYNE REID,

Author of "The Desert Home," "The Young Yagers," etc. etc. etc.

WITH ILLUSTRATIONS.

BOSTON:
TICKNOR AND FIELDS.
M DCCC LXVI.

TO MY EARLY INSTRUCTOR,

THE REVEREND DAVID M'KEE,

OF ANAGHLONE.

CONTENTS.

vi CONTENTS.

THE PLANT–HUNTERS.

CHAPTER I.

THE PLANT-HUNTER.

"A PLANT-HUNTER! what is that?

"We have heard of fox-hunters, of deer-hunters, of bear and buffalo-hunters, of lion-hunters, and of 'boy-hunters;' of a plant-hunter never.

"Stay! Truffles are plants. Dogs are used in finding them; and the collector of these is termed a truffle-hunter. Perhaps this is what the Captain means?"

No, my boy reader. Something very different from that. My plant-hunter is no fungus-digger. His occupation is of a nobler kind than contributing merely to the capricious palate of the gourmand. To his labors the whole civilized world is indebted—yourself among the rest. Yes, you owe him gratitude for many a bright joy. For the varied sheen of your garden you are indebted to him. The gorgeous dahlia that nods over the flower-bed—the brilliant peony that sparkles on the parterre—the lovely camelia that greets you in

the greenhouse,—the kalmias, the azaleas, the rhododendrons, the starry jessamines, the gerania, and a thousand other floral beauties, are, one and all of them, the
gifts of the plant-hunter. By his agency England—
cold cloudy England—has become a garden of flowers,
more varied in species and brighter in bloom than
those that blossomed in the famed valley of Cashmere.
Many of the noble trees that lend grace to our English
landscape,—most of the beautiful shrubs that adorn
our villas, and gladden the prospect from our cottage-
windows, are the produce of his industry. But for him,
many fruits, and vegetables, and roots, and berries, that
garnish your table at dinner and dessert, you might
never have tasted. But for him these delicacies might
never have reached your lips. A good word, then, for
the plant-hunter!

And now, boy reader, in all seriousness I shall tell
you what I mean by a "plant-hunter." I mean a person who devotes all his time and labor to the collection
of rare plants and flowers—in short, one who makes
this occupation his *profession*. These are not simply
"botanists"—though botanical knowledge they must
needs possess—but, rather, what has hitherto been
termed "botanical collectors."

Though these men may not stand high in the eyes of
the scientific world—though the closet-systematist may
affect to underrate their calling, I dare boldly affirm
that the humblest of their class has done more service
to the human race than even the great Linneus himself.
They are, indeed, the botanists of true value, who have
not only imparted to us a knowledge of the world's
vegetation, but have brought its rarest forms before our

very eyes—have placed its brightest flowers under our very noses, as it were—flowers, that but for them had been still " blushing unseen," and " wasting their sweetness on the desert air."

My young reader, do not imagine that I have any desire to underrate the merits of the scientific botanist. No, nothing of the sort. I am only desirous of bringing into the foreground a class of men whose services in my opinion the world has not yet sufficiently acknowledged—I mean the botanical collectors—the *plant-hunters*.

It is just possible that you never dreamt of the existence of such a profession or calling, and yet from the earliest historic times there have been men who followed it. There were plant-collectors in the days of Pliny, who furnished the gardens of Herculaneum and Pompeii ; there were plant-collectors employed by the wealthy mandarins of China, by the royal sybarites of Delhi and Cashmere, at a time when our semi-barbarous ancestors were contented with the wild flowers of their native woods. But even in England the calling of the plant-hunter is far from being one of recent origin. It dates as early as the discovery and colonization of America ; and the names of the Tradescants, the Bartrams, and the Catesbys—true plant-hunters—are among the most respected in the botanical world. To them we are indebted for our tulip-trees, our magnolias, our maples, our robinias, our western *platanus*, and a host of other noble trees, that already share the forest, and contest with our native species, the right to our soil.

At no period of the world has the number of plant-hunters been so great as at present. Will you believe it, hundreds of men are engaged in this noble and useful calling? Among them may be found representatives of all the nations of Europe—Germans in greatest number; but there are Swedes and Russ as well, Danes and Britons, Frenchmen, Spaniards, and Portuguese, Swiss and Italians. They may be found pursuing their avocation in every corner of the world—through the sequestered passes of the Rocky Mountains, upon the pathless prairies, in the deep barrancas of the Andes, amid the tangled forests of the Amazon and the Orinoco, on the steppes of Siberia, in the glacier valleys of the Himalaya—everywhere—everywhere amid wild and savage scenes, where the untrodden and the unknown invite to fresh discoveries in the world of vegetation. Wandering on with eager eyes, scanning with scrutiny every leaf and flower—toiling over hill and dale—climbing the steep cliff—wading the dank morass or the rapid river—threading his path through thorny thicket, through "chapparal" and "jungle."—sleeping in the open air—hungering, thirsting, risking life amidst wild beasts, and wilder men,—such are a few of the trials that chequer the life of the plant-hunter.

From what motive, you will ask, do men choose to undergo such hardships and dangers?

The motives are various. Some are lured on by the pure love of botanical science; others by a fondness for travel. Still others are the *employés* of regal or noble patrons—of high-born botanical amateurs. Not a few are the emissaries of public gardens and arboretums; and yet another few—perchance of humbler names and more limited means, though not less zealous in their well-beloved calling,—are collectors for the "nursery."

Yes; you will no doubt be astonished to hear that

the plain "seedsman" at the town end, who sells you your roots and bulbs and seedlings, keeps in his pay a staff of plant-hunters—men of botanical skill, who traverse the whole globe in search of new plants and flowers, that may gratify the heart and gladden the eyes of the lovers of floral beauty.

Need I say that the lives of such men are fraught with adventures and hair-breadth perils? You shall judge for yourself when I have narrated to you a few chapters from the experience of a young Bavarian botanist,—Karl Linden—while engaged in a *plant-hunting* expedition to the Alps of India—the stupendous mountains of the Himalaya.

CHAPTER II.

KARL LINDEN.

KARL LINDEN was a native of Upper Bavaria, near the Tyrolese frontier. Not high-born, for his father was a gardener; but, what is of more importance in modern days, well brought up and well educated. A gardener's son may still be a gentleman; and so may a gardener himself, for that matter, or he may not. There are many senses to this much-abused title. It so happens, that young Linden was a gentleman in the *true* sense; that is, he was possessed of a feeling heart, a nice sense of honesty and honor, and was, notwithstanding his humble lineage, an educated and accomplished youth. His father, the gardener, was a man of ambitious spirit, though quite unlettered; and, having himself often experienced the disadvantage of this condition, he resolved that his son never should.

In most parts of Germany, education is considered a thing of value, and is eagerly sought after. It is provided liberally for all classes; and the Germans, as a people, are perhaps the best educated in the world. It is partly owing to this fact, and partly to their energetic industry, that they exercise so great an influence in the affairs of the world; in the arts and sciences, in music, painting, and the study of nature—above all, in a knowledge of botany. I cannot believe that the Germans stand highest as an *intellectual* race, but only as an *educated* people. What a pity I could not add, that they are a free people ; but in that their condition differs less from our own than we fondly imagine.

At nineteen years of age, young Karl Linden did not consider them as free as they deserved to be. He was then a student in one of the universities ; and, naturally enough, had imbibed those principles of patriotic liberty, that, in 1848, were stirring in the German heart.

He did more than advocate his faith by empty words. Joined with his college compatriots, he endeavored to have it carried into practice ; and he was one of those brave students, who, in 1848, gave freedom to Baden and Bavaria.

But the hydra league of crowned heads was too strong to be so easily broken ; and, among other youthful patriots, our hero was forced to flee from his native land.

An exile in London—"a refugee," as it is termed— he scarce knew what to do. His parent was too poor to send him money for his support. Besides, his father was not over well pleased with him. The old man was one of those who still clung to a belief in the divine right of kings, and was contented with the " powers that be," no matter how tyrannical they be. He was angry with Karl, for having made a fool of himself by turning patriot, or " rebel," as it pleases crowned monsters to term it. He had intended him for better things ; a secretary to some great noble, a post in the

Custom-house, or, may be, a commission in the body-guard of some petty tyrant. Any of these would have fulfilled the ambitious hopes of Karl's father. The latter, therefore, was displeased with the conduct of his son. Karl had no hope from home, at least until the anger of the old man should die out.

What was the young refugee to do? He found English hospitality cold enough. He was free enough; that is, to wander the streets and beg.

Fortunately, he bethought him of a resource. At intervals, during his life, he had aided his father in the occupation of gardening. He could dig, plant, and sow. He could prune trees, and propagate flowers to perfection. He understood the management of the greenhouse and hothouse, the cold-pit and the forcing-pit; nay, more—he understood the names and nature of most of the plants that are cultivated in European countries; in other words, he was a botanist. His early opportunities in the garden of a great noble, where his father was superintendent, had given him this knowledge; and, having a taste for the thing, he had made botany a study.

If he could do no better, he might take a hand in a garden, or a nursery, or some such place. That would be better than wandering idly about the streets of the metropolis, and half-starving in the midst of its profuse plenty.

With such ideas in his mind, the young refugee presented himself at the gate of one of the magnificent " nurseries," in which great London abounds. He told his story; he was employed.

It was not long before the intelligent and enterpris-

ing proprietor of the establishment discovered the botanical knowledge of his German *protégé.* He wanted
just such a man. He had "plant-hunters" in other
parts of the world; in North and South America, in
Africa, in Australia. He wanted a collector for India;
he wanted to enrich his stock from the flora of the
Himalayas, just then coming into popular celebrity,
on account of the magnificent forms of vegetation discovered there, by the great "plant-hunters" Royle and
Hooker.

The splendid pine-trees, arums, and screw-pines;
the varied species of bambusa, the grand magnolias
and rhododendrons, which grow so profusely in the
Himalaya valleys, had been described, and many of
them introduced into European gardens. These plants
were therefore the rage; and, consequently, the *deside-
rata* of the nurseryman.

What rendered them still more interesting and valuable was, that many of those beautiful exotics would
bear the open air of high latitudes, on account of the
elevated region of their native habitat possessing a
similarity of temperature and climate to that of northern Europe.

More than one "botanical collector" was at this time
despatched to explore the chain of the Indian Alps,
whose vast extent offered scope enough for all.

Among the number of these plant-hunters, then, was
our hero, Karl Linden.

CHAPTER III.

CASPAR, OSSAROO, AND FRITZ.

An English ship carried the plant-hunter to Calcutta, and his own good legs carried him to the foot of the Himalaya Mountains. He might have travelled there in many other ways—for perhaps in no country in the world are there so many modes of travelling as in India. Elephants, camels, horses, asses, mules, ponies, buffaloes, oxen, zebus, yaks, and *men*, are all made use of to transport the traveller from place to place. Even dogs, goats, and sheep, are trained as beasts of burden!

Had Karl Linden been a Government emissary, or the *employé* of some regal patron, he would very likely have travelled in grand style—either upon an elephant in a sumptuous howdah, or in a palanquin with relays of bearers, and a host of coolies to answer to his call.

As it was, he had no money to throw away in such a foolish manner. It was not *public* money he was spending, but that of private enterprise, and his means were necessarily limited. He was not the less likely to accomplish the object for which he had been sent out. Many a vast and pompous expedition has gone forth regardless either of expense or waste—aye, many a one that has returned without having accomplished the object intended. "Too many cooks spoil the dinner," is a familiar old adage, very applicable to exploring expeditions; and it is a question, whether unaided individual enterprise has not effected more in the way of scientific and geographical discovery, than has been done by the more noisy demonstrations of governments. At all events, it is certain enough, that the exploring expeditions to which we are most indebted for our geognostic knowledge are those that have been fitted out with the greatest economy. As an example, I may point to the tracing of the northern coasts of America—which, after costing enormous sums of money, and the lives of many brave men, has been done, after all, by the Hudson's Bay Company with a simple boat's crew, and at an expense, that would not have franked one of our grand Arctic exploring expeditions for a week!

I might point to the economic mode by which the Americans are laying open their whole continent—a *single* officer having lately been sent to descend the Amazon alone, and explore its extensive valley from the Andes to the Atlantic. This was performed, and a copious report delivered to the American government and to the world at an expense of a few hundred dollars; whereas an English exploration of similar importance would have cost some thousands of pounds, with perhaps a much scantier return for the outlay.

As with the American explorer, so was it with our plant-hunter. There was no expensive equipment or crowd of idle attendants. He reached the Himalayas on foot, and on foot he had resolved to climb their vast slopes and traverse their rugged valleys.

But Karl Linden was not alone. Far from it. He was in company with him he held dearest of all others in the world—his only brother. Yes, the stout youth by his side is his brother Caspar, who had joined him in his exile, and now shares the labors and perils of his expedition. There is no great difference between them in point of size, though Caspar is two years the younger. But Caspar's strength has not been wasted by too much study. He has never been penned up within the walls of a college or a city ; and, fresh from his native hills, his stout build and bright ruddy cheek present a con-trast to the thinner form and paler visage of the student.

Their costumes are in keeping with their looks. That of Karl exhibits the sombre hue of the man of learning, while on his head he wears the proscribed "Hecker hat." Caspar's dress is of a more lively style, and consists of a frock of Tyrolese green, a cap of the same color, with long projecting peak, over-alls of blue velveteen, and Blucher boots.

Both carry guns, with the usual accoutrements of sportsmen. Caspar's gun is a double-barrelled fowling-piece,—while that of Karl is a rifle of the species known as a "Swiss yäger."

A true hunter is Caspar, and although still but a boy, he has often followed the chamois in its dizzy path among his native mountains. Of letters he knows little, for Caspar has not been much to school ; but in matters of hunter-craft he is well skilled. A brave and cheerful youth is Caspar—foot-free and untiring— and Karl could not have found in all India a better assistant.

But there is still another individual in the train of the plant-hunter—the *guide, Ossaroo.* It would take pages to describe Ossaroo; and he is worthy of a full description: but we shall leave him to be known by his deeds. Suffice it to say, that Ossaroo is a Hindoo of handsome proportions, with the swarth complexion, large beautiful eyes, and luxuriant black hair, which characterize his race. He is by caste a "shikarree," or hunter, and is not only so by hereditary descent, but he is one of the noted "mighty hunters" in the province to which he belongs. Far and wide is his name known —for Ossaroo possesses, what is somewhat rare among his indolent countrymen, an energy of mind, combined with strength and activity of body, that would have given him distinction anywhere; but among a people where such qualities are extremely rare, Ossaroo is of course a hunter-hero—the Nimrod of his district.

Ossaroo's costume and equipments differ entirely from those of his fellow-travellers. A white cotton tunic, and wide trousers, sandals, a scarlet sash around the waist, a check shawl upon the head, a light spear in the hand, a bamboo bow, a quiver of arrows on his back, a long knife stuck behind the sash, a shoulder-belt sustaining a pouch, with various trinket-like implements suspended over his breast. Such is the *coup d'œil* presented by the shikarree.

Ossaroo had never in his life climbed the mighty Himalayas. He was a native of the hot plains—a hunter of the jungles—but for all that the botanist had engaged him for a *guide.* It was not so much a guide to enable them to find their route, as one who could assist them in their daily duties, who knew the way of life peculiar to this part of the world, who knew how to *keep house in the open air*, Ossaroo was the very man of all others.

Moreover the expedition was just to his mind. He had long gazed upon the gigantic Himalaya from the distant plains—he had looked upon its domes and peaks glittering white in the robes of eternal snow, and had often desired to make a hunting excursion thither. But no good opportunity had presented itself, although through all his life he had lived within sight of those stupendous peaks. He, therefore, joyfully accepted the offer of the young botanist, and became " hunter and guide " to the expedition.

There was still another of the hunter-race in that company—one as much addicted to the chase as either Ossaroo or Caspar. This was a quadruped as tall as a mastiff dog, but whose black-and-tan color and long pendulous ears bespoke him of a different race—the race of the hound. He was, in truth, a splendid hound, whose heavy jaws had ere now dragged to the ground many a red stag, and many a wild Bavarian boar. A dog to be valued was Fritz, and highly did his master esteem him. Caspar was that master. Caspar would not have exchanged Fritz for the choicest elephant in all India.

CHAPTER IV.

IS IT BLOOD?

BEHOLD the plant-hunter and his little party *en route!*

It was the same day on which they had engaged the guide Ossaroo, and this was their first journey together. Each carried his knapsack and blanket strapped to his back—and as each was to be his own travelling attendant, there was not much extra baggage. Ossaroo was some paces in the advance, and Karl and Caspar habitually walked side by side, where the nature of the path would permit. Fritz usually trotted along in the rear, though he sometimes busked up to the side of the guide, as if by instinct he recognized the born hunter. Although the acquaintance was but a short one, already had Fritz become a favorite with the " shikarree."

As they trudged along, the attention of Caspar was drawn to some red spots that appeared at intervals upon the path. It was a smooth road, and a very small object could be discerned upon it. The spots had all the appearance of blood-spots, as if quite freshly dropped !

" Blood it is," remarked Karl, who was also observing the spots.

" I wonder whether it's been a man or a beast," said Caspar, after an interval.

"Well, brother," rejoined Karl, "I think it must have been a beast, and a pretty large one too ; I have been noticing it for more than a mile, and the quantity of blood I've observed would have emptied the veins of a giant. I fancy it must have been an elephant that has been bleeding."

"But there's no trace of an elephant," replied Caspar ; "at least no tracks that are fresh ; and this blood appears to be quite newly spilled."

"You are right, Caspar," rejoined his brother.

"It cannot have been an elephant, nor a camel neither. What may it have been, I wonder ? "

At this interrogatory both the boys directed their glances along the road, in the direction in which they were going, hoping to discover some explanation of the matter. There was no object before them as far as they could see except Ossaroo. The Hindoo alone was upon the road. The blood could not be from him —surely not? Such a loss of blood would have killed the shikarree long ago. So thought Karl and Caspar.

They had fixed their eyes, however, upon Ossaroo, and just at that moment they saw him lean his head to one side, as though he had spat upon the ground. They marked the spot, and what was their astonishment on coming up and discovering upon the road another red spot exactly like those they had been noticing. Beyond a doubt Ossaroo was spitting blood !

To make sure, they watched him a little longer, and about a hundred yards farther on they saw him repeat his red expectoration !

They became considerably alarmed for the life of their guide.

"Poor Ossaroo!" exclaimed they, "he cannot live much longer after the loss of so much blood!"

And as this remark was made, both ran forward call-upon him to stop.

The guide wheeled round, and halted, wondering what was the matter. He quickly unslung his bow and placed an arrow to the string, fancying that they were attacked by some enemy. The hound, too, catching the alarm, came scampering up, and was soon upon the ground.

"What's the matter, Ossaroo?" demanded Karl and Caspar in a breath.

"Matter, Sahibs! me knowee noting—matter."

"But what ails you? are you ill?"

"No, Sahibs! me not ill—why my lords askee?"

"But this blood? See?"

They pointed to the red saliva on the road.

At this the shikarree burst out laughing, still further perplexing his interrogators. His laughter was not intended to be disrespectful to the young "Sahibs," only that he was unable to restrain himself on perceiving the mistake they had made.

"Pawnee, Sahibs," said he, drawing from his pouch a small roll like a cartridge of tobacco-leaves, and taking a bite off the end of it, to convince them that it was it—the "pawn"—which had imparted to his saliva such a peculiar color.

The boys at once comprehended the nature of their mistake. The roll shown them by Ossaroo was the celebrated *betel;* and Ossaroo himself was a "betel-chewer," in common with many millions of his countrymen, and still more millions of the natives of Assam,

Burmah, Siam, China, Cochin China, Malacca, the
Philippine, and other islands of the great Indian Archipelago.

Of course the boys were now curious to know what
the betel was, and the shikarree proceeded to give them
full information about this curious commodity.

The "betel," or "pawn" as it is called by the Hindoos, is a compound substance, and its component parts
are a leaf, a nut, and some quicklime. The leaf is
taken from an evergreen shrub, which is cultivated in
India for this very purpose. Ossaroo stated that it is
usually cultivated under a shed made of bamboos, and
wattled all around the sides to exclude the strong rays
of the sun. The plant requires heat and a damp atmosphere, but exposure to the sun or dry winds would
wither it, and destroy the flavor and pungency of the
leaf. It requires great care in the cultivation, and every
day a man enters the shed by a little door and carefully
cleans the plants. The shed where it grows is usually
a favorite lurking-place for poisonous snakes, and this
diurnal visit of the betel-grower to his crop is rather a
dangerous business; but the article is so profitable, and
the mature crop yields such a fine price, that both the
labor and the danger are disregarded. Ossaroo chanced
to have some of the leaves in his pouch still in an entire
state. He only knew them as " pawn-leaves," but the
botanist at once recognized a rare hothouse plant, belonging to the pepper tribe, *Piperaceæ.* It is in fact a
species of *Piper,* the *Piper-betel,* very closely allied to
the climbing shrub which produces the common black
pepper of commerce, and having deep green oval and
sharply-pointed leaves of very similar appearance to

the leaves of the latter. Another species called *Piper siriboa* is also cultivated for the same purpose. So much for one of the component parts of this singular Oriental "quid."

"Now," continued Ossaroo, facing to one side of the path and pointing upwards, "if Sahibs lookee up, dey see de pawn-nut."

The boys looked as directed, and beheld with interest a grove of noble palms, each of them rising to the height of fifty feet, with a smooth cylindrical shank, and a beautiful tuft of pinnated leaves at the top. These leaves were full two yards in breadth, by several in length. Even the pinnæ, or leaflets, were each over a yard long. Just below where the leaves grew out from the stem, a large bunch of nuts of a reddish orange color, and each as big as a hen's egg, hung downward. These were the famous *betel-nuts*, so long recorded in the books of Oriental travellers. Karl recognized the tree as the *Areca catechu*, or betel-nut palm—by many considered the most beautiful palm of India.

Of the same genus *Areca* there are two other known species, one also a native of India, the other an American palm, and even a still more celebrated tree than the betel-nut, for it is no other than the great "cabbage-palm" of the West Indies (*Areca oleracea*). This last tree grows to the height of two hundred feet, with a trunk only seven inches in diameter! This beautiful shaft is often cut down for the sake of the young heart-leaves near the top, that when dressed are eaten as a substitute for cabbage.

Ossaroo showed his young masters how the betel was prepared for chewing. The leaves of the betel pepper

2

are first spread out. Upon these a layer of lime is placed, moistened so as to keep it in its place. The betel-nut is then cut into very thin slices, and laid on top; and the whole is rolled up like a cheroot, and deposited with other similar rolls in a neat case of bamboo—to be taken out whenever required for chewing.

The nut is not eatable alone. Its flavor is too pungent, and too highly astringent on account of the tannin it contains; but along with the pepper-leaf and the lime, it becomes milder and more pleasant. Withal, it is too acrid for a European palate, and produces intoxication in those not used to it. An old betel-eater like Ossaroo does not feel these effects, and would smile at the idea of getting " tipsy " upon pawn.

A singular peculiarity of the betel-nut is that of its staining the saliva of a deep red color, so as to resemble blood. Ossaroo, who possessed a large share of intelligence, and who had travelled to the great city of Calcutta and other parts of India, narrated a good anecdote connected with this fact. The substance of his relation was as follows :—

A young doctor, fresh from Europe and from the university, had arrived in one of the Indian cities in a big ship. The morning after his arrival he was walking out on the public road near the suburbs, when he chanced to meet a young native girl who appeared to be spitting blood. The doctor turned and followed the girl, who continued to spit blood at nearly every step she took ! He became alarmed, thinking the poor girl could not live another hour, and following her home to her house, announced to her parents who he was, and assured them that, from the symptoms he had observed, their daughter had not many minutes to live ! Her parents in their turn grew alarmed, as also did the girl herself—for the skill of a great Sahib doctor was not to be doubted. The priest was sent for, but before he could arrive the young girl *actually died.*

Now it was from *fear* that the poor girl had died, and it was the doctor who had *frightened* her to death ! but neither parents, nor priest, nor the doctor himself, knew this at the time. The doctor still believed the girl had died of blood-spitting, and the others remained in ignorance that it was upon this he had founded his prognosis.

The report of such a skilful physician soon spread abroad. Patients flocked to him, and he was in a fair way of rapidly accumulating a fortune. But ere long he had observed other people with symptoms of the same complaint which had caused the death of the poor girl, and had learnt also that these symptoms proceeded from chewing the betel-nut. Had he been discreet he would have kept his secret to himself; but, unluckily for his good fortune he was a talker, and could not help telling his companions the whole affair. He related it rather as a good joke—for, sad to say, the life of a poor native is held but too lightly by Europeans.

In the end, however, it proved no joke to the doctor. The parents of the girl came to understand the matter, as well as the public at large, and vengeance was vowed against him by the friends of the deceased. His patients deserted him as rapidly as they had come ; and to get rid of the scandal, as well as to get out of the danger that surrounded him, he was but too glad to take passage home in the same ship that had brought him out.

CHAPTER V.

THE FISHING-BIRDS.

OUR travellers were following up one of the tributaries of the Burrampooter, which, rising in the Himalayas, and running southward joins the latter near its great bend. The plant-hunter designed to penetrate the Bhotan Himalaya, because it had not yet been visited by any botanist, and its flora was reported to be very rich and varied. They were still passing through a settled part of the country, where fields of rice and sugar-cane, with groves of bananas, and various species of palm, were cultivated; some of the latter, as the cocoa-palm and betel, for their nuts, while others, as the large-leaved *Caryota*, for the wine which they produce.

The opium-poppy was also seen in cultivation, and mango-trees, and the great broad-leaved pawpaw, and black-pepper vines, with beautiful green leaves, trained against the stems of the palms. Jack-trees with their gigantic fruit, and figs, and nettle-trees, and the singular screw-pines, and euphorbias, and various species of the orange, were observed along the way.

The botanist saw many trees and plants, which he recognized as belonging to the Chinese flora, and he

could not help remarking many other things that reminded him of what he had read about China. In
fact, this part of India—for he was very near the borders of Assam—bears a considerable resemblance to
China, in its natural productions, and even the customs
of the people assimilate somewhat to those of the Celestial land. To make the resemblance more complete, the cultivation of the tea-plant has been introduced
into this part of the world, and is now carried on
with success.

But as our travellers proceeded, they became witnesses of a scene which brought China more vividly
before their minds than anything they had yet observed.

On rounding a clump of trees they came in view of
a moderate-sized lake. On the water, near the edge
of this lake, they perceived a man in a small light boat.
He was standing up, and held in his hands a long slender pole, with which he was poling the boat out towards
the centre of the lake.

Our travellers, Ossaroo excepted, uttered exclamations of surprise, and came at once to a halt.

What had caused them such astonishment? Not the
boat, nor the man in it, nor yet the long bamboo pole.
No. Such were common objects seen every day on
their journey. It was none of these that had brought
them to so sudden a stop, and caused them to stand
wondering. It was the fact that along both sides of
the boat—on the very edge or gunwale—was a row
of large birds as big as geese. They were white-
throated, white-breasted birds, mottled over the wings
and back with dark brown, and having long crooked

necks, large yellow bills, and broad tails rounded at the tips.

Although the man was standing up in his boat, and working his long pole over their heads, now on one side, then on the other, the birds appeared so tame that they did not heed his manœuvres; and yet not one of them seemed to be fastened, but merely perched upon the edge of the skiff! Now and then one would stretch its long neck over the water, turn its head a little to one side, and then draw it in again, and resume its former attitude. Such tame birds had never been seen. No wonder the sight astonished the Bavarian boys. Both turned to Ossaroo for an explanation, who gave it by simply nodding towards the lake, and uttering the words,—

"He go fishee."

"Ah! a fisherman!" rejoined the botanist.

"Yes, Sahib—you watchee, you see."

This was explanation enough. The boys now remembered having read of the Chinese mode of fishing with cormorants; and even at the distance at which they saw them, they could perceive that the birds on the boat were no other than cormorants. They were the species known as *Phalacrocorax Sinensis;* and although differing somewhat from the common cormorant, they possessed all the characteristic marks of the tribe,—the long flat body, the projecting breast-bone, the beak curving downward at the tip, and the broad rounded tail.

Desirous of witnessing the birds at work, our travellers remained stationary near the shore of the lake. It was evident the fisherman had not yet commenced

operations, and was only proceeding towards his ground.

After a short while he reached the centre of the lake; and then, laying aside his long bamboo, he turned his attention to the birds. He was heard giving them directions—just as a sportsman might do to his pointer or spaniel—and the next moment the great birds spread their shadowy wings, rose up from the edge of the boat, and after a short flight, one and all of them were seen plunging into the water.

Now our travellers beheld a singular scene. Here a bird was observed swimming along, with its keen eye scanning the crystal below—there the broad tail of another stood vertically upwards, the rest of its body hidden below the surface—yonder, a third was altogether submerged, the ripple alone showing where it had gone down—a fourth was seen struggling with a large fish that glittered in its pincer-like beak—a fifth had already risen with its scaly prey, and was bearing it to the boat; and thus the twelve birds were all actively engaged in the singular occupation to which they had been trained. The lake, that but the moment before lay tranquil and smooth as glass, was now covered with ripples, with circling eddies, with bubbles and foam, where the huge birds darted and plunged, and flapped about after their finny prey. It was in vain the fish endeavored to escape them—for the cormorant can glide rapidly through the water, and swim beneath with as much rapidity as upon the surface. Its keel-like breast-bone cuts the liquid element like an arrow, and with its strong wings for paddles, and its broad tail acting as a rudder, the bird is able to turn

sharply round, or shoot forward with incredible rapidity.

A singular circumstance came under the observation
of our travellers. When one of the birds had succeeded in bringing up a fish, which was larger than
common, and too large for its captor to convey to the
boat, several others might be seen rushing forward, to
render assistance in carrying the fish aboard !

You will wonder that these creatures—whose food is
the very prey they were capturing for their master—
did not swallow some of the fish they were taking. In
the case of the younger birds, and those not fully trained,
such little thefts do occasionally occur. But in such
cases the fisherman adopts a preventive precaution, by
fastening a collar round the necks of the birds—taking
care that it shall not descend to the thick part of the
throat, where it might choke them. With well-trained
old birds this precaution is unnecessary. No matter
how hungry the latter may be, they bring all they
"take" to their master, and are rewarded for their
honesty by the smaller and more worthless fish that
may have been caught.

Sometimes a bird becomes lazy, and sits upon the
water without attempting to do his duty. In such
cases, the fisherman approaches with his boat, stretches
forward his bamboo, strikes with violence close to
where the indolent individual is seated, and scolds him
for his laziness. This treatment seldom fails in its
effect ; and the winged fisher, once more roused by the
well-known voice of its master, goes to work with
renewed energy.

For several hours this fishing scene is kept up, until

the birds, becoming tired, are allowed to return and perch themselves on the boat; where their throat-straps are removed, and they are fed and caressed by their master.

Our travellers did not wait for this finale, but kept on their route; while Karl related to Caspar how that, not a great while ago, so late as the time of King Charles I., the common cormorant of Europe was trained to fish in the same way in several European countries, and especially in Holland; and that, at the present day, in some parts of China, this mode of fishing is followed to so great an extent, that the markets of some of the largest cities are supplied with fish caught altogether by cormorants.

. Certainly, no people exhibit more ingenuity in the training either of plants or animals, than do these same *oblique-eyed inhabitants* of the Celestial Empire.

2 *

CHAPTER VI.

THE TERÄI.

In approaching any great chain of mountains from the sea-level, you will find a large tract of country consisting of elevated hills and deep ravines, intersected by rapid streams and torrents. This tract is more or less broad, in proportion to the grandeur of the mountain chain; and, in the case of mountains of the first class, it is usually from twenty to fifty miles in breadth. Such a tract of country lies along both sides of the great chain of the Andes in South and North America, and also marks the approach to the Rocky Mountains and the Alleghanies. It is well known in Italy, under the Alps; and "Piedmont" is the French appellation for this sort of country, which is designated, in our lan guage, by an equally appropriate phrase, "foot-hills."

The "Alps of India" are not without this geological peculiarity. Along their whole southern flank, facing the hills of Hindustan, extends a belt of foot-hills, often above fifty miles in breadth; and characterized by steep ascents, deep dales and ravines, rapid foaming torrents, difficult paths and passes, and, consequently, by wild and picturesque scenery.

The lower part of this belt—that is, the portion which

lies contiguous to the hot plains, is known to Europeans as the " Teräi."

The Teräi is an irregular strip, of from ten to thirty miles in width, and extends along the whole base of the Himalayas, from the Sutledge River, on the west, to Upper Assam. Its character is peculiar. It differs both from the plains of India and from the Himalaya Mountains, possessing a botany and zoology almost totally distinct from either. It differs from both, in the malarious and unhealthy character of its climate, which is one of the deadliest in the world. In consequence of this, the Teräi is almost uninhabited ; the few scattered settlements of half-savage Mechs, its only inhabitants, lying remote and distant from each other.

Most of the Teräi is covered with forest and thick jungle ; and, notwithstanding its unhealthy climate, it is the favorite haunt of the wild beasts peculiar to this part of the globe. The tiger, the Indian lion, the panther and leopard, the cheetah, and various other large *felidæ*, roam through its jungly coverts ; the wild elephant, the rhinoceros, and gyal, are found in its forests ; and the sambur and axis browse on its grassy glades. Venomous snakes, hideous lizards, and bats, with the most beautiful of birds and butterflies, all find a home in the Teräi.

Several days' marching carried our travellers beyond the more settled portions of the country, and within the borders of this wild, jungle-covered district. On the day they entered the Teräi, they had made an early start of it ; and, therefore, arrived at their camping-ground some hours before sunset. But the young botanist, filled with admiration at the many singular and novel forms of vegetation he saw around him, resolved to remain upon the ground for several days.

Our travellers had no tent. Such an incumbrance would have been troublesome to them, travelling, as they were, afoot. Indeed, all three had their full loads to carry, as much as they could well manage, without the additional weight of a tent. Each had his blanket, and various other *impedimenta ;* but one and all of them had often slept without roof or canvas, and they could do so again.

At their present halting-place, they had no need for either. Nature had provided them with a cover quite equal to a canvas-tent. They had encamped under a canopy of thick foliage, the foliage of the *banyan* tree.

Young reader, you have heard of the great banyan of India ; that wonderful tree, whose branches, after spreading out from the main trunk, send down roots to the earth, and form fresh stems, until a space of ground is covered with a single tree, under whose shade a whole regiment of cavalry may bivouac, or a great public meeting be held ! No doubt, you have read of such a tree, and have seen pictures of one ? I need not, therefore, describe the banyan very particularly. Let me say, however, that it is a fig-tree ; not the one that produces the eatable fig, of which you are so very fond, but another species of the same genus—the genus *Ficus.* Now, of this genus there are a great many species ; as many, perhaps, as there are of any other genus of trees. Some of them are only creeping and climbing plants ; adhering to rocks and the trunks of other trees, like vines or ivy. Others, like the banyan, are among the largest trees of the forest. They are chiefly con-

fined to tropical countries, or hot regions lying on the
borders of the tropics; and they are found in both
hemispheres, that is, both in America and the Old
World. Some splendid species belong also to Australia. All of them possess, more or less, the singular
habit of throwing out roots from their branches, and
forming new stems, like the banyan; and frequently
they embrace other trees in such a manner, as to hide
the trunks of the latter completely from view!

This curious spectacle was witnessed by our travellers where they had encamped. The banyan which
they had chosen as their shelter was not one of the
largest—being only a young tree, but out of its top rose
the huge fan-shaped leaves of a palm-tree of the kind
known as the palmyra palm (*Borassus flagelliformis*).
No trunk of the palm-tree was visible; and had not
Karl Linden been a botanist, and known something of
the singular habit of the banyan, he would have been
puzzled to account for this odd combination. Above
spread the long radiating fronds of the palmyra directly
out of the top of the trunk of the fig, and looking so
distinct from the foliage of the latter as to form a very
curious sight. The leaves of the banyan being ovate,
and somewhat cordate or heart-shaped, of course presented quite a contrast to the large stiff fronds of the
palmyra.

Now the puzzle was, how the palm got there. Naturally one would suppose that a seed of the palm had
been deposited on the top of the banyan, and had there
germinated and thrown out its fronds.

But how did the palm seed get to the top of the fig?
Was it planted by the hand of man? or carried thither

by a bird? It could not well have been by the latter
mode—since the fruit of the palmyra is as large as a
child's head, and each one of the three seeds it contains
as big as a goose's egg! No bird would be likely to
carry about such a bulky thing as that. If there were
only one palm-tree growing from the top of one banyan,
it might be conjectured that some one had so planted it;
but there are many such combinations of these trees
met with in the forests of India, and also in districts entirely uninhabited. How then was this union of the two
trees to be accounted for?

Of our three travellers Caspar alone was puzzled.
Not so Karl and Ossaroo. Both were able to explain
the matter, and Karl proceeded to offer the elucidation.

" The fact is," said the botanist, " that the palm has
not grown out of the fig, but *vice versa.* The banyan
is the true parasite. A bird—wood-pigeon, or mino-
bird, or tree-pheasant perhaps—has carried the berries
of the fig-tree, and deposited them in the axil of the
palmyra. This the smallest birds may easily do, since
the fruit of the banyan is not larger than a diminutive
cherry. Once in its place the seed has germinated,
and sent its roots downward along the trunk of the
palm until they have reached the ground. These roots
have then flattened around the stem of the palm, until
they have enveloped it completely, with the exception
of the top, as you see. Afterwards the fig has thrown
out lateral branches, until the whole has assumed the
appearance of a banyan-tree with a fan-palm growing
out of its trunk !"

This was the true explanation. Ossaroo added some
remarks stating that the Hindoo people always regard

such a union of the two trees with great veneration, and believe it to be a holy marriage instituted by Providence. For himself, Ossaroo—not being a very strict sectarian, nor much given to religion in any form—laughed at the superstition, and called it "humbug."

CHAPTER VII.

TAPPING THE PALMYRA.

ALMOST the first thing done by Ossaroo after he had got relieved of his baggage was to climb the banyan. This he was able to do with ease, as the trunk, in consequence of the peculiar mode of its growth, was full of ridges and inequalities, and moreover Ossaroo could climb like a cat.

But what wanted he up the tree? Was he after the fruit? It could not be that, for the figs were not yet ripe, and even had they been quite mellow, they are but poor eating. Maybe he was going up for the nuts of the palmyra? No—it could not be that either, for these were not shaped. The great flower-spathe had not yet opened, and was only beginning to burst its green envelopes. Had the nuts been formed, and still in their young state, they would have afforded delicate eating. As already stated, the palmyra nuts grow to the size of a child's head. They are three-cornered, rounded off at the corners, consisting of a thick succulent yellowish rind, each containing three seeds as large as goose-eggs. It is the seeds that are eaten when young and pulpy; but if allowed to ripen, they become quite hard and blue-colored, and are then insipid and uneatable. But it could not be the seed either which Ossaroo was after, since there were no seeds, nor nuts —only the flower, and that still hidden in its great spadix.

The boys watched Ossaroo narrowly. He had carried up with him a bamboo-joint which he had cut from a very thick cane. It was open at one end, and formed a vessel that would hold rather more than a quart. Another thing they had observed him to take with him ; and that was a stone about as big as a paving-stone. Still another implement he carried up the tree —his long knife.

In a few seconds the shikarree had reached the top of the banyan ; and clutching the great leaf-stalks of the palm, he climbed up among its huge fronds. Here he was observed to lay hold of the spathe of the flower, and bending it against the trunk, he commenced hammering away with the stone, evidently with the intention of crushing the young inflorescence. With a few blows he succeeded in doing this effectually. He then drew the knife from his scarf, and, with an adroit cut, detached the upper half of the flower-spike, which fell neglected to the ground.

The bamboo vessel was next brought into service. This he fixed on the spathe in such a manner that the incised end remained inside the hollow of the cane. Both flower-spike and cane were then tied to one of the leaf-stalks of the palm, so that the bamboo hung vertically bottom downward ; and this arrangement having been completed, the shikarree flung down his hammering stone, replaced his knife under his belt, and descended from the tree.

"Now, Sahibs," said he, as soon as he had reached terra firma, "you waitee hour—you drinkee Indoo champagne."

In an hour or so his promise was fulfilled. The bamboo joint was released and brought down; and, sure enough, it was found to be full of a cool clear liquor, of which all of them drank, esteeming it equal to the best champagne. In fact, there is no more seducing and delicious drink in all India than the sap of the palmyra palm; but it is also very intoxicating, and is used too freely by the natives of the country where this splendid tree flourishes.

Sugar can also be manufactured from this sap, simply by boiling it down. When sugar is to be made, the tree is tapped in a similar manner; but it is necessary to have a little lime in the vessel while collecting the liquid, else it would ferment, and thus spoil it for sugar-boiling.

The reason why Ossaroo was so ready in tapping this particular tree, was because the banyan which enveloped its trunk offered him an excellent means of getting at it. Otherwise it would have been no easy matter to have ascended the smooth slender shaft of a palmyra, rising thirty or forty feet without knot or branch. Of course Ossaroo, as soon as the bamboo was empty, once more climbed up and readjusted it to the "tap," knowing that the sap would continue to run. This it does for many days, only that each day it is necessary to cut a fresh slice from the top of the flower-stalk, so as to keep the pores open and free.

Though the day had been hot, as soon as twilight came on the coolness of the air rendered it necessary for our travellers to kindle a fire. Ossaroo was not long in striking a light out of his tinder-box, and having set fire to some dry leaves and moss, a blaze was soon produced. Meanwhile Karl and Caspar had broken some branches from a dead tree that lay near the spot, and carrying them up in armfuls, piled them upon the burning leaves. A roaring fire was created in a few minutes, and around this the party seated themselves, and commenced cooking their supper of rice, with some pieces of dried meat, which they had brought along from the last village.

Whilst engaged in this occupation, so agreeable to men who are hungry, the botanist, whose eye was always on the alert for matters relating to his favorite calling, remarked that the wood out of which their fire had been made burned very much like oak. On taking up one of the fagots, and cutting it with his knife, he was astonished to find that it *was* oak in reality—for there is no mistaking the grain and fibre of this giant of the northern forests. What astonished him was the existence of oak-trees in a country where the flora was altogether tropical. He knew that he might expect to find representatives of the oak family upon the sides of the Himalayas ; but he was still only at their foot, and in the region of the palms and bananas.

Karl knew not then, nor is it yet generally known, that many species of oaks are tropical trees—in fact, many kinds may be found in the torrid zone, growing even as low as the level of the sea. It is no less strange, that although there are no oaks in tropical South America and Africa, in Ceylon, or even in the peninsula of India itself, yet there are numerous species in East Bengal, the Moluccas, and the Indian islands—perhaps a greater number of species than grows in any other part of the world !

The sight of this old acquaintance, as they termed the oak, had a cheering effect upon the Bavarian boys ; and after supper they sat conversing upon the subject, determined as soon as it was day to look out for some of the living trees as further confirmation of the strange fact they had observed.

They were about thinking of wrapping themselves up in their blankets, and retiring to rest, when an incident occurred that kept them awake for another hour or two.

CHAPTER VIII.

THE SAMBUR STAG.

" See !" cried Caspar, who was more sharp-eyed than Karl.

" Look ! look yonder ! two lights, I declare ! "

" Indeed, yes," replied Karl; "I see them—bright round lights ! What can they be ? "

" An animal !" answered Caspar ; "I can affirm that much. Some wild beast, I fancy ! "

They regarded the strange object with some uneasiness, for they knew they were in the haunts of dangerous wild beasts.

" Maybe a tiger?" suggested Karl.

" Or a panther ? " added his brother.

" I hope neither one nor the other," said Karl.

He was interrupted by Ossaroo, who had now observed the shining spots, and who with a single word reassured the whole party.

" Samboo," said the shikarree.

Both knew that Ossaroo meant by " Samboo," the great deer or stag known to Europeans as the sambur deer. It was the eyes of a deer, then, glancing back the blaze of the oak fagots, that had alarmed them.

Their fears were suddenly changed to feelings of joy.

They had a double motive for being pleased at the
sight. To shoot and bring down the deer would be
such excellent sport; besides, a fresh venison steak was
a delicacy which both could appreciate.

All of them, Ossaroo included, were too well accustomed to the habits of hunters to act rashly. Any
sudden movement among them might frighten the
game; and if it bounded off into the forest, or even
turned its head, it could no longer be seen in the pitchy
darkness that surrounded them. The shining eyes were
all of it that were visible; and if the creature had but
chosen to *shut its eyes* it might have stood there till
the morning light, without the least chance of being
aimed at.

The animal, however, was too full of its own curiosity
to adopt this precaution. Instead, it remained where it
had been first observed—its great round orbs uncovered
to their full extent and gleaming in the light like a pair
of "bull's-eyes."

Caspar in a whisper cautioned the others to remain
silent and not to move hand or finger. He, himself,
gradually dropped his arm, until he was able to grasp
his large double-barrelled gun; and then, raising the
piece slowly to a level, took aim and fired. He very
prudently did not aim for the centre spot between the
eyes. Had it been a bullet that was in his gun he might
have done so; but he knew that his piece was only loaded
with shot, and shot—even though they were "buck-shot"
—might not penetrate the hard thick skull of a stag so
strong as the sambur. Instead of aiming for the eyes,
therefore, he took sight at least a foot below them, and
in a direct line below. He had already conjectured,

from the even set of the eyes, that the deer was standing full front towards the camp-fire, and his object was
to send the shot into its breast and throat.

The instant after he had delivered the first barrel,
although the shining eyes went out like the snuffing of
candles, he fired the second, so as to take advantage of
a random shot.

He might have spared his load, for the first had done
the business ; and the noise of kicking and sprawling
among the dry leaves told that the deer was knocked
over, and, if not killed, at least badly wounded.

The dog Fritz had already leaped forth ; and before
the hunters could procure a torch and reach the spot,
the huge hound had seized the quarry by the throat,
and finished its struggles by strangling it to death.

They now dragged the carcass up to the light of the
fire, and it was just as much as the three of them could
manage—for the sambur deer is one of the largest animals of its kind, and the one that had fallen into their
hands was a fine old buck, with a pair of immense
antlered horns, of which no doubt in his lifetime he had
been excessively proud.

The sambur deer is one of the most distinguished
of the deer tribe. Although not equal in size to
the American wapiti (*Cervus Canadensis*), he is much
superior to the stag or red-deer of Europe. He is an
active, bold, and vicious animal ; and, when bayed, a
dangerous antagonist either to dogs or hunters. His
coat is close, the hair harsh, of a brown color, and
slightly grizzled. Around the neck it is long and
shaggy, but particularly upon the under line of the
throat, where it forms a mane similar to that of the

American wapiti.   Another mane runs along the back
of the neck, adding to the fierce bold appearance of the
animal.   A blackish band encircles the muzzle, and
the usual " crupper mark" around the tail is small and
of a yellowish color.

This is the description of the common sambur deer
(*Cervus hippelaphus*) best known to•Europeans, and
among Anglo-Indian sportsmen called " stag " ; but it
is to be observed that in different parts of Asia there
are many different species and varieties of the sambur.
Zoologists usually class them in a group called *Rusa ;*
and one or other of this group may be found in every
district of India from Ceylon to the Himalayas, and
from the Indus to the islands of the Indian Archipelago.•
They haunt in timber, and usually by the banks of
streams or other waters.

America has long been regarded as the favorite region of the deer tribe, as Africa is the true home of the
antelopes.   This belief, however, seems to be rather an
incorrect one, and has arisen, perhaps, from the fact
that the American species are better known to Europeans.   It is true that the largest of the deer—the
moose (*Cervus alces*)—is an inhabitant of the American continent in common with Northern Europe and
Asia; but the number of species on that continent, both
in its northern and southern divisions, is very limited.
When the zoology of the East—I mean of all those
countries and islands usually included under the term
East Indies—shall have been fully determined, we
shall no doubt find not only twice, but three times the
number of species of deer that belongs to America.

When we consider the vast number of educated

Englishmen—both in the army and in the civil service —who have idled away their lives in India, we cannot help wondering at the little that is yet known in relation to the *fauna* of the Oriental world. Most of the Indian officers have looked upon the wild animals of that country with the eye of the sportsman rather than of the naturalist. With them a deer is a deer, and a large ox-like animal a buffalo, or it may be a gayal, or a jungle cow, or a gour,.or a gyall; but which of all these is an ox, or whether the four last-mentioned bovine quadrupeds are one and the same species, remains to be determined. Were it not that these gentlemen have had spirit enough occasionally to send us home a skin or a set of horns, we might remain altogether ignorant of the existence of the creature from which these trophies were taken. Verily science owes not much to the Honorable East India Company. We are not blind to such noble exceptions as Sykes, Hodgson, and others; and, if every province of India had a resident of their character, a fauna might soon be catalogued that would astonish even the spectacled *savant.*

CHAPTER IX.

A NIGHT MARAUDER.

OSSAROO soon stripped the stag of its skin, cut the carcass into quarters, and hung them on the limb of a tree. Although the party had already supped, the excitement which had been occasioned by the incident gave them a fresh appetite; and venison steaks were broiled over the oak-wood cinders, and eaten with a relish. These were washed down by fresh draughts of the delicious palm-wine; and then the travellers, having gathered some of the hanging moss (*Usnea*), and strewed it near the fire, rolled themselves in their blankets, and went to sleep.

About midnight there was a camp alarm. The sleepers were awakened by the dog Fritz; who, by his angry baying and fierce demonstrations, showed that some creature must have approached the fire that had no business to be there. On rousing themselves they thought they heard footsteps at a little distance, and a low growl as of some wild beast; but it was not easy to distinguish any sound in particular, as at this season the tropical forest is full of noises—so loud that it is often difficult for persons to hear each other in conversation. What with the chirruping of cicadas, the croaking of swamp-frogs, the tinkling of tree-toads, and the hooting and screeching of owls and night-hawks, the Indian forest is filled with a deafening din throughout the whole night.

Fritz ceased barking after a time; and they all went to sleep again, and slept till morning.

As soon as day broke, they were up, and set about preparing breakfast. Fresh fagots were piled upon the fire, and preparations made for a savoury roast of venison rib. Ossaroo climbed up to his tap, while Caspar went for the meat.

The quarters of the deer had been suspended upon a tree, at the distance of about fifty paces from the camp-fire. The reason of their being hung at such a distance was that a stream flowed there, and in order to clean the meat, they had carried it down to the water's edge A horizontal branch, which was about the proper height from the ground, had tempted Ossaroo, and he had chosen it for his "meat-rack."

An exclamation from Caspar now summoned the others to the spot.

"See!" cried he, as they came up, "one of the quarters gone!"

"Ha! there have been thieves!" said Karl. "That was what caused Fritz to bark."

"Thieves!" ejaculated Caspar. "Not men thieves! They would have carried off the four quarters instead of one. Some wild beast has been the thief!"

"Yes, Sahib, you speakee true," said the shikarree, who had now reached the spot; "he wild beast—he very wild beast—big tiger!"

At the mention of the name of this terrible animal,

both boys started, and looked anxiously around. Even Ossaroo himself exhibited symptoms of fear. To think they had been sleeping on the open ground so close to a tiger—the most savage and dreaded of all beasts—and this, too, in India, where they were constantly hearing tales of the ravages committed by these animals!

"You think it was a tiger?" said the botanist, interrupting Ossaroo.

"Sure, Sahib—lookee here!—Sahib, see him track!"

The shikarree pointed to some tracks in the selvidge of sand that lined the bank of the rivulet. There, sure enough, were the footprints of a large animal; and, upon inspecting them closely, they could easily be distinguished as those of a creature of the cat tribe. There were the pads or cushions smoothly imprinted in the sand, and the slight impression of the claws—for the tiger, although possessed of very long and sharp claws, can retract these when walking, so as to leave very little mark of them in the mud or sand. The tracks were too large to be mistaken for those either of a leopard or panther, and the only other animal to which they could appertain was the lion. There were lions in that district. But Ossaroo well knew how to distinguish between the tracks of the two great carnivora, and without a moment's hesitation he pronounced the robber to have been a tiger.

It now became a matter of serious consideration what they should do under the circumstances. Should they abandon their camp, and move forward? Karl was very desirous of spending a day or two in the neighborhood. He made no doubt of being able to find several new species of plants there. But with the knowledge of having such a neighbor they would not sleep very soundly. The tiger would, no doubt, return to the camp. He was not likely to stay away from a quarter where he had found such hospitable entertainment—such a good supper. He must have seen the rest of the venison, and would be sure to pay them another visit on the following night. True, they might kindle large fires, and frighten him off from their sleeping place; still, they would be under an unpleasant apprehension; and even during the day they had no confidence that he might not attack them—particularly if they went botanizing in the woods. The very places into which their occupation would lead them, would be those in which they were most likely to meet this dreaded neighbor. Perhaps, therefore, it would be best to pack up, and proceed on their journey.

While eating their breakfasts the thing was debated among them. Caspar, full of hunter-spirit, was desirous of having a peep at the tiger anyhow; but Karl was more prudent, if not a little more timid, and thought it was better to "move on." This was the opinion of the botanist; but he at length gave way to Caspar, and more particularly to Ossaroo, who proposed *killing* the tiger if they would only remain one night longer upon the ground.

"What! with your bow, Ossaroo?" asked Caspar; "with your poisoned arrows?"

"No, young Sahib," replied Ossaroo.

"I thought you would have but little chance to kill a great tiger with such weapons. How do you mean to do it then?"

"If Sahib Karl consent to stay till to-morrow, Ossaroo show you—he kill tiger—he catch 'im 'live.'"

"Catch him alive !—In a trap ?—In a snare ? "

· "No trapee—no snaree. You see. Ossaroo do what
he say—he take tiger 'live.'"

Ossaroo had evidently some plan of his own, and the
others became curious to know what it was. As the
shikarree promised that it was unattended with danger,
the botanist consented to remain, and let the trial be
made.

Ossaroo now let them into the secret of his plan ;
and as soon as they had finished eating their breakfasts,
all hands set to work to assist him in carrying it into
execution.

They proceeded as follows. In the first place, a
large number of joints of bamboo were obtained from
a neighboring thicket of these canes. The bark of the
banyan was then cut, and the canes inserted in such a
manner that the white milky sap ran into them. Each
joint was left closed at the bottom, and served as a
vessel to collect the juice, and such stems of the fig only
were tapped as were young and full of sap. As soon
as a sufficient quantity of the fluid had been distilled
into the canes, the contents of all were poured into the
cooking-pot, and hung over a slow fire. The sap was
then stirred—fresh juice being occasionally thrown in—
and in a short while the whole attained the toughness
and consistency of the best birdlime. It was, in fact,
the birdlime—the same that is used by the bird-
catchers of India, and quite equal to that manufactured
from the holly.

During the time that this was being prepared, Karl

and Caspar, by the directions of. Ossaroo, had climbed into the trees, and collected an immense quantity of leaves. These leaves were also taken from the banyan figs, and for this purpose they had selected those that grew on the youngest trees and shoots. Each leaf was as large as a tea-plate, and they were covered with a woolly pubescence, peculiar only to the leaves upon the younger trees—for as the banyan grows old its leaves become harder and smoother on the surface.

The fig-leaves having been gathered to his hand, and the birdlime made ready, Ossaroo proceeded to carry out his design.

The two remaining quarters of the venison still hung on the tree. These were permitted to remain—as a bait to the singular trap that Ossaroo was about to set —only that they were raised higher from the ground in order that the tiger might not too readily snatch them away, and thus defeat the stratagem of the hunter.

The venison having been hung to his liking, Ossaroo now cleared the ground for a large space around—directing his assistants to carry off all the brush and dead wood to a distance from the spot. This was quickly done, and then the shikarree put the finishing stroke to his work. This occupied him for two hours at least, and consisted in anointing all the fig-leaves that had been gathered with a coat of birdlime, and spreading them over the ground, until they covered a space of many yards in circumference. In the centre of this space hung the venison; and no creature could have approached within yards of it without treading upon the smeared leaves. The leaves had been anointed upon both sides, so that they adhered slightly to the

grass, and a breeze of wind could not have disarranged
them to any great extent.

When all was fixed to their satisfaction, Ossaroo and
the others returned to the camp-fire, and ate a hearty
dinner. It was already late in the day, for they had
been many hours at work, and they had not thought of
dining until their arrangements were complete. Nothing more remained to be done, but to await the result
of their stratagem.

CHAPTER X.

A TALK ABOUT TIGERS.

I NEED not describe a tiger. You have seen one, or the picture of one. He is the great *striped* cat. The large *spotted* ones are not tigers. They are either jaguars, or panthers, or leopards, or ounces, or cheetahs, or servals. But there is no danger of your mistaking the tiger for any other animal. He is the largest of the feline tribe—the lion alone excepted—and individual tigers have been measured as large as the biggest lion. The shaggy mane that covers the neck and shoulders of an old male lion gives him the appearance of being of greater dimensions than he really is. Skin him and he would not be larger than an old he-tiger also divested of his hide.

Like the lion, the tiger varies but little in form or color. Nature does not sport with these powerful beasts. It is only upon the meaner animals she plays off her eccentricities. The tiger may be seen with the ground color of a lighter or deeper yellow, and the stripes or bars more or less black; but the same general appearance is preserved, and the species can always be recognized at a glance.

The range or habitat of the tiger is more limited than

3 *

that of the lion. The latter exists throughout the whole of Africa, as well as the southern half of Asia; whereas the tiger is found only in the southeastern countries of Asia, and some of the larger islands of the Indian Archipelago. Westwardly his range does not extend to this side of the Indus river, and how far north in Asia is uncertain. Some naturalists assert that there are tigers in Asia as far north as the Obi River. This would prove the tiger to be not altogether a tropical animal, as he is generally regarded. It is certain that tigers once did inhabit the countries around the Caspian Sea. There lay Hyrcania; and several Roman writers speak of the Hyrcanian tigers. They could not have meant any of the spotted cats,—ounce, panther, or leopard,—for the Romans knew the difference between these and the striped or true tiger. If, then, the tiger was an inhabitant of those trans-Himalayan regions in the days of Augustus, it is possible it still exists there, as we have proofs of its existence in Mongolia and northern China at the present day.

Were we to believe some travellers, we should have the tiger, not only in Africa, but in America. The jaguar is the tiger (*tigre*) of the Spanish Americans; and the panther, leopard, and cheetah, have all done duty as "tigers" in the writings of old travellers in Africa.

The true home of this fierce creature is the hot jungle covered country that exists in extended tracts in Hindostan, Siam, Malaya, and parts of China. There the tiger roams undisputed lord of the thicket and forest; and although the lion is also found in these countries, he is comparatively a rare animal, and, from being but seldom met with, is less talked about or feared.

We who live far away from the haunts of these great carnivora, can hardly realize the terror which is inspired by them in the countries they infest.

In many places human life is not safe ; and men go out upon a journey, with the same dread of meeting a tiger, that we would have for an encounter with a mad dog. This dread is by no means founded upon mere fancies or fabricated stories. Every village has its true tales of tiger attacks and encounters, and every settlement has its list of killed or maimed. You can scarce credit such a relation ; but it is a well-known fact that whole districts of fertile country have from time to time been abandoned by their inhabitants out of pure fear of the tigers and panthers which infested them ! Indeed, similar cases of depopulation have occurred in South America, caused by a far less formidable wild beast— the jaguar.

In some parts of India the natives scarce attempt resistance to the attack of the tiger. Indeed, the superstition of his victims aids the fierce monster in their destruction. They regard him as being gifted with supernatural power, and sent by their gods to destroy ; and under this conviction yield themselves up, without making the slightest resistance.

In other parts, where races exist possessed of more energy of character, the tiger is hunted eagerly, and various modes of killing or capturing him are practised in different districts.

Sometimes a bow is set with poisoned arrows, and a cord attached to the string. A bait is then placed on

the ground, and arranged in such a way that the tiger,
on approaching it, presses against the cord, sets the
bow-string free, and is pierced by the arrow—the poison
of which eventually causes his death.

A spring-gun is set off by a similar contrivance, and
the tiger shoots himself.

The log-trap or "dead fall"—often employed by
American backwoodsmen for capturing the black bear—
is also in use in India for trapping the tiger. This consists of a heavy log or beam so adjusted upon the top
of another one by a prop or "trigger," as to fall and
crush whatever animal may touch the trigger. A bait
is also used for this species of trap.

Hunting the tiger upon elephants is a royal sport in
India, and is often followed by the Indian rajahs, and
sometimes by British sportsmen—officers of the East
India Company. This sport is, of course, very exciting; but there is nothing of a *ruse* practised in it. The
hunters go armed with rifles and spears; and attended
by a large number of natives, who beat the jungle and
drive the game within reach of the sportsmen. Many
lives are sacrificed in this dangerous sport; but those
who suffer are usually the poor peasants employed as
beaters; and an Indian rajah holds the lives of a score
or two of his subjects as lightly as that of a tiger
itself.

It is said the Chinese catch the tiger in a box-trap,
which they bait simply with a looking-glass. The tiger,
on approaching the looking-glass, perceives his own
shadow, and mistaking it for a rival, rushes forward to
the trap, frees the trigger, and is caught. It may be
that the Chinese practised such a method. That part is

likely enough ; but it is not likely that they take many tigers in this way.

Perhaps you may be of opinion that the plan which Ossaroo was about to follow was quite as absurd as that of the Chinese. It certainly did sound very absurd to his companions, when he first told them that it was his intention *to catch the tiger by birdlime !*

CHAPTER XI.

A TIGER TAKEN BY BIRDLIME.

THE plan of the shikarree was put to the test sooner than any of them expected. They did not look for the tiger to return before sunset, and they had re-solved to pass the night among the branches of the banyan in order to be out of the way of danger. The tiger might take it into his head to stroll into their camp; and although, under ordinary circumstances, these fierce brutes have a dread of fire, there are some of them that do not regard it, and instances have occurred of tigers making their attack upon men who were seated close to a blazing pile! Ossaroo knew of several such cases, and had, therefore, given his advice, that all of them should pass the night in the tree. It was true the tiger could easily scale the banyan if the notion occurred to him; but, unless they made some noise to attract his attention, he would not be likely to discover their where-abouts. They had taken the precaution to erect a plat-form of bamboos among the branches, so as to serve them for a resting-place.

After all, they were not under the necessity of resort-ing to this elevated roost,—at least for the purpose of passing the night there. But they occupied it for a while; and during that while they were witnesses to a scene that for singularity, and comicality as well, was equal to anything that any of them had ever beheld.

It wanted about half-an-hour of sunset, and they were all seated around the camp-fire, when a singular noise reached their ears. It was not unlike the "whirr" made by a thrashing-machine—which any one must have heard who has travelled through an agricultural district. Unlike this, however, the sound was not prolonged, but broke out at intervals, continued for a few seconds, and then was silent again.

Ossaroo was the only one of the party who, on hearing this sound, exhibited any feelings of alarm. The others were simply curious. It was an unusual sound. They wondered what was producing it—nothing more.

They quite shared the alarm of the shikarree, when the latter informed them that what they heard was neither more nor less than the "purr" of a tiger !

Ossaroo communicated this information in an ominous whisper, at the same instant crouching forward towards the main trunk of the banyan, and beckoning to the others to follow him.

Without a word they obeyed the sign, and all three climbed, one after the other, up the trunk, and silently seated themselves among the branches.

By looking through the outer screen of leaves, and a little downward, they could see the quarters of venison hanging from the limb, and also the whole surface of the ground where the glittering leaves were spread.

Whether the haunch which the tiger had stolen on the preceding night had not been sufficient for his supper, and he had grown hungry again before his usual feeding-time, is uncertain. But certain it is that Ossaroo, who understood well the habits of this striped robber, did not expect him to return so soon. He looked for him after darkness should set in. But the loud "purr-r-r" that at intervals came booming through the jungle, and each time sounding more distinctly, showed that the great cat was upon the ground.

All at once they espied him coming out of·the bushes, and ŏn the other side of the rivulet—his broad whitish throat and breast shining in contrast with the dark green foliage. He was crouching just after the manner of a house-cat when making her approach to some unwary bird—his huge paws spread before him, and his long back hollowed down—a hideous and fearful object to behold. His eyes appeared to flash fire, as he bent them upon the tempting joints hanging high up upon the branch of the tree.

After reconnoitring a little, he gathered up his long back into a curve, vaulted into the air, and cleared the rivulet from bank to bank. Then, without further pause, he trotted nimbly forward, and stopped directly under the hanging joints.

Ossaroo had purposely raised the meat above its for-mer elevation, and the lowest ends of the joints were full twelve feet from the ground. Although the tiger can bound to a very great distance in a horizontal direction, he is not so well fitted for springing vertically upwards, and therefore the tempting morsels were just beyond his reach. He seemed to be somewhat nonplussed at this—for upon his last visit he had found things rather different—but after regarding the joints for a moment or two, and uttering a loud snuff of discontent, he flattened his paws against the ground, and sprang high into air.

The attempt was a failure. He came back to the earth without having touched the meat, and expressed his dissatisfaction by an angry growl.

. In another moment, he made a second spring upwards. This time, he struck one of the quarters with his paw, and sent it swinging backwards and forwards, though it had been secured too well to the branch to be in any danger of falling.

All at once, the attention of the great brute became directed to a circumstance, which seemed to puzzle him not a little. He noticed that there was something adhering to his paws. He raised one of them from the ground, and saw that two or three leaves were sticking to it. What could be the matter with the leaves, to cling to his soles in that manner? They appeared to be wet, but what of that? He had never known wet leaves stick to his feet any more than dry ones. Perhaps it was this had hindered him from springing up as high as he had intended? At all events, he did not feel quite comfortable, and he should have the leaves off before he attempted to leap again. He gave his paw a slight shake, but the leaves would not go. He shook it more violently, still the leaves adhered! He could not make it out. There was some gummy substance upon them, such as he had never met with before in all his travels. He had rambled over many a bed of fig-leaves in his day, but had never set foot upon such sticky leaves as these.

Another hard shake of the paw produced no better effect. Still stuck fast the leaves, as if they had been pitch plasters; one covering the whole surface of his foot, and others adhering to its edges. Several had even fastened themselves on his ankles. What the deuce did it all mean?

As shaking the paw was of no use, he next attempted to get rid of them by the only other means known to him; that was by rubbing them off against his cheeks and snout. He raised the paw to his ears, and drew it along the side of his head. He succeeded in getting most of them off his foot in this way, but, to his chagrin, they now adhered to his head, ears, and jaws, where they felt still more uncomfortable and annoying. These he resolved to detach, by using his paw upon them; but, instead of doing so, he only added to their number, for, on raising his foot, he found that a fresh batch of the sticky leaves had fastened upon it. He now tried the other foot, with no better effect. It, too, was covered with gummy leaves, that only became detached to fasten upon his jaws, and stick there, in spite of all his efforts to tear them off. Even some of them had got over his eyes, and already half-blinded him! But one way remained to get rid of the leaves, that had so fastened upon his head. Every time he applied his paws, it only made things worse. But there was still a way to get them off—so thought he—by rubbing his head along the ground.

No sooner thought of than done. He pressed his jaws down to the earth, and, using his hind legs to push himself along, he rubbed hard to rid himself of the annoyance. He then turned over, and tried the same method with the other side; but, after continuing at this for some moments, he discovered he was only making matters worse; in fact, he found that both his eyes were now completely "bunged up," and that he was perfectly blind! He felt, moreover, that his whole head, as well as his body, was now covered, even to the tip of his tail.

By this time, he had lost all patience. He thought no longer of the venison. He thought only of freeing himself from the detestable plight in which he was placed. He sprang and bounded over the ground; now rubbing his head along the surface, now scraping it with his huge paws, and ever and anon dashing himself against the stems of the trees that grew around. All this while, his growling, and howling, and screaming, filled the woods with the most hideous noises.

Up to this crisis, our travellers had watched his every movement, all of them bursting with laughter; to which, however, they dare not give utterance, lest they might spoil the sport. At length, Ossaroo knew that the time was come for something more serious than laughter; and, descending from the tree with his long spear, he beckoned the others to follow with their guns.

The shikarree could have approached and thrust the tiger, without much danger; but, to make sure, the double-barrel, already loaded with ball, was fired at him, along with Caspar's rifle; and one of the bullets striking him between the ribs, put an end to his struggles, by laying him out upon the grass dead as a herring.

Upon examining him, they found that the fig-leaves so covered his eyes, as to render him completely blind. What prevented him from scratching them off with his huge claws was, that these were so wrapped up in the leafy envelope as to render them perfectly useless, and no longer dangerous, had any one engaged with him in close combat.

When the exciting scene was over, all of the party indulged in hearty laughter ; . for there was something extremely ludicrous, not only in the idea, but in the act itself, of trapping a royal tiger by so simple a con .trivance as birdlime.

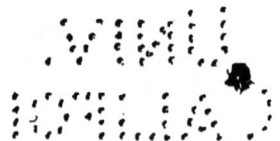

CHAPTER XII.

A RARE RAFT.

OSSAROO did not fail to skin the tiger, and to eat for his supper a large steak, cut off from his well-fleshed ribs. The others did not join him in this singular viand, although the shikarree assured them that tiger-beef was far superior to the venison of the sambur deer. There may have been truth in Ossaroo's asser-tion; for it is well known, that the flesh of several kinds of carnivorous animals is not only palatable, but delicate eating. Indeed, the delicacy of the meat does not seem at all to depend upon the food of the animal; since no creature is a more unclean feeder than the domestic pig, and what is nicer or more tender than a bit of roast pork? On the other hand, many animals, whose flesh is exceedingly bitter, feed only on fresh grass or sweet succulent roots and plants. As a proof of this, I might instance the tapir of South America, the quaggas and zebras of Africa, and even some ani-mals of the deer and antelope tribes, whose flesh is only eatable in cases of emergency.

The same fact may be observed in relation to birds. Many birds of prey furnish a dish quite equal to choice game. For one, the flesh of the large chicken-hawk of·America (eaten and eagerly sought after by the plantation negroes) is not much, if anything, inferior to that of the bird upon which it preys.

It was not for the "meat," however, that Ossaroo stripped the tiger of his skin, but rather for the skin itself; and not so much for the absolute value of the skin, for in India that is not great. Had it been a panther or leopard skin, or even the less handsome hide of the cheetah, its absolute value would have been greater. But there was an artificial value attached to the skin of a tiger, and that well knew the shikarree. He knew that there was a *bounty of ten rupees* for every tiger killed, and also that to obtain this bounty it was necessary to show the skin. True it was the East India Company that paid the bounty, and only for tigers killed in their territory. This one had not been killed under the British flag, but what of that? A tiger-skin was a tiger-skin; and Ossaroo expected·some day not distant to walk the streets of Calcutta; and, with this idea in his mind, he climbed up the great banyan, and hid his tiger-skin among its topmost branches, to be left there till his return from the mountains.

The next two days were spent in the same neighborhood, and the plant-hunter was very successful. The seeds of many rare plants, some of them quite new to the botanical world, were here obtained, and like the skin of the tiger deposited in a safe place, so that the collectors might not be burdened with them on their journey to the mountains. It was in this way that Karl had resolved upon making his collections, leaving the seeds and nuts he should obtain at various places upon his route; and, when returning, he trusted to be able to employ some Coolies to assist in getting them carried to Calcutta or some other sea-port.

On the fourth day the travellers again took the route, still facing due northward in the direction of the mountains. They needed no guide to point out their course, as the river which they had resolved upon following upwards was guide enough; usually they kept along its banks, but sometimes a thick marshy jungle forced them to abandon the water-edge and keep away for some distance into the back country, where the path was more safe and open.

About midday they arrived at the banks of a stream, that was a branch of the main river. This stream lay transversely to their route, and, of course, had to be crossed. There was neither bridge nor ford, nor crossing of any kind to be seen, and the current was both wide and deep. They followed it up for more than a mile; but it neither grew shallower nor yet more narrow. They walked up and down for a couple of hours, endeavoring to find a crossing, but to no purpose.

Both Caspar and Ossaroo were good swimmers, but Karl could not swim a stroke; and it was entirely on his account that they stayed to search for a ford. The other two would have dashed in at once, regardless of the swift current. What was to be done with Karl? In such a rapid running river it was as much as the best swimmer could do to carry himself across; therefore not one of the others could assist Karl. How then, were they to get over?

They had seated themselves under a tree to debate this question; and no doubt the habile Ossaroo would

soon have offered a solution to it, and got the young
Sahib across, but at that moment assistance arrived
from a very unexpected quarter.

There was a belt of open ground—a sort of meadow
upon the side opposite to where they were seated,
which was backed by a jungly forest.

Out of this forest a man was seen to emerge, and
take his way across the meadow in the direction of the
river. His swarthy complexion, and bushy black hair
hanging neglected over his shoulders—his dress consisting of a single blanket-like robe, held by a leathern
belt around the waist—his bare legs and sandalled feet
—all bore evidence that he was one of the half-savage
natives of the Terái.

His appearance created a great sensation, and astonished all the party—Ossaroo, perhaps, excepted. It
was not his wild look nor his odd costume that produced
this astonishment, for men who have travelled in Hindostan are not likely to be surprised by wild looks and
strange dresses. What astonished our travellers—and
it would have had a like effect upon the most stoical
people in the world—was that the individual who
approached was carrying a *buffalo upon his back!*
Not the quarter of a buffalo, nor the head of a buffalo,
but a whole one, as big, and black, and hairy, as an
English bull! The back of the animal lay against the
back of the man, with the head and horns projecting
over his shoulder, the legs sticking out behind, and the
tail dragging about his heels!.

How one man could bear up under such a load was
more than our travellers could divine; but not only did
this wild Mech bear up under it, but he appeared to

carry it with ease, and stepped as lightly across the meadow as if it had been a bag of feathers he was carrying!

Both Karl and Caspar uttered exclamations of sur-prise, and rapid interrogatories were put to Ossaroo for an explanation. Ossaroo only smiled significantly in reply, evidently able to explain this mysterious phe-nomenon; but enjoying the surprise of his companions too much to offer a solution of it as long as he could decorously withhold it.

The surprise of the boys was not diminished, when another native stepped out of the timber, buffalo on back, like the first; and then another and another—until half-a-dozen men, with a like number of buffaloes on their shoulders, were seen crossing the meadows!

Meanwhile the foremost had reached the bank of the river; and now the astonishment of the botanists reached its climax, when they saw this man let down the huge animal from his shoulders, embrace it with his arms, place it before him in the water, and then mount astride *upon its back!* In a moment more he was out in the stream, and his buffalo swimming under him, or rather he seemed to be pushing it along, using his arms and legs as paddles to impel it forward!

The others, on reaching the water, acted in a pre-cisely similar manner, and the whole party were soon launched, and crossing the stream together.

. It was not until the foremost Mech had arrived at the bank close to where our travellers awaited them, *lifted his buffalo out of the water, and reshouldered it,* that the latter learned to their surprise that what they had taken for buffaloes were nothing more than the

4

inflated skins of these animals that were thus employed as rafts by the rude but ingenious natives of the district !

The same contrivance is used by the inhabitants of the Punjaub and other parts of India, where fords are few and bridges cannot be built. The buffaloes are skinned, with the legs, heads, and horns left on, to serve as handles and supports in managing them. They are then rendered air-tight and inflated, heads, legs, and all ; and in this way bear such a resemblance to the animals from which they have been taken, that even dogs are deceived, and often growl and bark at them. Of course the quantity of air is far more than sufficient to buoy up the weight of a man. Sometimes, when goods and other articles are to be carried across, several skins are attached together, and thus form an excellent raft.

This was done upon the spot, and at a moment's notice. The Mechs, although a half-savage people, are far from uncivil in their intercourse with strangers. A word from Ossaroo, accompanied by a few pipes of tobacco from the botanist, procured the desired raft of buffalo-skins ; and our party, in less than half-an-hour, were safely deposited upon the opposite bank, and allowed to continue their journey without the slightest molestation.

CHAPTER XIII.

THE TALLEST GRASS IN THE WORLD.

As our travellers proceeded up-stream, they were occasionally compelled to pass through tracts covered with a species of jungle-grass, called "Dab-grass," which not only reached above the heads of the tallest of the party, but would have done so had they been giants! Goliath or the Cyclops might have, either of them, stood on tiptoe in a field of this grass, without being able to look over its tops.

The botanist was curious enough to measure some stalks of this gigantic grass, and found them full fourteen feet in height, and as thick as a man's finger near the roots! Of course no animal, except a giraffe, could raise its head over the tops of such grass as this; but there are no giraffes in this part of the world—these long-necked creatures being confined to the Continent of Africa. Wild elephants, however, are found here; and the largest of them can hide himself in the midst of this tall sward, as easily as a mouse would in an English meadow.

But there are other animals that make their layer in the dab-grass. It is a favorite haunt both of the tiger and Indian lion; and it was not without feelings of fear

that our botanical travellers threaded their way amidst
its tall canelike culms.

You will be ready to admit, that the dab-grass is a
tall grass.   But it is far from being the tallest in the
world, or in the East Indies either.   What think you
of a grass nearly five times as tall?   And yet in that
same country such a grass exists.   Yes—there is a
species of "panic-grass," the *Panicum arborescens,*
which actually grows to the height of fifty feet, with a
culm not thicker than an ordinary goose-quill!   This
singular species is, however, a climbing plant, growing
up amidst the trees of the forest, supported by their
branches, and almost reaching to their tops.

This panic-grass you will, no doubt, fancy *must be
the tallest grass in the world.*   But no.   Prepare yourself to hear that there is still another kind, not only
taller than this, but one that grows to the prodigious
height of a hundred feet!

You will guess what sort I am about to name.   It
could be no other than the giant *bamboo.   That is the
tallest grass in the world.*

You know the bamboo as a "cane;" but for all that
it is a true grass, belonging to the natural order of *gra-
mineæ,* or grasses, the chief difference between it, and
many others of the same order, being its more gigantic
dimensions.

My young reader, I may safely assert, that in all the
vegetable kingdom there is no species or form so valuable to the human race as the "grasses."   Among all
civilized nations bread is reckoned as the food of
primary importance, so much so as to have obtained
the sobriquet of "the staff of life;" and nearly every

sort of bread is the production of a grass. Wheat, barley, oats, maize, and rice, are all grasses; and so, too, is the sugarcane—so valuable for its luxurious product. It would take up many pages of our little volume to enumerate the various species of *graminea*, that contribute to the necessities and luxuries of mankind; and other pages might be written about species equally available for the purposes of life, but which have not yet been brought into cultivation.

Of all kinds of grasses, however, none possesses greater interest than the bamboo. Although not the most useful as an article of food, this noble plant serves a greater number of purposes in the economy of human life, than perhaps any other vegetable in existence.

What the palm-tree of many species is to the natives of South America or tropical Africa, such is the bamboo to the inhabitants of Southern Asia and its islands. It is doubtful whether nature has conferred upon these people any greater boon than this noble plant, the light and graceful culms of which are applied by them to a multitude of useful purposes. Indeed so numerous are the uses made of the bamboo, that it would be an elaborate work even to make out a list of them. A few of the purposes to which it is applied will enable you to judge of the valuable nature of this princely grass.

The young shoots of some species are cut when tender, and eaten like asparagus. The full-grown stems, while green, form elegant cases, exhaling a perpetual moisture, and capable of transporting fresh flowers for hundreds of miles. When ripe and hard, they are converted into bows, arrows, and quivers, lance-shafts, the masts of vessels, walking-sticks, the poles of palanquins, the floors and supporters of bridges, and a variety of similar purposes.   In a growing state the strong kinds are formed into stockades, which are impenetrable to any thing but regular infantry or artillery.   By notching their sides the Malays make wonderfully light scaling ladders, which can be conveyed with facility, where heavier machines could not be transported.   Bruised and crushed in water, the leaves and stems form Chinese paper, the finer qualities of which are only improved by a mixture of raw cotton and by more careful pounding. The leaves of a small species are the material used by the Chinese for the lining of their tea-chests.   Cut into lengths, and the partitions knocked out, they form durable water-pipes, or by a little contrivance are made into cases for holding rolls of paper.   Slit into strips, they afford a most durable material for weaving into mats, baskets, window-blinds, and even the sails of boats ; and the larger and thicker truncheons are carved by the Chinese into beautiful ornaments.   For building purposes the bamboo is still more important.   In many parts of India the framework of the houses of the natives is chiefly composed of this material.   In the flooring, whole stems, four or five inches in diameter, are laid close to each other, and across these, laths of split bamboo, about an inch wide, are fastened down by filaments of rattan cane.   The sides of the houses are closed in by the bamboos opened and rendered flat by splitting or notching the circular joints on the outside, chipping away the corresponding divisions within, and laying it in the sun to dry, pressed down with weights. Whole bamboos often form the upright timbers, and the house is generally roofed in with a thatch of narrow split bamboos, six feet long, placed in regular layers, each reaching within two feet of the extremity of that beneath it, by which a treble covering is formed. Another and most ingenious roof is also formed by cutting large straight bamboos of sufficient length to reach from the ridge to the eaves, then splitting them exactly in two, knocking out the partitions, and arranging them in close order with the hollow or inner sides uppermost; after which a second layer, with the outer or concave sides up, is placed upon the other in such a manner that each of the convex pieces falls into the two contiguous concave pieces covering their edges, thus serving as gutters to carry off the rain that falls on the convex layer.

Such are a few of the uses of the bamboo, enumerated by an ingenious writer; and these are probably not more than one tenth of the purposes to which this valuable cane is applied by the natives of India.

The quickness with which the bamboo can be cut and fashioned to any purpose is not the least remark able of its properties. One of the most distinguished of English botanists (Hooker) relates that a complete *furnished* house of bamboo, containing chairs and a table, was erected by his six attendants in the space of one hour !

Of the bamboos there are many species—perhaps fifty in all—some of them natives of Africa and South America, but the greater number belonging to southern Asia, which is the true home of these gigantic grasses. The species differ in many respects from each other— some of them being thick and strong, while others are light, and slender, and elastic. In nothing do the different species vary more than in size.   They are found growing of all sizes, from the dwarf . bamboo, as slender as a wheat-stalk, and only two feet high, to the *Bambusa maxima*, as thick as a man's body, and towering to the height of a hundred feet !

CHAPTER XIV.

THE MAN-EATERS.

OSSAROO had lived all his life in a bamboo country, and was well acquainted with all its uses. · Hardly a vessel or implement that he could not manufacture of bamboo canes of some kind or another, and many a purpose besides he knew how to apply them to. Had he been obliged to cross a tract of country where there was no water, and required a large vessel, or " canteen," to carry a supply, he would have made it as follows. He would have taken two joints of bamboo, each a couple of feet long and six or seven inches in diameter. These he would have trimmed, so that one of the nodes between the hollow spaces would serve as a bottom for each. In the node, or partition, at the top, he would have pierced a small hole to admit the water, which hole could be closed by a stopper of the pith of a palm or some soft wood, easily procured in the tropical forests of India. In case he could not have found bamboos with joints sufficiently long for the purpose it would have mattered little. Two or more joints would have been taken for each jar, and the partitions between them broken through, so as to admit the water into the hollow spaces within. The pair of "jars" he would have then

4 *

bound together at a very acute angle—something after the form of the letter **V**—and then to carry them with ease he would have strapped the bamboos to his back, the apex of the angle downwards, and one of the ends just peeping over each shoulder. In this way he would have provided himself with a water-vessel that for strength and lightness—the two great essentials—would have been superior to anything that either tinker or cooper could construct.

As it happened that they were travelling through a district where there was water at the distance of every mile or two, this bamboo canteen was not needed. A single joint holding a quart was enough to give any of the party a drink whenever they required it.

Now had the Mechs not arrived opportunely with their rafts of inflated buffalo-skins, there can be no doubt that Ossaroo would have found some mode of crossing the stream. A proof that he could have done so occurred but a few hours after, when our travellers found themselves in a similar dilemma. This time it was the main river, whose course they were following, that lay in the way. A large bend had to be got over, else they would have been compelled to take a circuitous route of many miles, and by a path which the guide knew to be difficult on account of some marshes that intervened.

Ossaroo proposed fording the river, but how was that to be done? It would be a longer swim than the other, and there were no natives with their skin-rafts—at least none were in sight. But there grew close by a clump of noble bamboos, and the guide pointed to them.

" Oh ! you intend to make a raft of the canes ? " inquired the botanist.

" Yes, Sahib," replied the shikarree.

" It will take a long time, I fear ? "

" No fearee, Sahib ; half hour do."

Ossaroo was as good as his promise. In half-an-hour not only one raft, but three—that is, a raft for each—was constructed and ready to be launched. The construction of these was as simple as it was ingenious. Each consisted of four pieces of bamboo, lashed together crossways with strips of rattan, so as to form a square in the centre just large enough to admit the body of a man. Of course, the bamboos, being hollow within, and closed at both ends, had sufficient buoyancy to sustain a man's weight above water, and nothing more was wanted.

Each of the party having adjusted his burden upon his back, stepped within the square space, lifted the framework in his hands, walked boldly into the river, and was soon floating out upon its current. Ossaroo had given them instructions how to balance themselves so as to keep upright, and also how to paddle with both hands and feet: so that, after a good deal of plashing and spluttering, and laughing and shouting, all three arrived safely on the opposite bank. Of course, Fritz swam over without a raft.

As the river had to be re-crossed on the other arm of the bend, each carried his raft across the neck or isthmus, where a similar fording was made, that brought them once more on the path they were following. Thus every day—almost every hour—our travellers were astonished by some new feat of their hunter-guide, and some new purpose to which the noble bamboo could be applied.

Still another astonishment awaited them. Ossaroo had yet a feat in store, in the performance of which the bamboo was to play a conspicuous part; and it chanced that upon the very next day, an opportunity occurred by which the hunter was enabled to perform this feat to the great gratification not only of his travelling companions, but to the delight of a whole village of natives, who derived no little benefit from the performance.

I have already said, that there are many parts of India where the people live in great fear of the tigers—as well as lions, wild elephants, panthers, and rhinoceroses. These people have no knowledge of proper fire-arms. Some, indeed, carry the clumsy matchlock, which, of course, is of little or no service in hunting; and their bows, even with poisoned arrows, are but poor weapons when used in an encounter with these strong savage beasts.

Often a whole village is kept in a state of terror for weeks or months by a single tiger who may have made his lair in the neighborhood, and whose presence is known by his repeated forays upon the cows, buffaloes, or other domesticated animals of the villagers. It is only after this state of things has continued for a length of time, and much loss has been sustained, that these poor people, goaded to desperation, at length assemble together, and risk an encounter with the tawny tyrant. In such encounters human lives are frequently sacrificed, and generally some one of the party receives a blow or scratch from the tiger's paw, which maims or lames him for the rest of his days.

But there is still a worse case than even this. Not unfrequently the tiger, instead of preying upon their cattle, carries off one of the natives themselves; and where this occurs, the savage monster, if not pursued and killed, is certain to repeat the offence. It is strange, and true as strange, that a tiger having once fed upon human flesh, appears ever after to be fonder of it than of any other food, and will make the most daring attempts to procure it. Such tigers are not uncommon in India, where they are known among the natives by the dreaded name of *man-eaters!*

It is not a little curious that the Caffres and other natives of South Africa, apply the same term to individuals of the lion species, known to be imbued with a similar appetite.

It is difficult to conceive a more horrible monster than a lion or tiger of such tastes ; and in India, when the presence of such an one is discovered, the whole neighborhood lives in dread. Often when a British post is near, the natives make application to the officers to assist them in destroying the terrible creature—well knowing that our countrymen, with their superior courage, with their elephants and fine rifles, are more than a match for the jungle tyrant. When no such help is at hand, the shikarrees, or native hunters, usually assemble, and either take the tiger by stratagem, or risk their lives in a bold encounter. In many a tiger-hunt had Ossaroo distinguished himself, both by stratagem and prowess, and there was no mode of trapping or killing a tiger that was not known to him.

He was now called upon to give an exhibition of his craft, which, in point of ingenuity, was almost equal to the stratagem of the limed fig-leaves.

CHAPTER XV.

THE DEATH OF THE MAN-EATER.

THE path which our travellers were following led them into one of the native villages of the Teräi, which lay in a sequestered part of the forest.   The inhabitants of this village received them with acclamations of joy. Their approach had been reported before they reached the place, and a deputation of the villagers met them on the way, hailing them with joyful exclamations and gestures of welcome.

Karl and Caspar, ignorant of the native language, and, of course, not comprehending what was said, were for some time at a loss to understand the meaning of these demonstrations.   Ossaroo was appealed to to furnish an explanation.

"A man-eater," he said.

"A man-eater!"

"Yes, Sahib; a man-eater in the jungle."

This was not sufficiently explicit.   What did Ossaroo mean?   A man-eater in the jungle?   What sort of creature was that?   Neither Karl nor Caspar had ever heard of such a thing before.   They questioned Ossaroo.

The latter explained to them what was a man-eater.

It was a tiger so called, as you already know, on account of its preying upon human beings. This one had already killed and carried off a man, a woman, and two children, beside large numbers of domestic animals. For more than three months it had infested the village, and kept the inhabitants in a state of constant alarm. Indeed, several families had deserted the place solely through fear of this terrible tiger; and those that remained were in the habit, as soon as night came on, of shutting themselves up within their houses, without daring to stir out again till morning. In the instance of one of the children, even this precaution had not served, for the fierce tiger had broken through the frail wall of bamboos, and carried the child off before the eyes of its afflicted parents!

Several times the timid but incensed villagers had assembled and endeavored to destroy this terrible enemy. They had found him each time in his lair; but, on account of their poor weapons and slight skill as hunters, he had always been enabled to escape from them. Indeed on such occasions the tiger was sure to come off victorious, for it was in one of these hunts that the man had fallen a sacrifice. Others of the villagers had been wounded in the different conflicts with this pest of the jungle. With such a neighbor at their doors no wonder they had been living in a state of disquietude and terror.

But why their joy at the approach of our travellers?

This was proudly explained by Ossaroo, who of course had reason to be proud of the circumstance.

It appeared that the fame of the shikarree, as a great tiger-hunter, had preceded him, and his name was known even in the Teräi. The villagers had heard that he was approaching, accompanied by two Feringhees, (so Europeans are called by the natives of India,) and they hoped, by the aid of the noted shikarree and the Feringhee Sahibs, to get rid of the dreaded marauder.

Ossaroo, thus appealed to, at once gave his promise to aid them. Of course the botanist made no objection, and Caspar was delighted with the idea. They were to remain all night at the village, since nothing could be done before night. They might have got up a grand battue to beat the jungle and attack the tiger in his lair, but what would have come of that? Perhaps the loss of more lives. None of the villagers cared to risk themselves in such a hunt, and that was not the way that Ossaroo killed his tigers.

Karl and Caspar expected to see their companion once more try his stratagem of the birdlime and the leaves; and such at first was his intention. Upon inquiry, however, he found that no birdlime was to be had. The villagers did not know how to prepare it, and there were no fig-trees about the neighborhood, nor holly, nor trees of any other kind out of which it could properly be made.

What was Ossaroo to do under these circumstances? Must he abandon the idea of destroying the man-eater, and leave the helpless villagers to their fate? No. His hunter pride would not permit that. His name as a great shikarree was at stake. Besides, his humanity was touched—for, although but a poor Hindoo, he possessed the common feelings of our nature. Karl and Caspar, moreover, had taken an interest in the thing, and urged him to do his best, promising him all the assistance it was in their power to give.

It was resolved, therefore, that, cost what it might, the tiger should be destroyed.

Ossaroo had other resources besides the birdlime and the battue, and he at once set to work to prepare his plan. He had an ample stock of attendants, as the villagers worked eagerly and ran hither and thither obedient to his nod. In front of the village there was a piece of open ground. This was the scene of operations.

Ossaroo first commanded four large posts to be brought, and set in the ground in a quadrangle of about eight feet in length and width. These posts when sunk firmly in their place stood full eight feet in height, and each had a fork at the top. On these forks four strong beams were placed horizontally, and then firmly lashed with rawhide thongs. Deep trenches were next dug from post to post, and in these were planted rows of strong bamboos four inches apart from each other—the bamboos themselves being about four inches in thickness. The earth was then filled in, and trodden firmly, so as to render the uprights immovable. A tier of similar bamboos was next laid horizontally upon the top, the ends of which, interlocking with those that stood upright, held the latter in their places. Both were securely lashed to the frame timbers—that had been notched for the purpose—and to one another, and then the structure was complete. It resembled an immense cage with smooth yellow rods, each four inches in diameter. The door alone was wanting, but it was not desirable to have a door. Although it was intended for a " trap cage," the " bird " for which it had been constructed was not to be admitted to the inside.

Ossaroo now called upon the villagers to provide him with a goat that had lately had kids, and whose young were still living. This was easily procured. Still another article he required, but both it and the goat had been "bespoke" at an earlier hour of the day, and were waiting his orders. This last was the skin of a buffalo, such a one as we have already seen used by these people in crossing their rivers.

When all these things had been got ready it was near night, and no time was lost in waiting. With the help of the villagers Ossaroo was speedily arrayed in the skin of the buffalo, his arms and limbs taking the place of the animal's legs, with the head and horns drawn over him like a hood, so that his eyes were opposite the holes in the skin.

Thus metamorphosed, Ossaroo entered the bamboo cage, taking the goat along with him. The stake, that had been kept out for the purpose of admitting them within the enclosure, was now set into its place as firmly as the others; and this done, the villagers, with Karl and Caspar, retired to their houses, and left the shikarree and his goat to themselves.

A stranger passing the spot would have had no other thoughts than that the cage-like enclosure contained a buffalo and a goat. On closer examination it might have been perceived that this buffalo held, grasped firmly in its fore-hoofs, a strong bamboo spear; and that was all that appeared odd about it—for it was lying down like any other buffalo, with the goat standing beside it.

The sun had set, and night was now on. The villagers had put out their lights, and, shut up within their houses, were waiting in breathless expectation. Ossaroo on his part, was equally anxious—not from the fear of any danger, for he had secured himself against that. He was only anxious for the approach of the man-eater, in order that he might have the opportunity to exhibit the triumph of his hunter-skill.

He was not likely to be disappointed. The villagers had assured him that the fierce brute was in the habit of paying them a nightly visit, and prowling around the place for hours together. It was only when he had succeeded in carrying off some of their cattle that he would be absent for days—no doubt his hunger being for the time satiated; but as he had not lately made a capture, they looked for a visit from him on that very night.

If the tiger should come near the village, Ossaroo had no fear that he could attract him to the spot. He had laid his decoy too well to fail in this. The goat, deprived of her young, kept up an incessant bleating, and the kids answered her from one of the houses of the village. As the hunter knew from experience that the tiger has a particular relish for goat-venison, he had no fear but that the voice of the animal would attract him to the spot, provided he came near enough to hear it. In this the villagers assured him he would not be disappointed.

He *was not disappointed;* neither was he kept long in suspense. He had not been more than half-an-hour in his buffalo disguise, before a loud growling on the edge of the forest announced the approach of the dreaded man-eater, and caused the goat to spring wildly about in the enclosure, uttering at intervals the most piercing cries.

This was just what Ossaroo wanted. The tiger, hearing the voice of the goat, needed no further invitation; but in a few moments was seen trotting boldly up to the spot. There was no crouching on the part of the terrible brute. He had been too long master there to fear anything he might encounter, and he stood in need of a supper. The goat that he had heard would be just the dish he should relish; and he had determined on laying his claws upon her without more ado. In another moment he stood within ten feet of the cage!

The odd-looking structure puzzled him, and he halted to survey it. Fortunately there was a moon, and the light not only enabled the tiger to see what the cage contained, but it also gave Ossaroo an opportunity of watching all his movements.

"Of course," thought the tiger, "it's an enclosure some of these simple villagers have put up to keep that goat and buffalo from straying off into the woods; likely enough, too, to keep me from getting at them. Well, they appear to have been very particular about the building of it. We shall see if they have made the walls strong enough."

With these reflections he drew near, and rearing upward caught one of the bamboos in his huge paw, and shook it with violence. The cane, strong as a bar of iron, refused to yield even to the strength of a tiger; and, on finding this, the fierce brute ran rapidly round the enclosure, trying it at various places, and searching for an entrance.

There was no entrance, however; and on perceiving that there was none, the tiger endeavored to get at the goat by inserting his paws between the bamboos. The

goat, however, ran frightened and screaming to the opposite side, and so kept out of the way. It would have
served the tiger equally well to have laid his claws upon
the buffalo, but this animal very prudently remained
near the centre of the enclosure, and did not appear
to be so badly scared withal. No doubt the coolness
of the buffalo somewhat astonished the tiger, but in
his endeavors to capture the goat, he did not stop to
show his surprise, but ran round and round, now dashing forcibly against the bamboos, and now reaching
his paws between them as far as his fore-legs would
stretch.

All at once the buffalo was seen to rush towards him,
and the tiger was in great hopes of being able to reach
the latter with his claws, when, to his astonishment, he
felt some hard instrument strike sharply against his
snout, and rattle upon his teeth, while the fire flew from
his eyes at the concussion. Of course it was the *horn*
of the buffalo that had done this; and now, rendered
furious by the pain, the tiger forgot all about the goat,
and turned his attention towards revenging himself upon
the animal who had wounded him. Several times he
launched himself savagely against the bamboos, but the
canes resisted all his strength. Just then it occurred to
him that he might effect an entrance by the top, and
with one bound he sprang upon the roof of the enclosure.
This was just what the buffalo wished, and the broad
white belly of his assailant stretched along the open
framework of bamboos, was now a fair mark for that
terrible horn. Like a gleam of lightning it entered between his ribs; the red blood spouted forth, the huge
man-eater screamed fiercely as he felt the deadly stab,

and then, struggling for a few minutes, his enormous body lay stretched across the rack silent,—motionless,— dead !

A signal whistle from Ossaroo soon brought the villagers upon the spot. The shikarree and the goat were set free. The carcass of the man-eater was dragged into the middle of the village amidst shouts of triumph, and the rest of the night was devoted to feasting and rejoicing. The "freedom of the city" was offered to Ossaroo and his companions, and every hospitality lavished upon them that the grateful inhabitants knew how to bestow.

CHAPTER XVI.

KARL'S ADVENTURE WITH THE LONG-LIPPED BEAR.

NEXT morning they were *en route* at an early hour; and having passed through some cultivated fields, they once more entered the wild primeval forest which covers most of the hills and valleys of the Teräi.

Their road during the whole day was a series of ascents and descents, now running along the bed of a stream; now upon its high bank, anon over some projecting ridge, and at intervals crossing the stream, sometimes by fording, and once or twice by natural bridges formed by the long trailing roots of various species of fig-trees.

Although they were gradually ascending to a higher elevation, the vegetation was still of a tropical character. Pothos plants, and broad-leaved arums, bamboos, wild plantains, and palms, were seen all along the way, while lovely orchidaceous flowers,—epiphytes and trailing plants,—hung down from the trunks and branches of the great trees, forming festoons and natural trellis-work, that stretched across the path and almost closed it up.

That was a busy day for the botanical collector. Many rare species were found in seed, and he gathered a load for all three, to be carried on to their halting place, and stored until their return from the mountains. Those species that were yet only in flower he noted down in his memorandum-book. They would be ripe for him on his way back.

About noon they halted to refresh themselves. The spot they had chosen was in a grove of purple magnolias, whose splendid flowers were in full bloom, and scented the air around with their sweet perfume. A crystal stream,—a mere rivulet,—trickled in its deep bed through the midst of the grove, and the movement of its waters seemed to produce a refreshing coolness in the surrounding atmosphere.

They had just unbuckled their packs, intending to lunch, and remain an hour or so on the ground, when some animal was heard moving among the bushes on the other side of the rivulet.

Caspar and Ossaroo, ever ready for the chase, immediately seized their weapons; and, crossing the stream, went in search of the animal, which they supposed would turn out to be a deer. Karl, therefore, was left by himself.

Now Karl felt very much jaded. He had worked hard in gathering his seeds, and nuts, and drupes, and berries, and pericarps, and he felt quite done up, and had some thoughts of remaining upon that spot for the night. Before giving up, however, he determined to try a refreshing medicine, which he had brought with him, and in which he had been taught to have great faith. This medicine was nothing more than a bottle of hot peppers pickled in vinegar, which Karl had been told by a friend was one of the finest remedies for fatigue that could be found in the world,—in fact, the sovereign

cure,—far excelling rum or brandy, or even the potent spirit of his native land, the kirschen-wasser. A drop or two of it mixed with a cup of water would impart instantaneous relief to the weary traveller, and enable him to continue his journey like a new man. So Karl's friend had told him, and he was now determined to give the pickled peppers a trial.

Taking the bottle in one hand, and his tin drinking-cup in the other, he descended to the bed of the rivulet to fill the cup with water.

The little stream ran in a deep cut or gully, and its bed was not more than a yard or two in width, but it was nearly empty—so that Karl as soon as he had clambered down the steep sloping bank, found dry footing among the pebbles.

He was just in the act of stooping to fill his cup, when he heard the voices of Caspar and Ossaroo farther up the stream, as if they were in pursuit of some animal. Presently a shot rang through the woods. Of course it was Caspar's gun, for Caspar was heard shouting in the direction whence the shot came.

Karl had raised himself erect, and was thinking, whether he could give any help to the hunters, by intercepting the animal if it came his way. He heard the voice of Caspar crying to him to "look out," and just at the moment he did "look out," and saw coming right down upon him a large animal covered with black shaggy hair, and a white patch upon its breast. At the first glance it had the look of a bear, but Karl noticed a hunch upon its back, which gave it a very peculiar appearance, and rendered him doubtful as to what sort of beast it was. He had no time to examine it very

5

minutely—although it was close enough, for when he
first set eyes upon it, it was within six paces of where
he stood. It was altogether too close to him, Karl
thought; and so far from endeavoring to intercept it,
he tried with all his might to get out of its way.

His first impulse was to rush up the bank. He saw
that the bear, or whatever it was, was resolved to keep
right on; and the only way to avoid an encounter
would be to leave the channel free. He therefore
made a dash at the bank, and tried to clamber out.
The clayey slope, however, chanced to be wet and
slippery, and before Karl could reach the top his feet
flew from under him, and he came back to the bottom
faster than he had gone up.

He now found himself face to face with the bear—
for it *was* a bear—and not six feet separated them
from each other. Neither could pass the other in the
narrow channel, and Karl knew that by turning down
he would soon be overtaken, and perhaps hugged to
death. He had no weapon—nothing in his hand but
the bottle of red peppers—what could he do?

There was not a moment left for reflection. The
bear reared upward with a savage growl, and rushed
forward to the attack. He had almost got his claws
upon the plant-hunter, when the latter mechanically
struck forward with the bottle, and, as good luck
guided it, hit his assailant fair upon the snout. A loud
smash, and the rattling of glass among the pebbles,
announced the fate of the bottle, and the red peppers,
vinegar, and all, went streaming about the head of the
bear.

The brute uttered a scream of terror—such as bears

will do when badly frightened—and, wheeling away from the conflict, headed up the sloping bank. He succeeded in his climbing better than Karl had done; for, in the twinkling of an eye, he had reached the top of the slope, and in the twinkling of another eye would have disappeared among the bushes, had not Caspar at this moment arrived upon the ground, and with his second barrel brought him rolling back into the channel.

The bear fell dead almost at Karl's feet, and the latter stepped forward to examine the carcass. What was his astonishment on perceiving that what he had taken for a hunch on the bear's back was a brace of young cubs, that had now rolled off, and were running round the body of their dam, whining, and snarling, and snapping like a pair of vixens! But Fritz at this moment rushed forward, and, after a short fierce struggle, put an end to their lively demonstrations.

Caspar now related that when he and Ossaroo first came in sight of the bear the cubs were upon the ground playing; but the moment he fired the first shot—which had not hit the old bear withal—she seized the cubs one after the other in her mouth, flung them upon her shoulders, and then made off!

The animal that had fallen before the bullet of Caspar's gun was the "long-lipped," or sloth-bear (*Ursus labiatus*). The first name has been given to this species on account of the capability it possesses of protruding the cartilage of its nose and its lips far in advance of its teeth, and by this means seizing its food. It is called "sloth" bear, because when first known it was supposed to belong to the sloths; and its long shaggy hair, its rounded back, and the apparently unwieldly and deformed contour of its whole body, gave some color to the idea. These marks of ugliness, combined with its sagacity—which enables the Indian jugglers to train it .to a variety of tricks—render this species of bear a favorite with them, and on this account it is also known by the name of the "Ours de jongleurs," or "Jugglers' bear."

The sloth-bear is long-haired and shaggy, of a deep black color, except under the throat, where there is a white mark shaped like the letter Y. It is nearly as large as the black bear of America, and its habits in a state of nature are very similar to this species. It will not attack man unless closely pressed or wounded; and had Karl been able to get out of her way, the old she would not have followed him, savage as she was from being shot at by Caspar.

No doubt the "pickle" had helped him out of a worse pickle. The peppery vinegar getting into the eyes of the bear quite confounded her, and caused her to turn tail. But for that Karl might have undergone a hug and a sharp scratch or two, and he might well be thankful—as he was—that he had escaped with no more serious damage than the loss of his precious peppers.

CHAPTER XVII.

OSSAROO IN TROUBLE.

FRITZ had scarce finished his battle with the young bears, with Karl and Caspar standing over him, when a loud shouting drew the attention of all to another quarter. The shouting evidently proceeded from Ossaroo, as the boys could distinguish his voice. The shikarree was in trouble—as they could easily understand by his shrill continued screams—and the words " Help! Sahibs, help !" which he repeatedly uttered.

What could be the matter with Ossaroo? Had another bear attacked him? Maybe a panther, or a lion, or a tiger? No matter what it was, both Karl and Caspar felt it to be their duty to hasten to his assistance ; and without more ado both of them started off in the direction whence came the shouts. Karl had got possession of his rifle, and Caspar hastily rammed a load into the right-hand barrel, so that both were in readiness to offer good help to the guide, if it should turn out to be a wild beast that was his assailant.

In a few moments, they came in sight of Ossaroo ; and, to their great relief, saw that no animal was near him. Neither bear nor panther, nor lion nor tiger, appeared upon the spot   Ossaroo, however still continued his noisy cries for help; and, to the astonishment of the boys, they saw him dancing about over the ground, now stooping his head downwards, now leaping up several feet, his arms all the while playing about, and striking out as if at some imaginary enemy!

What could it all mean? Had Ossaroo gone mad? Or had he become suddenly afflicted with the malady of St. Vitus? His movements were altogether of a comical nature; no mountebank could have danced about with more agility; and, but for the earnestness of his cries, evidently forced from him by fear, both Karl and Caspar would have burst out into a fit of laughter. They saw, however, that the shikarree was in some danger--from what, they could not tell; but they very naturally suspected that he had been attacked by a venomous serpent, and, perhaps, already bitten by it. It might still be attacking him, *perhaps under his clothes*, and that was why they could not perceive it.

This idea restrained them from laughter, for, if their conjecture proved correct, it would be no laughing matter for poor Ossaroo; and, with fear in their hearts, both the boys rushed forward to the spot.

On getting nearer, however, the odd behavior of the shikarree was explained, and the enemy with which he was contending, and which had hitherto remained invisible, came under their view. Around the head of Ossaroo there appeared a sort of misty halo, encircling him like a glory; which, on closer view, the boys perceived was neither more nor less than a *swarm of bees!*

The whole matter was cleared up. Ossaroo had

been assailed by bees; and it was they that were making him dance and fling his arms about in so wild a
manner!

Karl and Caspar had forborne to laugh, so long as
they believed their guide to be in real danger; but
now that they saw what it was, they could no more
restrain their mirth, and both simultaneously broke out
into a fit of cachinnation, that caused the woods to ring
again.

. On seeing how his young companions sympathized
with his distress, Ossaroo was by no means pleased.
The stings of the bees had nettled the Hindoo's temper, and the laughter of the boys exasperated him
still more. He resolved, therefore, that they should
both have a taste of the same trouble; and, without
saying another word, he rushed between the two; of
course, carrying the swarm of bees along with him.

This unexpected manœuvre on the part of the guide,
at once put an end to the merriment of his companions; and the next moment, instead of enjoying a laugh
at Ossaroo's expense, both of themselves exhibited a
spectacle equally ludicrous. The bees, on perceiving
these new enemies, at once separated into three distinct
swarms, each swarm selecting its victim; so that not
only Ossaroo, but Karl and Caspar as well, now danced
over the ground like acrobats. Even Fritz was attacked by a few—enough to make him scamper around,
and snap at his own legs as if he had suddenly gone
mad!

Karl and Caspar soon learned, that what had so
lately amused them was by no means· a thing to be
amused at. They were stung about the face, and found

the stings to be exceedingly virulent and painful. Besides, the number of their assailants rendered the affair
one of considerable danger. They began to feel that
there was peril as well as pain.

Where was it to end? All their demonstrations
failed to drive off the bees. Run where they would,
the enraged insects followed them, buzzing about their
ears, and alighting whenever an opportunity offered.
Where was it to end?

It was difficult to tell when and how the scene
would have been brought to a termination, had it not
been for Ossaroo himself. The cunning Hindoo had
bethought him of a plan, and, calling to the others to
follow him, was seen to run forward in a direct line
through the woods.

Karl and Caspar started after, in hopes of finding
relief from their tormentors.

In a few minutes, Ossaroo approached the bank of
the stream, at a place where it was dammed up, and
formed a reach of deep water—a pool. Without hesitating a moment, the Hindoo plunged into the water.
The boys, flinging down their guns, imitated his example; and all three stood side by side, neck-deep in the
pool. They now commenced ducking their heads under, and continued this, at intervals; until at length the
bees, finding themselves in danger of being drowned,
gave up the attack, and, one after another, winged their
way back into the woods.

After remaining long enough in the pool, to make
sure that their enemies had gone quite away, the three
smarting hunters climbed out, and stood dripping upon
the bank. They would have laughed at the whole

adventure, but the pain of the stings put them out of all humor for enjoying a joke; and, out of sorts altogether, they quietly wended their way back to the place of their temporary encampment.

On their way, Ossaroo explained how he had chanced to provoke the attack of the bees. On hearing the report of Caspar's gun, and the noise of the conflict between Fritz and the bears, he had started in great haste to get up to the spot, and give assistance. In running forward, he scarce looked before him; and was dashing recklessly through among trees, when his head came in contact with a large bees' nest, which was suspended upon a vine that stretched across the path. The nest was constructed out of agglutinated mud, and attached only slightly to the vine; and Ossaroo, having become entangled in the latter, shook it so violently that the nest fell down, broke into pieces, and set the whole swarm of angry bees about his ears. It was just then that he had been heard crying out, and that Karl and Caspar had run to his rescue; which act both of them now said they very much regretted. They were hardly in earnest, however; and Ossaroo, having procured an herb from the woods, the sap of which soon alleviated the pain of the stings, in a short time the tempers of all three were restored to their usual equanimity.

5 *

.

CHAPTER XVIII.

THE AXIS AND PANTHER.

THE maternal solicitude displayed by the bear in endeavoring to carry her young out of danger, had quite won the admiration of the plant-hunters; and now that the excitement of the conflict was over, they experienced some pangs of regret at having killed the creature. But the thing was done, and could not be helped. Besides, as Ossaroo informed them, these bears are esteemed a great nuisance in the country. Descending from their mountain retreats, or issuing out of the jungle during the season of the crops, they commit very destructive depredations upon the produce of the farmer, often entering his very garden without fear, and in a single night laying waste the contents of a whole enclosure. On hearing this, both Karl and Caspar were more contented with what they had done. Perhaps, reflected they, had these two cubs lived to grow up, they or their mother might have devastated the paddy-field of some poor jemindar, or farmer, and he and his family might have been put to great distress by it.

Whether or not their reasoning was correct, it satisfied the two boys, and quieted their consciences about the killing of the bears. But as they continued their journey, they still conversed of the curious circumstance of the old one carrying off her cubs in the manner she was doing. Karl had read of such a habit in animals —which is common to many other sorts along with the bears—such as the great ant-eater of South America, the opossum, and most kinds of monkeys. Both agreed that it was a pretty trait in the character of the lower animals, and proved even the most savage of them capable of tender affection.

It chanced that upon that same day they had another illustration of this very nature, and one that by good fortune did not have so tragical an ending.

They had finished their day's journey, and were reclining under a great *talauma* tree—a species of magnolia, with very large leaves—by the edge of a little glade. They had not yet made any preparations for their camp. The day's march had been a severe one, for they were now among the foot-hills of the great Himalaya chain ; and though they appeared to travel as much down hill as up they were in reality ascending, and by evening they were really more than five thousand feet above the plains of India. They had arrived in a new zone of vegetation, among the great forests of magnolias which gird the middle parts of the mountains. It is in this part of the world that the remarkable genus of magnolia is found in its greatest vigor and variety ; and many species of these trees, in forests of vast extent, cover and adorn the declivities of the lower Himalayas. There are the white-flowered magnolias, at an elevation of from four thousand to eight thousand feet, which are then replaced by the still more gorgeous purple magnolia (*Magnolia Campbellia*)—the latter being the most superb species known, its brilliant corollas often arraying the sloping sides of the hills as with a robe of purple. Here, too, our travellers observed chestnut-trees of rare species, and several kinds of oak —laurels also, not in the form of humble shrubs, but rising as tall trees, with straight smooth boles, to the height of the oaks themselves. Maples, too, were seen mingling in the forest, and the tree rhododendrons growing forty feet high !

What appeared singular to the eyes of the botanist, was the mingling of many European forms of plants among those of a strictly tropical character. For instance, there were birches, willows, alders, and walnut-trees, growing side by side with the wild plantain, the Wallich palm, and gigantic bamboos ; while the great *Cedrela Toona*, figs of several species, *melastomas,* balsams, *pothos* plants, peppers, and gigantic climbing vines and orchids, were intermixed with speedwell, common bramble, forget-me-not, and stinging-nettles, just such. as might have been met with in a European field! Tree ferns were seen rising up and towering high above the common brake-fern of the English moors ; while the wild strawberry of Britain was seen covering the ground in patches of large extent. Its fruit, however, in the Himalayas is quite insipid, but a fine yellow raspberry—one of the most luscious fruits met with in these mountains—was found growing in the same districts, as if to compensate for the absence of flavor in the strawberry.

Under one of these magnificent magnolias, whose large wax-like corollas filled the air with their odorous perfume, our travellers had just stretched themselves—

intending, after a few minutes of rest, to make the necessary arrangements for passing the night there.

Ossaroo was chewing his betel-nut, and Karl and Caspar, both very tired, were doing nothing and saying as little. Fritz, too, lay along the ground, with his tongue out, and panting after the hot day's rambling among the bushes.

Just at that moment, Caspar, whose sharp hunter eye was always on the alert, caught Karl by the sleeve, and in a hurried whisper, said,—

"See, Karl! see!—Isn't it a beauty?"

As Caspar said this, he pointed to an animal that had just come out of the jungle, and stood within a few feet of its edge. The creature in question had the shape, size, and general appearance of a fallow-deer, and its slender limbs and well proportioned body bespoke it to be a near kin to that animal. In color, however, it essentially differed from the fallow-deer. Its ground color was much the same, but it was spotted all over with snow-white spots that gave it a very beautiful appearance. It looked somewhat like the young of the fallow-deer, and might have been taken for an overgrown fawn. Karl, however, knew what it was.

"A spotted deer," he replied, also in a whisper. "It is the *axis*. Hold back Fritz, and let us watch it a moment."

Karl had guessed correctly what kind of animal it was. It was the axis, one of the best known of the Indian deer, and closely allied to the *Rusa* group of Asia as well as to the fallow-deer of Europe. There are several species of the axis in eastern Asia, more or less marked with spots, and in no part are they more

common than in the country through which the plant-
hunters were passing—the country of the Ganges and
the Burrampooter.

Caspar caught Fritz as desired, and held him fast ;
and the travellers, without making any noise, sat watching the movements of the axis.

To their surprise, another axis now showed itself
upon the ground, but this one was of such small dimensions that they saw at once it was the young of the
first.   It was a tiny little fawn, but a few days old, and
speckled all over with similar snow-white spots.

The deer, unconscious of the presence of the travellers, walked several paces out upon the meadow, and
commenced browsing upon the grass.   The little fawn
knew not, as yet, how to eat grass ; and occupied itself
by skipping and playing about its mother, like a kid.

The hunters, all speaking in whispers, now counselled
among themselves as to what they should do.   Ossaroo
would have liked a bit of venison for supper, and, certainly, the fawn was a tempting *morceau.*   Caspar voted
to kill ; but Karl, of gentler nature, opposed this design.

" A pity ! " he said.   " Look, brother, how gentle
they appear ?   Remember how we felt after killing the
savage bear, and this would be far worse."

While engaged in this undertone discussion, a new
party made his appearance upon the scene, which drove
all thoughts of killing the deer out of the minds both of
Caspar and Ossaroo.

This intruder was an animal quite as large as the
axis, but of an entirely different form.   Its ground-
colour was not unlike that of the deer, with a deeper

tinge of yellow, and it, too, was spotted all over the body. Herein, however, a striking contrast existed between the two. As already stated, the spots upon the axis were snow-white; while those upon the new comer were just the reverse—black as jet. Spots they could hardly be termed, though, at a distance, they presented that appearance. When closely viewed, however, it would have been seen that they were rather rosettes, or rings; the centre part being of the same yellowish ground-color as the rest of the body.

The animal had a stout, low body; short, but strong limbs; a long, tapering tail, and a cat-like head. The last is not to be wondered at, since it was in reality a cat. It was the *panther*.

The attention of the hunters was at once taken away from the axis, and became fixed on the great spotted cat, which all three knew to be a panther; next to the lion and tiger, the most formidable of Asiatic *felidæ*.

All knew that the Indian panther often attacks man; and it was, therefore, with no very comfortable feelings that they hailed his appearance. The boys grasped their guns more firmly, and Ossaroo his bow, ready to give the panther the volley, should he approach within range.

The latter, however, had no design of molesting the travellers. He was unaware of their presence. His whole attention was occupied with the axis; upon whose ribs, or, perhaps, those of the fawn, he intended to make his supper.

With crouching gait and silent tread he approached his intended victims, stealing along the edge of the jungle. In a few seconds, he was near enough to spring, and, as yet, the poor doe browsed unconsciously. He was just setting his paws for the leap, and, in all probability, would have pounced next moment upon the back of the deer, but, just in the nick of time, Caspar chanced to sneeze. It was not done designedly, or with any intention of warning the deer; for all three of the hunters were so absorbed in watching the manœuvres of the panther, that they never thought of such a thing. Perhaps the powerful odor of the magnolia blossoms had been the cause; but, whether or no, Caspar sneezed.

That sneeze was a good thing. It saved the tender mother and her gentle fawn from the fangs of the ferocious panther. She heard it, and, raising her head on the instant, glanced round. The crouching cat came under her eyes; and, without losing a second of time, she sprang up to the fawn, seized the astonished little creature in her mouth, and, bounding like an arrow across the glade, was soon out of sight, having disappeared into the jungle on the opposite side!

The panther, who had either not heard or not regarded the sneeze, sprang out, as he had intended, but missed his aim. He ran a few stretches, rose into the air, and, a second time, came down without touching the deer; and then, seeing that the latter had sped beyond his reach, according to the usual habit of all the *felidæ*, he desisted from farther pursuit. Trotting back whence he had come, he entered the jungle before the hunters could get within shooting distance of him, and was never more seen by any of the three.

As they returned to camp, Karl congratulated Caspar for having sneezed so opportunely; though Caspar acknowledged that it was quite accidental, and that, for his part, he would rather he had not sneezed at all, and that he had either got a shot at the panther, or had a bit of the fawn for his supper.

CHAPTER XIX.

THE PESTS OF THE TROPICS.

MUCH has been said and written in praise of the bright sun and the blue skies of tropical countries; and travellers have dilated largely upon the magnificent fruits, flowers, and foliage of tropical forests. One who has never visited these southern climes is disposed to indulge in very fanciful dreams of enjoyment there. Life would seem to be luxurious; every scene appears to be *couleur de rose*.

But Nature has not designed that any portion of her territory should be favored beyond the rest to such an extreme degree; and, perhaps, if a just comparison were instituted, it would be found that the Esquimaux, shivering in his hut of snow, enjoys as much personal happiness as the swarth southerner, who swings in his hammock under the shade of a banyan or a palm-tree.

The clime of the torrid zone, with its luxuriant vegetation, is also prolific of insect and reptile life; and, from this very circumstance, the denizen of a hot country is often subject to a greater amount of personal discomfort than the dweller in the Arctic zone. Even the scarcity of vegetable food, and the bitter, biting frost, are far easier to endure than the plague of tipulary insects and reptiles, which swarm between Cancer and Capricorn.

It is a well-known fact, that there are large districts in tropical America where human life is scarce endurable, on account of the mosquitos, gnats, ants, and other insects.

Thus writes the great Prussian geognosist :—

" Persons who have not navigated the rivers of equinoctial America can scarcely conceive how, at every instant, without intermission, you may be tormented by insects flying in the air, and how the multitudes of these little animals may render vast regions almost uninhabitable. Whatever fortitude be exercised to endure pain without complaint, whatever interest may be felt in the objects of scientific research, it is impossible not to be constantly disturbed by the mosquitos, zancudos, jejens, and tempraneros, that cover the face and hands, pierce the clothes with their long, needle-formed suckers ; and, getting into the mouth and nostrils, occasion coughing and sneezing, whenever any attempt is made to speak in the open air.

" In the missions of the Orinoco, in the villages on the banks of the river, surrounded by immense forests, the *plaga de las moscas,* or plague of the mosquitos, affords an inexhaustible subject of conversation. When two persons meet in the morning, the first questions they address to each other are : ' How did you find the zancudos during the night?' ' How are we to-day for the mosquitos?'

" An atmosphere filled with venomous insects always appears to be more heated than it is in reality. We were horribly tormented in the day by mosquitos and the jejen (a small venomous fly), and at night by the zancudos, a large species of gnat, dreaded even by the natives.

"At different hours of the day you are stung by different species. Every time that the scene changes, and, to use the simple expression of the missionaries, other insects 'mount guard,' you have a few minutes— often a quarter of an hour, of repose. The insects that disappear have not their places instantly supplied by their successors. From half-past six in the morning till five in the afternoon the air is filled with mosquitos. An hour before sunset a species of small gnats—called tempraneros, because they appear also at sunrise—take the place of the mosquitos. Their presence scarcely lasts an hour and a half. They disappear between six and seven in the evening. After a few minutes' repose, you feel yourself stung by zancudos, another species of gnat, with very long legs. The zancudo, the proboscis of which contains a sharp-pointed sucker, causes the most acute pain, and a swelling that remains several weeks.

"The means that are employed to escape from these little plagues are very extraordinary. At Maypures the Indians quit the village at night to go and sleep on the little islets in the midst of the cataracts. There they enjoy some rest, the mosquitos appearing to shun air loaded with vapors.

"Between the little harbor of Higuerote and the mouth of the Rio Unare the wretched inhabitants are accustomed to stretch themselves on the ground, and pass the night buried in the sand three or four inches deep, leaving out the head only, which they cover with a handkerchief.

"At Mandanaca we found an old missionary, who told us with an air of sadness that he had had his 'twenty years of mosquitos' in America. He desired us to look at his legs, that we might be able to tell one day beyond sea 'what the poor monks suffer in the forests of Cassiquiare.' Every sting leaving a small darkish brown spot, his legs were so speckled that it was difficult to recognize the whiteness of his skin, through the spots of coagulated blood!"

Just such torments as the great Prussian traveller suffered from insects in the forests of South America, our plant-hunters had to endure while passing through the humid woods of the Lower Himalayas. By night and by day the air seemed filled with insects, in countless swarms,—large and small moths, cockchafers, glow-flies, cockroaches, winged ants, may-flies, flying earwigs, beetles, and "daddy long-legs." They experienced the bite of ants or the stings of mosquitos every moment, or they were attacked by large ticks, a species of which infests the bamboo, and which is one of the most hateful of insects. These the traveller cannot avoid coming in contact with while brushing through the forest. They get inside his dress, often in great numbers, and insert their proboscis deeply, but without pain. Buried head and shoulders, and retained by its barbed lancet, this tick can only be extracted with great force, and the operation is exceedingly painful.

But of the tortures to which they were subjected by insects and reptiles, there was one more disagreeable and disgusting than all the rest, and on their first experience of it the three were quite horrified.

It happened to them on the very day after their ad-venture with the bear and the bees. They had walked several miles for their morning stage, and the sun hav-ing grown quite hot, they agreed to rest for some hours till afternoon. Having thrown off their packs and ac-coutrements, all three lay down upon the grass close by the edge of a little stream, and under the shadow of a spreading tree. The fatigue of the walk, combined with the heated atmosphere, had rendered them drowsy, and one and all of them fell fast asleep.

Caspar was the first to awake. He did not feel quite comfortable during his sleep. The mosquitos or some other kind of insects appeared to be biting him, and this had prevented him from sleeping soundly. He awoke at length and sat upright. The others were still asleep close by, and the eyes of Caspar by chance rested upon Ossaroo, whose body was more than half naked, the slight cotton tunic having fallen aside and exposed his breast to view; besides, his legs were bare, as the shikarree had rolled up his trousers on account of the damp grass they had been passing through. What was the astonishment of Caspar at perceiving the naked part of Ossaroo's body mottled with spots of dark and red—the latter being evidently blotches of blood! Caspar perceived that some of the dark spots were in motion, now lengthening out, and then closing up again into a smaller compass; and it was only after he had drawn closer, and examined these objects more minutely that he was able to determine what they were. They were *leeches! Ossaroo was covered with leeches!*

Caspar uttered a cry that awoke both of his com-panions on the instant.

Ossaroo was not a little disgusted with the fix he found himself in, but Karl and Caspar did not waste much time in condoling with him, for upon examination they found that they themselves had fared no better, both of them being literally covered with the same bloodthirsty reptiles.

A scene now ensued that would not be easy to de- scribe. All three pulled off their garments, and went to work to extract the leeches with their fingers—for there was no other mode of getting rid of the trouble- some intruders—and after a full half-hour spent in picking one another clean, they rapidly dressed again, and took the route, desirous of getting away from that spot as quickly as possible.

Of all the pests of warm Oriental climates, there are none so troublesome to the traveller, or so disgusting, as these land-leeches. They infest the humid woods on the slopes of the Himalaya Mountains from about two thousand to eleven thousand feet of elevation; but they are not confined to the Himalayas alone, as they are common in the mountain forests of Ceylon, Sumatra, and other parts of the Indies. There are many species of them—and even upon the Himalayas more than one kind—the small black species swarming above the ele- vation of three thousand feet, while a large yellow kind, more solitary, is found farther down. They are not only troublesome and annoying, but dangerous. They often crawl into the fauces, noses, and stomachs of human beings, where they produce dreadful sufferings and even death. Cattle are subject to their attacks; and hundreds perish in this way—the cause of their death not being always understood, and usually attrib- uted to some species of vermin.

It is almost impossible to keep them off the person while travelling through a track of woods infested by them. If the traveller only sit down for a moment, they crawl upon him without being perceived. They are exceedingly active, and move with surprising rapidity. Indeed, some fancy they have the power to spring from the ground. Certain it is that they possess the powers of contraction and extension to a very great degree. When fully extended they appear as thin as a thread, and the next moment they can clue themselves up like a pea. This power enables them to pass rapidly from point to point, and also to penetrate into the smallest aperture. They are said to possess an acute sense of smell, and guided by this they approach the traveller the moment he sits down. They will crowd up from all quarters, until fifty or a hundred crawl upon one person in a few minutes' time, so that one is kept busy in removing them as fast as they appear.

They occur in greatest numbers in moist shady woods, and cover the leaves when heavy dew is on them. In rain they are more numerous than at other times, and then they infest the paths; whereas in dry weather they betake themselves into the streams, or the thickly-shaded interior of the jungle.

Those who know not their haunts, their love of blood, their keenness and immense numbers, cannot understand the disgust and annoyance experienced from them by travellers. They get into the hair, hang by the eyelids, crawl up the legs, or down the back, and fasten themselves under the instep of the foot; and if not removed, gorge themselves with blood till they roll off. Often the traveller finds his boots filled with these hideous creatures when arrived at the end of his day's journey. Their wound at the time produces no pain, but it causes a sore afterwards, which is frequently months in healing, and leaves a scar that remains for years!

Many antidotes are adopted, and tobacco-juice or snuff will keep them off when applied over the skin; but in passing through moist woods and the long wet jungle grass, such applications require to be continually renewed, and it becomes so troublesome and vexatious to take these precautions, that most travellers prefer wearing long boots, tucking in their trousers, and then keeping a good look-out for these insidious crawlers.

CHAPTER XX.

THE MUSK-DEER.

A FEW days' more journeying up the mountains brought our travellers to the limits of the forest. They once more looked upon the snowy peaks of the great central chain towering up into the clouds. I say once more—for they had already seen these peaks from the plains of India while still more than a hundred miles distant from them ; but, as they approached nearer, and while advancing through the foot-hills, the snow-covered mountains had no longer been in sight !

This may appear a puzzle, but it is very easily explained. When very near to a house you will be unable to see the steeple of a church that is behind it ; whereas by going to a greater distance from the house, the higher steeple comes at once before your eyes.

So is it with mountains. From a great distance their highest peaks are those that may be seen, but as you draw nearer, their lower range, or foot-hills, subtend the angle of vision ; and it is only after having passed through, or over these, that you again behold the more elevated summits.

Our travellers were now in sight of the snowy summits of the Himalayas, several of which rose to the stupendous height of five miles above the level of the sea—one or two even exceeding this elevation.

Of course it was not the design of the plant-hunters to attempt to climb to the tops of any of these gigantic mountains. That they well knew would not be possible, as it is almost certain that at such an elevation a human being could not live. Karl, however, was determined to proceed as far as vegetation extended; for he believed that many rare and choice plants might be found even as high as the snow-line; and indeed there are several species of beautiful rhododendrons, and junipers, and pines, which grow only in what may be termed the "Arctic zone" of the Himalayas.

With this idea, then, the travellers kept on—each day getting higher, and farther into the heart of the great chain.

For two or three days they had been climbing through wild desolate valleys, quite without inhabitants; yet they were able to find plenty of food, as in these valleys there were animals of various kinds, and with their guns they had no difficulty in procuring a supply of meat. They found the "talin," a species of wild goat, the male of which often attains to the weight of three hundred pounds, and a fine species of deer known in the Himalayas as the "serow." They also shot one or two wild sheep, known by the name of "burrell," and an antelope called "gooral," which is the "chamois" of the Indian Alps.

It may be as well here to remark, that in the vast extended chain of the Himalayas, as well as throughout the high mountain steppes of Asia, there exist wild sheep and wild goats, as well as deer and antelopes, of a

great many species that have never been described by
naturalists.   Indeed, but little more is known of them
than what has been obtained from the notes of a few
enterprising English sportsmen.   It would be safe to
conjecture that there are in Asia a dozen species of
wild sheep, and quite as many belonging to the goat-
tribe ; and when that continent shall be thoroughly
explored by scientific travellers, a very large addition
will be made to the catalogue of ruminant animals.
Nearly every extensive valley or chain of the Asiatic
mountains possesses some species of the sheep or goat-
tribe peculiar to itself, and differing from all others of
the same genus ; and in ascending the stupendous
heights of the Himalayas you find that every stage of
elevation has its peculiar species.   Some dwell in dense
forests, others in those that are thin and open.   Some
prefer the grassy slopes, while others affect the barren
ridges of rock.   There are those that are found only
upon the very limits of vegetation, spending most of
their lives within the region of eternal snow.   Among
these are the famed ibex and the large wild sheep
known as the *Ovis ammon.*

There was none of the Himalayan animals that in-
terested our travellers more than the curious little creature known as the " musk-deer."   This is the animal
from which the famous scent is obtained ; and which
is consequently a much persecuted creature.   It dwells
in the Himalayan Mountains, ranging from an elevation of about eight thousand feet to the limits of perpetual snow, and is an object of the chase to the hunters
of these regions, who make their living by collecting
the musk and disposing of it to the merchants of the

plains. The animal itself is a small creature, less in size than our fallow-deer, and of a speckled brownish gray color, darker on the hind-quarters. Its head is small, its ears long and upright, and it is without horns.

A peculiarity exists in the males which renders them easy to be distinguished from other animals of the deer kind. They have a pair of tusks in the upper jaw projecting downwards, each full three inches in length, and about as thick as a goose's quill. These give to the animal altogether a peculiar appearance. The males only yield the musk, which is found in grains, or little pellets, inside a sac or pod in the skin, situated near the navel; but what produces this singular substance, or what purpose it serves in the economy of the animal, it is not easy to say. It has proved its worst foe. But for the musk this harmless little deer would be comparatively a worthless object of the chase; but as it is, the valuable commodity has created for it a host of enemies, who follow no other occupation but that of hunting it to the death.

The plant-hunters had several times seen musk-deer as they journeyed up the mountain; but as the animal is exceedingly shy, and one of the swiftest of the deer kind, they had not succeeded in getting a shot. They were all the more anxious to procure one, from the very difficulty which they had met with in doing so.

One day as they were proceeding up a very wild ravine, among some stunted juniper and rhododendron bushes, they started from his lair one of the largest musk-deer they had yet seen. As he kept directly on, and did not seem to run very fast, they determined to pursue him. Fritz, therefore, was put upon his trail, and the others followed as fast as they were able to get over the rough ground.

They had not gone far, when the baying of the dog told them that the chase had forsaken the ravine in which they had first started it, and had taken into a lateral valley.

On arriving at the mouth of this last, they perceived that it was filled by a glacier. This did not surprise them, as they had already seen several glaciers in the mountain valleys, and they were every hour getting farther within the region of these icy phenomena.

A sloping path enabled them to reach the top of the glacier, and they now perceived the tracks of the deer. Some snow had fallen and still lay unmelted upon the icy surface, and in this the foot-prints of the animal were quite distinct.

Fritz had stopped at the end of the glacier, as if to await further instructions; but without hesitation the hunters climbed up on the ice, and followed the trail.

CHAPTER XXI.

THE GLACIER.

For more than a mile they toiled up the sloping glacier which all the way lay between two vertical cliffs.

That the musk-deer was still in advance of them, they had evidence from the · imprint of its tracks. Even without this evidence they could not doubt that the game was still before them. It would have been impossible for it to have scaled the cliffs on either side, so far as they had yet seen them; and as far before them as they could see, both sides appeared equally steep and impracticable.

As the hunters advanced, the cliffs gradually converged; and at the distance of a few hundred yards before them, appeared to close in—as if the ravine ended there, and there was no outlet in that direction. In fact they appeared to be approaching the apex of a very acute angle, the sides of which were formed by the black granite cliffs.

This singular formation was just what the hunters desired. If the valley ended in a *cul-de-sac*, then the game would be hemmed in by their approach, and they might have a chance of obtaining a shot.

In order the more surely to accomplish this, they separated, and deployed themselves into a line which extended completely across the valley. In this formation they continued to advance upward.

When they first adopted this plan, the ravine was about four hundred yards in width—so that less than one hundred lay between 'each two of them. These equal distances they preserved as well as they could, but now and then the cracks in the icy mass, and the immense boulders that lay over its surface, obliged one or other of them to make considerable detours. As they advanced, however, the distance between each two grew less, in consequence of the narrowing of the valley, until at length a space of only fifty yards separated one from the other. The game could not now pass them without affording a fine opportunity for all to have a shot; and with the expectation of soon obtaining one, they kept on in high spirits.

All at once their hopes appeared to be frustrated. The whole line came to a halt, and the hunters stood regarding each other with blank looks. Directly in front of them yawned an immense crevasse in the ice, full five yards in width at the top, and stretching across the glacier from cliff to cliff.

A single glance into this great fissure convinced them that it was impassable. Their hunt was at an end. They could go no farther. Such was the conviction of all.

The glacier filled the whole ravine from cliff to cliff. There was no space or path between the ice and the rocky wall. The latter rose vertically upward for five hundred feet at least, and no doubt extended downward to as great a depth. Indeed, by looking into the fissure, they could trace the wall of rock to an immense distance downward, ending in the green cleft of the ice below. To look down into that terrible abyss made their heads reel with giddiness; and they could only do so with safety by crawling up to the edge of the lye, and peeping over.

A glance convinced one and all of them that the crevasse was impassable.

But how had the deer got over it? Surely it had not leaped that fearful chasm?

But surely it had. Close by the edge its tracks were traced in the snow, and there, upon the lower side of the cleft, was the spot from which it had sprung. On the opposite brink the disarrangement of the snow told where it had alighted, having cleared a space of sixteen or eighteen feet! This, however, was nothing to a musk-deer, that upon a deal level often bounds to more than twice that length; for these animals have been known to spring down a slope to the enormous distance of sixty feet!

The leap over the crevasse, therefore, fearful as it appeared in the eyes of our hunters, was nothing to the musk-deer, who is as nimble and sure-footed as the chamois itself.

"Enough!" said Karl, after they had stood for some minutes gazing into the lye. "There's no help for it; we must go back as we came—what says Ossaroo?"

"You speakee true, Sahib—no help for we—we no get cross—too wide leapee—no bridge—no bamboo for makee bridge—no tree here."

Ossaroo shook his head despondingly as he spoke.

6 *

He was vexed at losing the game—particularly as the buck was one of the largest, and might have yielded an ounce or two of musk, which, as Ossaroo well knew, was worth a guinea an ounce in the bazaars of Calcutta.

The Hindoo glanced once more across the lye, and then turning round, uttered an exclamation, which told that he was beaten.

"Well, then, let us go back!" said Karl.

"Stay, brother!" interrupted Caspar, "a thought strikes me. Had we not better remain here for a while? The deer cannot be far off. It is, no doubt, up near the end of the ravine; but it won't stay there long. There appears to be nothing for it to eat but rocks or snow, and it won't be contented with that. If there's no outlet above, it must come back this way Now I propose we lie in wait for it a while, and take it as it comes down again. What say you to my plan?"

"I see no harm in trying it, Caspar," replied Karl. "We had better separate, however, and each hide behind a boulder, else it may see us, and stay back. We shall give it an hour."

"Oh!" said Caspar, "I think it'll tire of being cooped up in less time than that; but we shall see."

The party now spread themselves right and left along the lower edge of the crevasse—each choosing a large rock or mass of snowy ice as a cover. Caspar went to the extreme left, and even to the edge of the glacier, where a number of large rocks rested on its surface. Having entered among these, he was hidden from the others, but presently they heard him calling out,—

"Hurrah! come here!—a bridge! a bridge!"

Karl and Ossaroo left their hiding-places, and hastened to the spot.

On arriving among the boulders, they saw, to their delight, that one of the largest of these—an enormous block of gneiss—lay right across the crevasse, spanning it like a bridge, and looking as though it had been placed there by human hands! This, however, would have been impossible, as the block was full ten yards in length, and nearly as broad as it was long. Even giants could not have built such a bridge!

A little examination showed where it had fallen from the overhanging precipice—and it had rested on the glacier, perhaps, before the great cleft had yawned open beneath it. Its upper end overlapped the ice for a breadth of scarce two feet, and it seemed a wonder that so huge a weight could be sustained by such an apparently fragile prop. But there it rested; and had done so for years—perhaps for ages—suspended over the beetling chasm, as if the touch of a feather would precipitate it into the gulf below!

If Karl had been near, he might have warned his brother from crossing by such a dangerous bridge; but before he had reached the spot, Caspar had already mounted on the rock, and was hurrying over.

In a few moments he stood upon the opposite side of the crevasse; and, waving his cap in the air, shouted to the rest to follow.

The others crossed as he had done, and then the party once more deployed, and kept up the ravine, which grew narrower as they advanced, and appeared to be regularly closed in at the top, by a perpendicular wall. Surely the deer could not escape them much longer?

"What a pity," said Caspar, "we could not throw down that great stone and widen the crack in the ice, so that the deer could not leap over it! We should then have it nicely shut up here."

"Aye, Caspar," rejoined Karl, "and where should *we* be then? Shut up too, I fear."

"True, brother, I did not think of that. What a terrible thing it would be to be imprisoned between these black cliffs! It would, I declare."

The words had scarce issued from Caspar's lip, when a crash was heard like the first bursting of a thunder-clap, and then a deafening roar echoed up the ravine, mingled with louder peals, as though the eternal mountains were being rent asunder!

The noise reverberated from the black cliffs; eagles, that had been perched upon the rocks, rose screaming into the air; beasts of prey howled from their lurking-places; and the hitherto silent valley was all at once filled with hideous noises, as though it were the doom of the world!

.

CHAPTER XXII.

THE GLACIER SLIDE.

"AN avalanche!" cried Karl Linden, as the first crash fell upon his ear; but on turning, he saw his mistake.

"No," he continued, with a look of terror, "it is not an avalanche! My God! my God! *the glacier is in motion!*"

He did not need to point out the spot. The eyes of Caspar and Ossaroo were already turned upon it.— Away down the ravine as far as they could see the surface of the glacier appeared in motion, like sea-billows; huge blocks of ice were thrown to the top and rolled over, with a rumbling crashing noise, while large blue fragments raised high above the general surface, were grinding and crumbling to pieces against the faces of the cliffs. A cloud of snow-spray, rising like a thick white mist, filled the whole ravine—as if to conceal the work of ruin that was going on—and underneath this ghostly veil, the crushing and tearing for some moments continued. Then all at once the fearful noises ceased, and only the screaming of the birds, and the howling of beasts, disturbed the silence of the place.

Pale, shuddering, almost paralyzed by fear, the hunters had thrown themselves on their hands and knees, expecting every moment to feel the glacier move beneath them,—expecting to sink beneath the surface, or be crushed amidst the billows of that icy sea. So long as the dread sounds echoed in their ears, their hearts were filled with consternation, and long after the crashing and crackling ceased, they remained the victims of a terrible suspense; but they felt that that portion of the glacier upon which they were did not move. It still remained firm; would it continue so?

They knew not the moment it, too, might commence sliding downward, and bury them under its masses, or crush them in some deep crevasse.

O heavens! the thought was fearful. It had paralyzed them for a moment; and for some time after the noises had ceased, they remained silent and motionless. Indeed, absurd as it may seem, each dreaded to stir, lest the very motion of his body might disturb the icy mass upon which he was kneeling!

Reflection soon came to their aid. It would never do to remain there. They were still exposed to the danger. Whither could they retreat? Up the ravine might be safer? Above them the ice had not yet stirred. The ruin had all been below—below the crevasse they had just crossed.

Perhaps the rocks would afford a footing? They would not move, at all events, even if the upper part of the glacier should give way; but was there footing to be found upon them?

They swept their eyes along the nearest cliff. It offered but little hope. Yes—upon closer inspection there was a ledge—a very narrow one, but yet capable of giving refuge to two or three men; and, above all, it was easy of access. It would serve their purpose.

Like men seeking shelter from a heavy shower, or running to get out of the way of some impending danger, all three made for the ledge; and after some moments spent in sprawling and climbing against the cliff, they found themselves standing safely upon it.— Small standing-room they had. Had there been a fourth, the place would not have accommodated him. There was just room enough for the three side by side, and standing erect.

Small as the space was, it was a welcome haven of refuge. It was the solid granite, and not the fickle ice. It looked eternal as the hills; and, standing upon it, they breathed freely.

But the danger was not over, and their apprehensions were still keen. Should the upper part of the glacier give way, what then? Although it could not reach them where they stood, the surface might sink far below its present level, and leave them on the cliff—upon that little ledge on the face of a black precipice !

Even if the upper ice held firm, there was another thought that now troubled them. Karl knew that what had occurred was a *glacier slide*—a phenomenon that few mortals have witnessed. He suspected that the slide had taken place in that portion of the glacier below the crevasse they had just crossed. If so, the lye would be widened, the huge gneiss rock that bridged it gone, and their *retreat down the glacier cut off!*

Upward they beheld nothing but the beetling cliffs meeting together. No human foot could scale them.— If no outlet offered in that direction, then, indeed, might the jesting allusion of Caspar be realized. They might be imprisoned between those walls of black granite, with nought but ice for their bed, and the sky for their ceiling. It was a fearful supposition, but all three did not fail to entertain it.

As yet they could not tell whether their retreat downwards was in reality cut off. Where they stood an abutment of the cliff hid the ravine below. They had rushed to their present position, with the first instinct of preservation. In their flight, they had not thought of looking either toward the crevasse or the gneiss rock.— Other large boulders intervened, and they had not observed whether it was gone. They trembled to think of such a thing.

The hours passed; and still they dared not descend to the glacier. Night came on, and they still stood upon their narrow perch. They hungered, but it would have been of no use to go down to the cold icy surface. That would not have satisfied their appetite.

All night long they remained standing upon the narrow ledge; now on one foot, now on the other, now resting their backs against the granite wall, but all night, without closing an eye in sleep. The dread of the capricious ice kept them on their painful perch.

They could bear it no longer. With the first light of morning they determined upon descending.

The ice had remained firm during the night. No farther noises had been heard. They gradually recovered confidence; and as soon as the day began to break, all three left the ledge, and betook themselves once more to the glacier.

At first they kept close to the cliff; but, after a while,

ventured out far enough to get a view of the ravine below.

Caspar mounted upon a rocky boulder that lay upon the surface of the glacier. From the top of this he could see over the others. *The crevasse was many yards wide. The bridge-rock was gone!*

CHAPTER XXIII.

THE PASS.

THE philosophy of the movement of glaciers is but ill understood, even by the most accomplished geologists. It is supposed that the under surface of these great icy masses is detached from the ground by the thaw which continually takes place there, caused by the radiating heat of the earth. Water is also an agent in loosening their hold; for it is well known that currents of water, —sometimes large streams,—run under the glaciers. The icy mass thus detached, and resting on an inclined surface, is carried down by its own weight.

Sometimes only a very small portion of a glacier moves, causing a fissure above the part that has given way; and at other times these fissures are closed up, by the sliding of that portion next above them. An unusually hot summer produces these effects upon the glacier ice, combined with the falling of avalanches, or mountain slides, which, with their weight, serve to impel the icy mass downwards.

The weight of our three hunters was but as a feather, and could have had no effect in giving motion to the glacier; but it is possible that the gneiss rock was just upon the balance when they crossed it. Thawed around its surface, it had no cohesion with the ice on which it rested ; and, as a feather turns the scale, their crossing upon it may have produced a motion, which resulted in its fall.

So vast a mass hurled into the great cleft, and acting as a driven wedge, may have been the feather's touch that imparted motion to a section of the glacier, already hanging upon the balance, and ready to slide down-wards.

Whether or not they had any agency in producing this fearful phenomenon, our travellers reflected not at the time. They were far too much terrified at the re-sult to speculate upon causes. One after another they mounted upon the great boulder, and satisfied them-selves of the facts that the crevasse had widened,—the bridge-rock had disappeared,—and their retreat was cut off !

After a little, they ventured closer to the fearful chasm. They climbed upon a ledge of the precipice, that gave them a better view of it.

From this elevation they could partially see into the cleft. At the surface it was many yards wide. It ap-peared to be hundreds of feet in depth. Human agency could not have bridged it. All hope of getting back down the glacier was at an end ; and with consterna-tion in their looks, they turned their faces away, and commenced ascending towards the head of the ravine.

They advanced with timid steps. They spoke not at all, or only in low murmuring voices. They looked right and left, eagerly scanning the precipice on both sides. On each side of them towered the black cliffs, like prison walls, frowning and forbidding. No ledge of any size appeared on either; no terrace, no sloping ravine, that might afford them a path out of that dark valley. The cliffs, sheer and smooth, presented no hold for the human foot. The eagles, and other birds that screamed over their heads, alone could scale them.

Still they had not lost hope. The mind does not yield to despair without full conviction. As yet they were not certain that there was no outlet to the ravine; and until certain they would not despair.

They observed the tracks of the musk-deer as they went on. But these were no longer fresh; it was the trail of yesterday.

They followed this trail with renewed hopes,—with feelings of joy. But it was not the joy of the hunter who expects ere long to overtake his game. No, directly the reverse. Hungry as all three were, they *feared* to overtake the game; they dreaded the discovery of fresh tracks!

You will wonder at this; but it is easily explained. They had reasoned with themselves, that if there existed any outlet above, the deer would have gone out by it. If the contrary, the animal would still be found near the head of the ravine. Nothing would have been less welcome than the sight of the deer at that moment.

Their hopes rose as they advanced. No fresh tracks appeared upon the glacier. The trail of the musk-deer still continued onward and upward. The creature had not halted, nor even strayed to either side. It had gone straight on, as though making for some retreat already known to it. Here and there it had made detours; but these had been caused by lyes in the ice, or boulders, that lay across the path.

With beating hearts the trackers kept on ; now scanning the cliffs on each hand, now bending their eyes in advance.

At length they saw themselves within a hundred paces of the extreme end of the ravine, and yet no opening appeared. The precipice rose high and sheer as ever, on the right, on the left, before their faces. Nor break nor path cheered their eyes.

Where could the deer have gone ? The ground above was pretty clear of *débris*. There were some loose rocks lying on one side. Had it hidden behind these ? If so, they would soon find it ; for they were within a few paces of the rocks.

They approached with caution. They had prepared their weapons for a shot. Despite their fears, they had still taken some precautions. Hunger instigated them to this.

Caspar was sent on to examine the covert of rocks, while Karl and the shikarree remained in the rear to intercept the deer if it attempted to retreat down the ravine.

. Caspar approached with due caution. He crawled silently up to the boulders. He placed himself close to the largest ; and, raising his head, peeped over it.

There was no deer behind the rock, nor any traces of it in the snow.

He passed on to the next, and then to the next. This brought him into a new position, and near the head of the ravine ; so that he could now see the whole surface of the glacier.

There was no musk-deer to be seen ; but a spectacle greeted his eyes far more welcome than the sight of the largest herd of deer could have been to the keenest hunter ; and a cry of joy escaped him on the instant.

He was seen to start out from the rocks, shouting as he ran across the ravine,—

" Come on, brother ! we are safe yet ! There's a pass ! there's a pass ! "

CHAPTER XXIV.

THE LONE MOUNTAIN VALLEY.

A PASS there was, sure enough, that opened between the cliffs like a great gate. Why they had not perceived it sooner was because the gorge bent a little to the right before opening to this outlet; and, of course, the bend from a distance appeared to be the termination of the ravine.

A hundred yards from the bend brought them into the great gate between the cliffs, and there a view opened before their eyes that filled their hearts with joy and admiration.

Perhaps in all the world they could not have looked upon a more singular landscape. Right before their faces, and somewhat below the level on which they stood, lay a valley. It was nearly of a circular shape, and, perhaps, a league or more in circumference. In the middle of this valley was a lake several hundred yards in diameter. The whole bottom of the valley appeared to be a plane, but slightly elevated above the water level, consisting of green meadows, beautifully interpersed with copses of shrubbery and clumps of trees, with foliage of rich and varied colors. What appeared to be droves of cattle and herds of deer were browsing on the meadows, or wandering around the copses ; while flocks of waterfowl disported themselves over the blue water of the lake.

So park-like was the aspect of this sequestered valley, that the eyes of our travellers instinctively wandered over its surface in search of human dwellings or the forms of human beings ; and were only astonished at not perceiving either. They looked for a house,—a noble mansion,—a palace to correspond to that fair park. They looked for chimneys among the trees—for the ascending smoke. No trace of all these could be detected. A smoke there was, but it was not that of a fire. It was a white vapor that rose near one side of the valley, curling upward like steam. This surprised and puzzled them. They could not tell what caused it, but they could tell that it was not the smoke of a fire.

But the form of the valley—its dimensions—its central lake—its green meadows and trees—its browsing herds—its wild fowl might have been seen elsewhere. All these things might occur, and do occur in many parts of the earth's surface without the scene being regarded as singular or remarkable. It was not these that have led us to characterize the landscape in question as one of the most singular in the world. No—its singularity rested upon other circumstances.

One of these circumstances was, that around the valley there appeared a dark belt of nearly equal breadth, that seemed to hem it in as with a gigantic fence. A little examination told that this dark belt was a line of cliffs, that, rising up from the level bottom on all sides, fronted the valley and the lake. In other words, the valley was surrounded by a precipice. In the distance it appeared only a few yards in height, but that might be a deception of the eye.

Above the black line another circular belt encompassed the valley. It was the sloping sides of bleak barren mountains. Still another belt higher up was formed by the snowy crests of the same mountains—here in roof-like ridges, there in rounded·domes, or sharp cone-shaped peaks, that pierced the heavens far above the line of eternal snow.

There seemed to be no way of entrance into this singular basin except over the line of black cliff. The gap in which our travellers stood, and the ravine through which they had ascended appeared to be its only outlet; and this, filled as it was by glacier ice, raised the summit of the pass above the level of the valley; but a sloping descent over a vast *débris* of fallen rocks—the "moraine" of the glacier itself—afforded a path down to the bottom of the valley.

For several minutes all three remained in the gap, viewing this strange scene with feelings that partook of the nature of admiration—of wonder—of awe. The sun was just appearing over the mountains, and his rays, falling upon the crystallized snow, were refracted to the eyes of the spectators in all the colors of the rainbow. The snow itself in one place appeared of a roseate color, while elsewhere it was streaked and mottled with golden hues. The lake, too—here rippled by the sporting fowl, there lying calm and smooth—reflected from its blue disk the white cones of the mountains, the darker belting of the nearer cliffs, or the green foliage upon its shores.

7

For hours Karl Linden could have gazed upon that fairy-like scene. Caspar, of ruder mould, was entranced by its beauty; and even the hunter of the plains—the native of palm-groves and cane fields—confessed he had never beheld so beautiful a landscape. All of them were well acquainted with the Hindoo superstition concerning the Himalaya Mountains. The belief that in lonely valleys among the more inaccessible peaks, the Brahmin gods have their dwelling and their home; and they could not help fancying at that moment that the superstition might be true. Certainly, if it were true, some one of these deities, Vishnu, or Siva, or even Brahma himself, must dwell in that very valley that now lay before them.

But poetical and legendary sentiment soon vanished from the minds of our travellers. All three were hungry—hungry as wolves—and the ruling thought at the moment was to find the means for satisfying their appetites.

With this intent, therefore, they strode forward out of the gap, and commenced descending towards the bottom of the valley.

CHAPTER XXV.

GRUNTING OXEN.

THERE were several kinds of animals in sight, but it was natural that the hungry hunters should choose those that were nearest for their game. The nearest also chanced to be the largest—though in the flock there were individuals of different sizes, from the bigness of a large ox to that of a Newfoundland dog. There were about a dozen in all, evidently of one kind, and the difference in size and other respects arose from a difference of age and sex.

What sort of animals they were, not one of the party could tell. Even Ossaroo did not know them. He had never seen such creatures on the plains of India. It was evident to all, however, that they were some species of oxen or buffaloes, since they bore a general resemblance to animals of the family of *bovidæ*. First there was the great massive bull, the patriarch of the herd, standing nearly as tall as a horse, and quite as tall reckoning from the top of the stately hump on his shoulders. His curved horns spreading outward rose from a mass of thick curled hair, giving him the fierce aspect which characterizes animals of the buffalo kind. But his chief peculiarity lay in the drapery of long silky hair,

that from his sides, flanks, neck, belly, and thighs, hung
downward until its tips almost dragged upon the grass.
This singular appendage gave the animal the appearance of being short-legged, and the massive thickness
of the legs themselves added to the effect.

Karl could not help remarking in the old bull a considerable resemblance to the rare musk-ox of America;
an animal with which he was acquainted, from having
seen stuffed specimens in the museums. He noted,
however, that there was one point in which the musk-
ox differed essentially from the species before him—in
regard to the tail. The musk-ox is almost tailless; or,
rather, his tail is so small as to be quite inconspicuous
amidst the long masses of hair that adorn his croup;
whereas the strange creature before them was remarkable for the large development of this appendage,
which swept downward, full and wide, like the tail of
a horse. The color of the bull's body appeared black
in the distance, though, in reality, it was not black, but
of a dark, chocolate brown; the tail, on the contrary,
was snow-white, which, from this contrast in color,
added to the singularity of the animal's appearance.

There was but one large bull in the herd; evidently
the lord and master of all the others. These consisted
of the females or cows, and the young. The cows were
much smaller, scarce half the size of the old bull;
their horns less massive, and the tails and long hair less
full and flowing.

Of the young, there were some of different ages;
from the half-grown bull or heifer, to the calves lately
dropped; which last were tearing about over the
ground, and gambolling by the feet of their mothers.

About these little creatures there was a peculiarity. The long hair upon their flanks and sides had not yet made its appearance; but their whole coat was black and curly, just like that of a water-spaniel, or New-foundland dog. In the distance, they bore a striking resemblance to these animals; and one might have fancied the herd to be a flock of buffaloes, with a number of black dogs running about in their midst.

"Whatever they be," remarked Caspar, "they look like they might be eatable. I think they're beef of some kind."

"Beef, venison, or mutton—one of the three," rejoined Karl.

Ossaroo was not particular at that moment. He could have picked a rib of wolf-meat, and thought it palatable.

"Well, we must stalk them," continued Karl. "I see no other way of getting near them but by crawling through yonder copse."

The speaker pointed to a grove, near which the animals were browsing.

Caspar and Ossaroo agreed with this suggestion, and all three, having now reached the bottom of the descent, commenced their stalk.

Without any difficulty, they succeeded in reaching the copse; and then, creeping silently through the underwood, they came to that edge of it which was closest to the browsing herd. The bushes were evergreens—rhododendrons—and formed excellent cover for a stalk; and, as yet, the game had neither seen, nor heard, nor smelt the approaching enemy. They were too distant for the arrows of Ossaroo, therefore Ossaroo could do nothing; but they were within excellent range of the rifle and double-barrel, loaded, as the latter was, with large buck-shot.

Karl whispered to Caspar to choose one of the calves for the first barrel, while he himself aimed at the larger game.

The bull was too distant for either bullet or buck-shot.   He was standing apart, apparently acting as sentry to the herd, though this time he did not prove a watchful guardian.   He had some suspicion, however, that all was not right; for, before they could fire, he seemed to have caught an alarm, and, striking the ground with his massive hoofs, he uttered a strange noise, that resembled the grunting of a hog.   So exactly did it assimilate to this, that our hunters, for the moment, believed there were pigs in the place, and actually looked around to discover their whereabouts.

A moment satisfied them, that the grunting came from the bull; and, without thinking any more about it, Karl and Caspar levelled their pieces, and fired.

The reports reverberated through the valley; and the next moment the whole herd, with the bull at their head, were seen going in full gallop across the plain. Not all of them, however.   A calf, and one of the cows, lay stretched upon the sward, to the great delight of the hunters, who, rushing forth from their cover, soon stood triumphant over the fallen game.

A word or two passed between them.   They had determined on first cooking the calf, to appease their hunger, and were about proceeding to skin it, when a long, loud grunting sounded in their ears; and, on looking around, they beheld the great bull coming full tilt towards them, his head lowered to the ground, and his large, lustrous eyes flashing with rage and vengeance. He had only retreated a short distance, fancying, no doubt, that his whole family was after him; but, on missing two of its members, he was now on his return to rescue or revenge them.

Strange as was the animal to all three, there was no mistaking his prowess. His vast size, his wild, shaggy front and sweeping horns, the vengeful expression of his eyes, all declared him a powerful and dangerous assailant. Not one of the hunters thought for a moment of withstanding such an assault; but, shouting to each other to run for their lives, all three started off as fast as their legs would carry them.

They ran for the copse, but that would not have saved them had it been mere copsewood. Such a huge creature as their pursuer would have dashed through copsewood as through a field of grass; and, in reality, he did so, charging through the bushes, goring them down on all sides of him, and uttering his loud grunting like a savage boar.

It so happened that there were several large trees growing up out of the underwood, and these, fortunately, were not difficult to climb. The three hunters did not need any advice, as to what they should do under the circumstances. Each had an instinct of his own, and that instinct prompted him to take to a tree; where, of course, he would be safe enough from an animal, whose claws, if it had any, were encased in hoofs.

The bull continued for some minutes to grunt and charge backward and forward among the bushes, but, not finding any of the party, he at length returned to the plain, where the dead were lying. He first approached the cow, and then the calf, and then repeatedly passed from one to the other, placing his broad muzzle to their bodies, and uttering his grunting roar, apparently in a more plaintive strain than before.

After continuing these demonstrations for a while, he raised his head, looked over the plain, and then trotted sullenly off in the direction in which the others had gone.

Hungry as were the hunters, it was some time before they ventured to come down from their perch. But hunger overcame them at length, and descending, they picked up their various weapons—which they had dropped in their haste to climb—and, having loaded the empty barrels, they returned to the game.

These were now dragged up to the edge of the timber —so that in case the bull should take it into his head to return, they might not have so far to run for the friendly trees.

The calf was soon stripped of its skin—a fire kindled —several ribs broiled over the coals, and eaten in the shortest space of time. Such delicious veal not one of the three had ever tasted in his life. It was not that their extreme hunger occasioned them to think so, but such was really the fact, for they were no longer ignorant of what they were eating. They now knew what sort of animals they had slain, and a singular circumstance had imparted to them this knowledge. As the bull charged about in front of the thicket, Ossaroo from his perch on the tree had a good view of him, and one thing belonging to the animal Ossaroo recognized as an old acquaintance—it was *his tail!* Yes, that tail was not to be mistaken. Many such had Ossaroo seen and handled in his young days. Many a fly had he brushed away with just such a one, and he could have recognized it had he found it growing upon a fish

When they returned to the quarry, Ossaroo pointed to the tail of the dead cow—not half so full and large as that of the bull, but still of similar character—and with a significant glance to the others, said,—

" Know 'im now, Sahibs—*Chowry.*"

7 *

CHAPTER XXVI.

THE YAKS.

WHAT Ossaroo meant was that he knew the tail; but he was as ignorant of the animal to which it was attached, as if the latter had been a dragon or a comet. Ossaroo saw that the tail was a "chowry," in other words, a fly-flapper, such as is used in the hot countries of India for brushing away flies, mosquitos, and other winged insects. Ossaroo knew it, for he had often handled one to fan the old sahib, who had been his master in the days of his boyhood.

The word chowry, however, at once suggested to the plant-hunter a train of ideas. He knew that the chowries of India were imported across the Himalayas from Chinese Tartary and Thibet; that they were the tails of a species of oxen peculiar to these countries, known as the yak, or grunting ox. Beyond a doubt then the animals they had slain were "yaks."

Karl's conjecture was the true one. It was a herd of wild yaks they had fallen in with, for they were just in the very country where these animals exist in their wild state.

Linneus gave to these animals the name of *Bos grunniens,* or grunting ox—seeing that they were clearly a species of the ox. It would be difficult to conceive a more appropriate name for them ; but this did not satisfy the modern closet-naturalists—who, finding certain differences between them and other *bovidæ*, must needs form a new genus, to accommodate this one species, and by such means render the study of zoölogy more difficult. Indeed, some of these gentlemen would have a genus for every species, or even variety—all of which absurd classification leads only to the multiplication of hard names and the confusion of ideas.

It is a great advantage to the student, as well as to the simple reader, when the scientific title of an animal is a word which conveys some idea of its character, and not the latinized name of Smith or Brown, Hofenshaufer or Wislizenus ; but this title should usually be the specific one given to the animal. Where a genus exists so easily distinguished from all others as in the case of the old genus "*bos*," it is a great pity it should be cut up by fanciful systematists into *bos, bubalus, bison, anoa, poëphagus, ovibos*, and such like. The consequence of this subdividing is that readers who are not naturalists, and even some who are, are quite puzzled by the multitude of names, and gain no clear idea of the animal mentioned. All these titles would have been well enough as specific names, such as *Bos bubalus, Bos bison, Bos grunniens*, &c., and it would have been much simpler and better to have used them so. Of course if there were many species under each of these new genera, then the case would be different, and subdivision might lead to convenience. As it is, however, there are only one or two species of each, and in the case of some of the genera, as the musk-ox (*ovibos*) and the yak or grunting ox, only one. Why then multiply names and titles ?

These systematists, however, not satisfied with the generic name given by the great systematist Linneus, have changed the name of the *Bos grunniens* to that of *Poëphagus grunniens*, which I presume to mean the "grunting poa-eater," or the "grunting eater of poa grass!"—a very specific title indeed, though I fancy there are other kinds of oxen as well of the yak who indulge occasionally in the luxury of poa grass.

Well, this yak, or syrlak, or grunting ox, or poa-eater, whatever we may call him, is a very peculiar and useful animal. He is not only found wild in Thibet and other adjacent countries, but is domesticated, and subjected to the service of man. In fact, to the people of the high cold countries that stretch northward from the Himalayas he is what the camel is to the Arabs, or the reindeer to the people of Lapland. His long brown hair furnishes them with material out of which they weave their tents and twist their ropes. His skin supplies them with leather. His back carries their merchandise or other burdens, or themselves when they wish to ride; and his shoulder draws their plough and their carts. His flesh is a wholesome and excellent beef, and the milk obtained from the cows—either as milk, cheese, or butter—is one of the primary articles of food among the Thibetian people.

The tails constitute an article of commerce, of no mean value. They are exported to the plains of India, where they are bought for several purposes—their principal use being for "chowries," or fly-brushes, as already observed. Among the Tartar people they are worn in the cap as badges of distinction, and only the chiefs and distinguished leaders are permitted the privilege of wearing them. In China, also, they are similarly worn by the mandarins, first having been dyed of a bright red color. A fine full yak's tail will fetch either in China or India quite a handsome sum of money.

There are several varieties of the yak. First, there is the true wild yak—the same as those encountered by our travellers. These are much larger than the domestic breeds, and the bulls are among the most fierce and powerful of the ox tribe. Hunting them is often accompanied by hair-breadth 'scapes and perilous encounters, and large dogs and horses are employed in the chase.

The tame yaks are divided into several classes, as the ploughing yak, the riding yak, &c., and these are not all of the dark brown color of the original race, but are met with dun-colored, mottled red, and even pure white. Dark brown or black, however, with a white tail, is the prevailing color. The yak-calf is the finest veal in the world; but when the calf is taken from the mother, the cow refuses to yield milk. In such cases the foot of the calf is brought for her to lick, or the stuffed skin to fondle, when she will give milk as before, expressing her satisfaction by short grunts like a pig.

The yak when used as a beast of burden will travel twenty miles a-day, under a load of two bags of rice or salt, or four or six planks of pine-wood slung in pairs along either flank. Their ears are generally pierced by their drivers, and ornamented with tufts of scarlet worsted. Their true home is on the cold table-lands of Thibet and Tartary, or still higher up among the mountain valleys of the Himalayas, where they feed on grass or the smaller species of carices. They love to browse upon steep places, and to scramble among rocks; and their favorite places for resting or sleeping are on the tops of isolated boulders, where the sun has full play upon them. When taken to warm climates, they languish, and soon die of disease of the liver. It is possible, however, that they could be acclimated in many European countries, were it taken in hand by those who alone have the power to make the trial in a proper manner—I mean the governments of these countries. But such works of utility are about the last things that the tyrants of the earth will be likely to trouble their heads with.

CHAPTER XXVII.

CURING THE YAK-MEAT.

OUR travellers found the yak-veal excellent, and the three consumed a quarter of it for their breakfasts before their appetites were satisfied.

This business being brought to a conclusion, they held a council as to what was best to be done next. Of course they had already made up their minds to spend some days in this beautiful valley in plant-hunting. From the glance they had had of it, Karl had no doubt that its *flora* and *sylva* were exceedingly rich and varied. Indeed, while passing through the underwood he had noticed many curious kinds that were quite new to him, and he would be likely enough to find some altogether unknown to the botanical world. These thoughts filled him with joyful anticipations—bright visions of future triumph in his beloved science passed before his mind's eye, and he felt for the moment contented and happy.

The peculiar situation of the valley led him to expect a peculiar flora, surrounded as it was by snowy mountains—isolated apparently from other fertile tracts, and sheltered from every wind by the lofty ridges that encircled it. Among other peculiarities he had observed plants of almost tropical genera, although the altitude could not be less than 15,000 feet, and the snowy mountains that towered above it were some of the highest peaks of the Himalayas! These tropical forms had puzzled him not a little, considering the altitude at which he observed them; and to account for the apparent anomaly was one of the thoughts that was passing through his mind at the moment.

As for Caspar, he was pleased to know that his brother desired to remain there for some days. He had less interest in the rare plants, but he had observed that the place was very well stocked with wild animals, and he anticipated no little sport in hunting them.

It is just possible that Ossaroo sighed for the warm plains, for the palm-groves and bamboo thickets, but the shikarree liked the look of the game, and could spend a few days well enough in this region. Moreover, the atmosphere of the valley was much warmer than that of the country in which they had been travelling for several days past. Indeed, the difference was so great as to surprise all three of them, and they could only account for the higher temperature by supposing that it arose from the sheltered situation of the valley itself.

Having determined on remaining, therefore it became necessary to make some provision against hunger. Though the game seemed plenty enough, they might not always be so successful in stalking it; and as the yak cow offered them beef enough to last for some days, it would not do to let the meat spoil. That must be looked to at once.

Without further ado, therefore, they set about preserving the meat. Having no salt this might appear to

be a difficult matter, and so it would have been to the
northern travellers. But Ossaroo was a man of the
tropics—in whose country salt was both scarce and
dear—and consequently he knew other plans for curing
meat besides pickling it. He knew how to cure it by
the process called "jerking." This was a simple operation, and consisted in cutting the meat into thin slices,
and either hanging it upon the branches of trees, or
spreading it out upon the rock—leaving the sun to do
the rest.

It happened, however, that on that day the sun did
not shine very brightly, and it was not hot enough for
jerking meat. But Ossaroo was not to be beaten so
easily. He knew an alternative which is adopted in
such cases. He knew that the meat can be jerked by
the fire as well as by the sun, and this plan he at once
put into operation. Having gathered a large quantity
of fagots, he kindled them into a fire, and then hung the
beef upon scaffolds all around it—near enough to be
submitted to the heat and smoke, but not so near as
that the meat should be either broiled or burnt. When
it should hang thus exposed to the fire for a day or so,
Ossaroo assured his companions it would be cured and
dried so as to keep for months without requiring a
pinch of salt.

The skinning of the yak, and then cutting its flesh
into strips—the erection of the scaffold-poles, and string-
ing up of the meat, occupied all hands for the space of
several hours, so that when the job was finished it was
past mid-day.

Dinner had then to be cooked and eaten, which occupied nearly another hour; and although it was not

yet quite nightfall, they were all so sleepy from their long vigil, and so tired with standing upon the ledge, that they were glad to stretch themselves by the fire and go to rest.

The cold air, as evening approached, caused them to shiver; and now for the first time they began to think of their blankets, and other matters which they had left at their last camp. But they only thought of them with a sigh. The road, to where these had been left, could no longer be traversed. It would no doubt be necessary for them to make a long detour over the mountains, before they could get back to that camp.

Ossaroo had prepared a substitute for one of the blankets at least. He had stretched the yak-skin upon a frame, and placed it in front of the fire, so that by night it was dry enough for some of the party to wrap their bodies in. Sure enough, when Caspar was enveloped in this strange blanket—with the hairy side turned inward—he obtained in it, as he himself declared, one of the pleasantest and soundest sleeps he had ever slept in his life.

All three rested well enough; but had they only known of the discovery that awaited them on the morrow, their sleep would not have been so sound, nor their dreams so light.

CHAPTER XXVIII.

THE BOILING SPRING.

THEY ate their breakfasts of boiled yak-steak, wash-ing it down with a draught of water. They had not even a cup to hold the water. They knelt down and drank it out of the lake. The water was clear enough, but not as cold as they might have expected at such an elevation. They had noticed this on the preceding day, and now expressed their surprise at finding it so warm. They had no thermometer with which to test it, but it was evidently of much higher temperature than the air!

Whence came this water? It could not be from the melting snow—else it would certainly have been colder than it was. Perhaps there was a spring some-where? Perhaps there was a hot spring?

This was not at all improbable, for, strange to say, hot springs are numerous on the Himalaya Mountains —often bursting out amidst ice and snow, and at very great elevations.

Karl had read of such springs, and this it was that led him to infer the existence of one in the valley. How else could the water be warm?

Now they recollected that on the previous morning they had noticed a singular cloud of vapour that hung over the tops of the trees on one side of the valley. It was no longer visible, after they had descended from the elevation at which they then were; but they remembered the direction in which it had been seen, and now went in search of it.

They soon reached the spot, and found it just as they had conjectured. A hot spring was there, bubbling out from among the rocks, and then running off in a rivulet towards the lake. Caspar thrust his hand into the water, but drew it back again with an exclamation that betokened both pain and surprise. The water was almost boiling!

"Well," said he, "this is convenient at all events. If we only had a teapot, we should need no kettle. Here's water on the boil at all hours!"

"Ha!" ejaculated Karl, as he dipped his fingers into the hot stream; "this explains the high temperature of the valley, the rich luxuriant vegetation, the presence of plants of the lower region; I thought that there was some such cause. See, yonder grow magnolias! How very interesting!. I should not wonder if we meet with palms and bamboos!".

Just at that moment the attention of the party was called away from the hot spring. A noble buck came bounding up until he was within twenty yards of the spot, and then halting in his tracks, stood for some moments gazing at the intruders.

There was no mistaking this creature for any other animal than a stag. The vast antlers were characteristics that left no room to doubt of his species. He was about the size of the European stag or red deer, and his branching horns were very similar. His color, too, was reddish gray with a white mark around the croup, and his form and proportion were very like to those of the English stag. He was, in fact, the Asiatic representative of this very species—known to naturalists as the *Cervus Wallichii*.

At sight of the party around the spring, he exhibited symptoms more of surprise than of fear. Perhaps they were the first creatures of the kind his great large eyes had ever glanced upon. He knew not whether they might prove friendly or hostile.

Simple creature! He was not to remain long in doubt as to that point. The rifle was brought to bear upon him, and the next moment he was prostrate upon the ground.

It was Karl who had fired, as Caspar with the double-barrel was standing at some distance off. All three, however, ran forward to secure the game, but, to their chagrin, the stag once more rose to his feet and bounded off among the bushes, with Fritz following at his heels. They could see that he went upon three legs, and that the fourth—one of the hind ones—was broken and trailing upon the ground.

The hunters started after, in hopes of still securing the prize ; but after passing through the thicket they had a view of the buck still bounding along close by the bottom of the cliffs, and as yet far ahead of the hound. It was near the cliff where the animal had been wounded, for the hot spring was close in to the rocks that bounded that side of the valley.

The dog ran on after him, and the hunters followed as fast as they were able. Karl and Ossaroo kept along the bottom of the cliff, while Caspar remained

out in the open valley, in order to intercept the game
should it turn outwards in the direction of the lake.

In this way they proceeded for more than half-a-mile
before seeing anything more of the stag. At length
the loud baying of Fritz warned them that he had
overtaken the game, which was no doubt standing to
bay.

This proved to be the case. Fritz was holding the
buck at bay close to the edge of a thicket; but the
moment the hunters came in sight, the stag again
broke, dashed into the thicket, and disappeared as
before.

Another half-mile was passed before they found the
game again, and then the dog had brought him to bay a
second time; but just as before, when the hunters were
approaching, the stag made a rush into the bushes, and
again got off.

It was mortifying to lose such noble game after having been so sure of it, and all determined to follow out
the chase if it should last them the whole day. Karl
had another motive for continuing after the deer. Karl
was a person of tender and humane feelings. He saw
that the ball had broken the creature's thigh-bone, and
he knew the wound would cause its death in the end.
He could not think of leaving it thus to die by inches,
and was anxious to put an end to its misery. With
this view as well as for the purpose of obtaining the
venison, he continued the chase.

The stag gave them another long run, before it was
again brought up; and again, for the third time, it
broke and made off.

They began to despair of being able to come up with

it. All this while the deer had kept along the base of
the cliffs, and the hunters as they ran after it could not
help noticing the immense precipice that towered above
their heads. It rose to the height of hundreds of feet,
in some places with a slanting face, but generally almost
as vertical as a wall. The chase of the wounded stag,
however, occupied too much their attention to allow of
their observing anything else very minutely; and so
they pressed on without halting anywhere—except for
a moment or so to gain breath. Six or seven times had
they seen the wounded stag, and six or seven times had
Fritz brought him to bay, but Fritz for his pains had
only received several severe scores from the antlers of
the enraged animal.

The hunters at length approached the great gap in
the cliff, through which they had first entered the valley,
but the chase was carried past this point and continued
on as before.

Once more the loud barking of the dog announced
that the deer had come to a stand; and once more the
hunters hurried forward.

This time they saw the stag standing in a pool of
water up to the flanks. The ground gave Caspar an
opportunity to approach within a 'few yards without
being observed by the game, and a discharge from the
double-barrel put an end to the chase.

CHAPTER XXIX.

AN ALARMING DISCOVERY.

You will naturally suppose that this successful termination of the chase gave great satisfaction to the hunters. It might have done so under other circumstances, but just then their minds became occupied by thoughts of a far different nature.

As they came up to the spot where the stag had fallen, and were preparing to drag it from the pool, their eyes rested upon an object which caused them to turn toward one another with looks of strange significance. This object was no other than the hot spring—the place where the chase had begun. Within less than a hundred yards of the spot where the stag had received his first wound was he now lying dead! The pool in fact was in the little rivulet that ran from the spring to the lake.

I have said that the hunters on observing this exchanged significant glances. One fact was evident to all of them—that they had got back to the spot whence they started. A very little reasoning taught them another fact—that in the pursuit of the stag they must have made the full circuit of the valley. They had not turned back anywhere—they had not crossed the

valley—they had not even been in sight of the lake
during the whole chase. On the contrary, Karl with
Ossaroo had kept continually along the bottom of the
cliffs, sometimes in the timber, and at intervals passing
across stretches of open ground.

What was there remarkable about all this? It only
proved that the valley was small, and of roundish form;
and that in about an hour's time any one might make
the circuit of it. What was there in this discovery that
should cause the hunters to stand gazing upon one
another with troubled looks? Was it surprise at the
stag having returned to die where he had received his
wound? Certainly there was something a little singular about that, but so trifling a circumstance could not
have clouded the brows of the hunters. It was not
surprise that was pictured in their looks—more serious
feelings were stirring within them. Their glances were
those of apprehension—the fear of some danger not
fully defined or certain. What danger?

The three stood, Ossaroo lightly grasping his bow,
but not thinking of the weapon; Karl holding his rifle
with its butt resting on the ground, and Caspar gazing
interrogatively in the face of his brother.

For some moments not one of them spoke. Each
guessed what the other was thinking of. The stag lay
untouched in the pool, his huge antlers alone appearing
above the surface of the water, while the dog stood baying on the bank.

Karl at length broke silence. He spoke half in soliloquy, as if his thoughts were busy with the subject.

"Yes, a precipice the whole way round. I saw no
break—no signs of one. Ravines there were, it is true,

8

but all seemed to end in the same high cliffs. You observed no outlet, Ossaroo?"

"No, Sahib; me fearee de valley shut up, no clear o
dis trap yet Sahib."

Caspar offered no opinion. He had kept farther out
from the cliffs, and at times had been quite out of sight
of them—the trees hiding their tops from his view.
He fully comprehended, however, the meaning of his
brother's observations.

"Then you think the precipice runs all around the
valley?" he asked, addressing the latter.

"I fear so, Caspar. I observed no outlet—neither
has Ossaroo; and although not specially looking for
such a thing, I had my eyes open for it; I had not forgotten our perilous situation of yesterday, and I wished
to assure myself. I looked up several gorges that ran
out of the valley, but the sides of all seemed to be precipitous. The chase, it is true, kept me from examining
them very closely; but it is now time to do so. If there
be no pass out of this valley, then are we indeed in
trouble. These cliffs are five hundred feet in height—
they are perfectly impassable by human foot. Come
on! let us know the worst."

"Shall we not draw out the stag?" inquired Caspar,
pointing to the game that still lay under the water.

"No, leave him there; it will get no harm till our
return: should my fears prove just, we shall have
time enough for that, and much else beside. Come
on!"

So saying Karl led the way toward the foot of the
precipice, the others following silently after.

Foot by foot, and yard by yard, did they examine the

beetling front of those high cliffs. They viewed them from their base, and then passing outward scanned them to the very tops. There was no gorge or ravine which they did not enter and fully reconnoitre. Many of these there were, all of them resembling little bays of the ocean, their bottoms being on the same level with the valley itself, and their sides formed by the vertical wall of granite.

At some places the cliffs actually hung over. Now and then they came upon piles of rock and scattered boulders—some of them of enormous dimensions. There were single blocks full fifty feet in length, breadth, and height; and there were also cairns, or collections of rocks, piled up to four times that elevation, and standing at such a distance from the base of the cliff, that it was evident they could not have fallen from it into their present position. Ice, perhaps, was the agent that had placed them where they lay.

None of the three were in any mood to speculate upon geological phenomena at that moment. They passed on, continuing their examination. They saw that the cliff was not all of equal height. It varied in this respect, but its lowest escarpment was too high to be ascended. At the lowest point it could not have been less than three hundred feet sheer, while there were portions of it that rose to the stupendous height of one thousand from the valley!

On went they along its base, carefully examining every yard. They had gone over the same path with lighter feet and lighter hearts. This time they were three hours in making the circuit; and at the end of these three hours they stood in the gap by which they

had entered, with the full and painful conviction that
that gap was the only outlet to this mysterious valley—
the only one that could be traversed by human foot!
The valley itself resembled the crater of some extinct
volcano, whose lava lake had burst through this gate-
like gorge, leaving an empty basin behind.

They did not go back through the glacier ravine.
They had no hope of escaping in that direction. That
they knew already.

From the gap they saw the white vapor curling up
over the spring. They saw the remaining portion of
the precipice that lay beyond. It was the highest and
most inaccessible of all.

All three sat down upon the rocks; and remained for
some minutes silent and in a state of mind bordering
upon despair.

CHAPTER XXX.

PROSPECTS AND PRECAUTIONS.

BRAVE men do not easily yield to despair. Karl was brave. Caspar, although but a mere boy, was as brave as a man. So was the shikarree brave—that is, for one of his race. He would have thought light of any ordinary peril—a combat with a tiger, or a gayal, or a bear; but, like all his race, he was given to superstition. He now firmly believed that some of his Hindoo gods dwelt in this valley, and that they were all to be punished for intruding into the sacred abode. There was nothing singular about his holding this belief. It was perfectly natural,—in fact, it was only the belief of his religion and his race.

Notwithstanding his superstitious fears, he did not yield himself up to destiny. On the contrary, he was ready to enter heart and soul into any plan by which he and his companions might escape out of the territory of Brahma, Vishnu, or Siva—whichsoever of these it belonged to.

It was in thinking over some plan that kept all three of them in silence, and with such thoughts Ossaroo was as busy as the others.

Think as they would, no feasible or practicable idea

could be got hold of.　There were five hundred feet of a cliff to be scaled.　How was that feat to be accomplished?

By making a ladder?　The idea was absurd.　No ladder in the world would reach to the quarter of such a height.　Ropes, even if they had had them, could be in no way made available.　These might aid in going *down* a precipice, but for going *up* they would be perfectly useless.

The thought even crossed their minds of cutting notches in the cliff, and ascending by that means! This might appear to be practicable, and viewing the matter from a distance it certainly does seem so.　But had you been placed in the position of our travellers,— seated as they were in front of that frowning wall of granite,—and told that you must climb it by notches cut in the iron rock by your own hand, you would have turned from the task in despair.

So did they; at least the idea passed away from their thoughts almost in the same moment in which it had been conceived.

For hours they sat pondering over the affair.　What would they not have given for wings; wings to carry them over the walls of that terrible prison?

All their speculations ended without result; and at length rising to their feet, they set off with gloomy thoughts toward the spot where they had already encamped.

As if to render their situation more terrible, some wild beasts,—wolves they supposed,—had visited the encampment during their absence, and had carried off every morsel of the jerked meat.　This was a painful discovery, for now more than ever should they require such provision.

The stag still remained to them. Surely it was not also carried off? and to assure themselves they hurried to the pool, which was at no great distance. They were gratified at finding the deer in the pool where it had been left; the water, perhaps, having protected it from ravenous beasts.

As their former camp ground had not been well chosen, they dragged the carcass of the deer up to the hot spring; that being a better situation. There the animal was skinned, a fire kindled, and after they had dined upon fresh venison-steaks, the rest of the meat Ossaroo prepared for curing,—just as he had done that of the yak,—but in this case he took the precaution to hang it out of reach of all four-footed marauders.

So careful were they of the flesh of the deer, that even the bones were safely stowed away, and Fritz had to make his supper upon the offal.

Notwithstanding their terrible situation, Karl had not abandoned one of the national characteristics of his countryman,—prudence. He foresaw a long stay in this singular valley. How long he did not think of asking himself; perhaps for life. He anticipated the straits in which they might soon be placed; food even might fail them; and on this account every morsel was to be kept from waste.

Around their night camp-fire they talked of the prospects of obtaining food; of the animals they supposed might exist in the valley; of their numbers and kinds, —they had observed several kinds; of the birds upon the lake and among the trees; of the fruits and berries;

of the roots that might be in the ground; in short, of every thing that might be found there from which they could draw sustenance.

They examined their stock of ammunition. This exceeded even their most sanguine hopes. Both Caspar's large powder-horn and that of his brother were nearly full. They had·used their guns but little since last filling their horns. They had also a good store of shot and bullets; though these things were less essential, and in case of their running short of them they knew of many substitutes, but gunpowder is the *sine quâ non* of the hunter.

Even had their guns failed them, there was still the unerring bow of Ossaroo, and it was independent of either powder or lead. A thin reed, or the slender branch of a tree, were nearly all that Ossaroo required to make as deadly a shaft as need be hurled.

They were without anxiety, on the score of being able to kill such animals as the place afforded. Even had they been without arrows, they felt confident that in such a circumscribed space they would have been able to circumvent and capture the game. They had no uneasiness about any four-footed creature making its escape from the valley any more than themselves. There could be no other outlet than that by which they had entered. By the ravine only could the four-footed denizens of the place have gone out and in; and on the glacier they had observed a beaten path made by the tracks of animals, before the snow had fallen. Likely enough the pass was well known to many kinds, and likely also there were others that stayed continually in the valley, and there brought forth their young. Indeed, it would have been difficult for a wild animal to have found a more desirable home.

The hope of the hunters was that many animals might have held this very opinion, and from what they had already observed, they had reason to think so.

Of course they had not yet abandoned the hope of being able to find some way of escape from their singular prison. No, it was too early for that. Had they arrived at such a conviction, they would have been in poor heart indeed, and in no mood for conversing as they did. The birds and the quadrupeds, and the fruits and roots, would have had but little interest for them with such a despairing idea as that in their minds. They still hoped, though scarce knowing why; and in this uncertainty they went to rest with the resolve to give the cliffs a fresh examination on the morrow.

8 *

CHAPTER XXXI.

MEASURING THE CREVASSE.

AGAIN, on the morrow, every foot of the precipitous bluffs was minutely scanned and examined. The circuit of the valley was made, as before. Even trees were climbed in order the better to view the face of the cliffs that soared far above their tops. The result was a full conviction, that to scale the precipice at any point was an utter impossibility.

Until fully convinced of this, they had not thought of going back through the gap that led to the glacier; but now that all hopes of succeeding elsewhere had vanished from their minds, they proceeded in that direction.

They did not walk towards it with the light brisk step of men who had hopes of success; but rather mechanically, as if yielding to a sort of involuntary impulse. As yet they had not examined the ice-chasm very minutely.

Awed by the terror of the glacier slide, they had retreated from the spot in haste. One glance at the crevasse was all they had given; but in that glance they had perceived the impossibility of crossing it. At the time, however, they were not aware of the resources that were so near. They were not aware that within less than five hundred yards of the spot grew a forest of tall trees. Indeed, it was not until they had fully reconnoitred the cliffs, and turned away from them in despair, that such a train of reasoning occurred to the mind of any of the three.

As they were entering the portals of that singular passage, the thought seemed for the first time to have taken shape. Karl was the first to give expression to it. Suddenly halting, he pointed back to the forest, and said,—

" If we could bridge it ! "

Neither of his companions asked him what he contemplated bridging. Both were at that moment busy with the same train of thought. They knew it was the crevasse.

" Those pine-trees are tall," said Caspar.

" Not tall enough, Sahib," rejoined the shikarree.

" We can splice them," continued Caspar.

Ossaroo shook his head, but said nothing in reply.

The idea, however, had begotten new hopes ; and all three walked down the ravine with brisker steps. They scanned the cliffs on either side as they advanced, but these they had examined before.

Treading with caution they approached the edge of the crevasse. They looked across. A hundred feet wide—perhaps more than a hundred feet—yawned that fearful gulf. They knelt down and gazed into the chasm. It opened far away into the earth—hundreds of feet below where they knelt. It narrowed towards the bottom. They could see the crystal cliffs, blue at the top, grow greener and darker as they converged towards each other. They could see huge boulders of rock and masses of icy snow wedged between them, and could hear far below the roaring of water. A torrent ran there—no doubt the superfluous waters of the lake escaping by this subglacial stream.

A sublime, but terrible sight it was; and although the nerves of all were strung to an extreme degree, it made them giddy to look into the chasm, and horrid feelings came over them as they listened to the unnatural echoes of their voices. To have descended to the bottom would have been a dread peril: but they did not contemplate such an enterprise. They knew that such a proceeding would be of no use, even could they have accomplished it. Once in the bottom of the chasm the opposite steep would still have to be climbed, and this was plainly an impossibility. They thought not of crossing in that way—their only hope lay in the possibility of bridging the crevasse; and to this their whole attention was now turned.

Such a project might appear absurd. Men of weaker minds would have turned away from it in despair; and so, too, might they have done, but for the hopelessness of all other means of escape. It was now life or death with them—at all events, it was freedom or captivity.

To give up all hope of returning to their homes and friends—to spend the remainder of their lives in this wild fastness—was a thought almost as painful as the prospect of death itself.

It was maddening to entertain such a thought, and as yet not one of them could bring himself to dwell upon the reality of so terrible a destiny. But the fact that such in reality would be their fate, unless they could discover some mode of escaping from their perilous situation, sharpened all their wits; and every plan was brought forward and discussed with the most serious earnestness.

As they stood gazing across that yawning gulf, the conviction entered their minds that *it was possible to bridge it.*

Karl was the first to give way to this conviction. Caspar, ever sanguine, soon yielded to the views of his brother; and Ossaroo, though tardily convinced, acknowledged that they could do no better than try. The scientific mind of the botanist had been busy, and had already conceived a plan—which though it would be difficult of execution, did not seem altogether impracticable. On one thing, however, its practicability rested —the width of the chasm. This must be ascertained, and how was it to be done?

It could not be guessed—that was clear. The simple estimate of the eye is a very uncertain mode of measuring—as was proved by the fact that each one of the three assigned a different width to the crevasse. In fact, there was full fifty feet of variation in their estimates. Karl believed it to be only a hundred feet in width, Ossaroo judged it at a hundred and fifty, while Caspar thought it might be between the two. How, then, were they to measure it exactly? That was the first question that came before them.

Had they been in possession of proper instruments, Karl was scholar enough to have determined the distance by triangulation; but they had neither quadrant nor theodolite; and that mode was therefore impossible.

I have said that their wits were sharpened by their

situation, and the difficulty about the measurement was soon got over. It was Ossaroo who decided that point.

Karl and Caspar were standing apart discussing the subject, not dreaming of any aid from the shikarree upon so scientific a question, when they perceived the latter unwinding a long string, which he·had drâwn from his pocket.

" Ho ! " cried Caspar, " what are you about, Ossaroo ? Do you expect to measure it with a string ? "

" Yes, Sahib ! " answered the shikarree.

" And who is to carry your line to the opposite side, I should like to know ? " inquired Caspar.

It seemed very ridiculous, indeed, to suppose that the chasm could be measured with a string—so long as only one side of it was accessible ; · but there was a *way* of doing it, and Ossaroo's native wit had suggested that way to him.

In reply to Caspar's question, he took one of the arrows from his quiver, and, holding it up, he said,—

" This, Sahib, this carry it."

" True ! true ! " joyfully exclaimed the brothers ; both of whom at once comprehended the design of the shikarree.

It cost Ossaroo but a few minutes to put his design into execution. The string was unwound to its full extent. There were nearly a hundred yards of it. It was stretched tightly, so as to clear it of snarls, and then one end was adjusted to the shaft of the arrow. The other end was made fast to a rock, and after that the bow was bent, and the arrow projected into the air.

A shout of joy was raised as the shaft was seen to fall upon the snowy surface on the opposite ·side ; and the tiny cord was observed, like the thread of a spider's web, spanning the vast chasm.

Ossaroo seized the string in his hand, drew the arrow gently along until it rested close to the opposite edge; and then marking the place with a knot, he plucked the arrow till it fell into the chasm, and hand over hand commenced winding up the string.

In a few moments he had recovered both cord and arrow; and now came the important part, the measurement of the string.

The hearts of all three beat audibly as foot after foot was told off; but a murmur of satisfaction escaped from all, when it was found that the lowest estimate was nearest the truth. The chasm was about a hundred feet wide!

CHAPTER XXXII.

THE HUT.

KARL felt confident they could bridge the crevasse. The only weapons they had were their knives, and a small wood hatchet which Ossaroo chanced to have in his belt when they set out in chase of the musk-deer. True they had their guns, but of what service could these be in making a bridge?

Ossaroo's knife, as already described, was a long-bladed one,—half knife, half sword,—in fact, a jungle knife. The hatchet was not larger than an Indian tomahawk; but with these weapons Karl Linden believed he could build a bridge of one hundred feet span!

He communicated to his companions his plan in detail, and both believed in its feasibility. I need hardly say that under such a belief their spirits rose again; and, though they felt that success was far from certain, they were once more filled with hope; and having taken all the necessary steps, in regard to measuring the narrowest part of the crevasse, and noted the ground well, they returned to the valley with lighter hearts.

The bridge was not to be the work of a day, nor a week, nor yet might a month suffice. Could they

only have obtained access to both sides of the chasm it
would have been different, and they could easily have
finished it in less time. But you are to remember that
only one side was allowed them to work upon, and from
this they would of necessity have to project the bridge
to the other. If they could even have got a cable
stretched across, this would have been bridge enough
for them, and they would have needed no other. A
cable, indeed! They would soon have found their way
over upon a cable or even a stout rope; but the stoutest communication they had was a slender string, and
only an arrow to hold it in its place!

The genius of Karl had not only projected the bridge,
but a mode of placing it across the chasm, though many
a contrivance would have to be adopted, before the
work could be finished. Much time would require to
be spent, but what of time when compared with the
results of failure or success?

The first thing they did was to build them a hut.
The nights were cold, and growing colder, for the
Himalaya winter was approaching, and sleeping in the
open air, even by the largest fire they might make, was
by no means comfortable. They built a rude hovel
therefore, partly of logs, and partly of stone blocks, for
it was difficult to procure logs of the proper length, and
to cut them with such tools as they had would have
been a tedious affair. The walls were made thick,
rough, and strong; the interstices were matted and
daubed with clay from the bed of the rivulet; the
thatch was a sedge obtained from the lake; and the
floor of earth was strewed with the leaves of the sweet-
smelling rhododendron. The hole was left for the

smoke to escape. Several granite slabs served for seats—tables were not needed—and for beds each of the party had provided himself with a thick mattress of dried grass and leaves. With such accommodations were the hunters fain to content themselves. They felt too much anxiety about the future to care for present luxuries.

They were but one single day in building the hut. Had there been bamboos at hand, Ossaroo would have constructed a house in half the time, and a much handsomer one. As it was, their hovel occupied them just a day, and on the next morning they set to work upon the bridge.

They had agreed to divide the labour; Karl with the axe, and Ossaroo with his large knife, were to work upon the timbers; while Caspar was to provide the food with his double-barrelled gun, helping the others whenever he could spare time.

But Caspar found another purpose for his gun besides procuring meat. Ropes would be wanted, long tough ropes; and they had already planned it, that these should be made from the hides of the animals that might be killed. Caspar, therefore, had an important part to play. Two strong cables would be required, so Karl told him, each about a hundred feet in length, besides many other ropes and cords. It would be necessary to hunt with some success before these could be obtained. More than one large hide, a dozen at least, would be required; but Caspar was just the man to do his part of the work, and procure them.

For the timbers, the trees out of which they were to be made had already been doomed. Even that morning four trees had been marked by the axe and girdled. These were pine trees, of the species known as Thibet pines, which grow to a great height, with tall trunks clear of branches full fifty feet from the ground. Of course it was not the largest trees that were chosen; as it would have cost too much labor to have reduced their trunks to the ·proper dimension, and particularly with such tools as the workmen had. On the contrary, the trees that were selected were those very near the thickness that would be required; and but little would have to be done, beyond clearing them of the bark and hewing the heavier ends, so as to make the scantling of equal weight and thickness all throughout their length. The splicing each two of them together would be an operation requiring the greatest amount of care and labor.

All their designs being fully discussed, each set about his own share of the work. Karl and Ossaroo betook themselves to the pine-forest, while Caspar prepared to go in search of the game.

CHAPTER XXXIII.

THE BARKING-DEER.

"Now," said Caspar to himself, as he shouldered his double-barrelled gun, and started forth, "now to find that same herd of grunters! They're the biggest animals here I fancy, and their beef's not bad—the veal isn't, I know. Besides, the hide of the old bull would make—let me see—how many yards of rope."

Here Caspar entered into a mental calculation as to what length of raw-hide rope, of two inches in diameter, might be twisted out of the yak bull's skin. Karl had said two inches in diameter would be strong enough for his purpose, provided the hide of the animal was as tough as ordinary cow's hide; and this the skin of the yak really is.

The young hunter, after much computation, having stripped the great bull of his skin, and spread it out upon the grass, and measured it—all in fancy of course —and cut it into strips of near three inches in width— had arrived at the conclusion that he would get about twenty yards of sound rope out of the hide.

Then he submitted the skins of the cows to a similar process of measurement. There were four of them— there had been five, but one was already killed. To each of the four Caspar allowed a yield of ten yards of rope—as each of them was only a little more than half the size of the bull—besides their skins would not be either so thick or so strong.

There were four half-grown yaks—young bulls and heifers. Caspar remembered the number well, for he had noted this while stalking them. To these he allowed still less yield than to the cows—perhaps thirty yards from the four. So that the hides of all—old bull, cows, and yearlings—would, according to Caspar's calculation, give a cable of ninety yards in length. What a pity it would not make a hundred—for that was about the length that Karl had said the cable should be. True, there were some young calves in the herd, but Caspar could make no calculation on these. Their skins might serve for other purposes, but they would not do for working up into the strong cable which Karl required.

"Maybe there is more than the one herd in the valley," soliloquized Caspar. "If so it will be all right. Another bull would be just the thing;" and with this reflection the hunter brought his double-barrel down, looked to his flints and priming, returned the gun to his shoulder, and then walked briskly on.

Caspar had no fear that he should be able to kill all the yaks they had seen. He was sure of slaughtering the whole herd. One thing certain, these animals could no more get out of the valley than could the hunter himself. If they had ever been in the habit of going out of it to visit other pastures, they must have gone by the glacier; and they were not likely to traverse that path any more. The hunter now had them at an advantage—in fact, they were regularly penned up for him!

After all, however, it was not such a pen. The valley was a full mile 'in width, and rather better in length. It was a little country of itself. It was far from being of an even or equal surface. Some parts were hilly, and great rocks lay scattered over the surface here and there, in some places forming great mounds several hundred feet high, with cliffs and ravines between them, and trees growing in the clefts. Then there were dark woods and thick tangled jungle tracts, where it was almost impossible to make one's way through. Oh, there was plenty of covert for game, and the dullest animal might escape from the keenest hunter in such places. Still the game could not go clear away; and although the yaks might get off on an occasion, they were sure to turn up again; and Caspar trusted to his skill to be able to circumvent them at one time or another.

Never in his life before had Caspar such motives for displaying his hunter skill. His liberty—that of all of them—depended on all his success in procuring the necessary number of hides; and this was spur enough to excite him to the utmost.

In starting forth from the hut, he had taken his way along the edge of the lake. Several opportunities offered of a shot at Brahmin geese and wild ducks but, in anticipation of finding the yaks, he had loaded both barrels of his gun with balls. This he had done in order to be prepared for the great bull, whose thick hide even buck-shot would scarce have pierced. A shot at the waterfowl, therefore, could not be thought of. There would be every chance of missing them with the bullet; and neither powder nor lead were such plentiful articles as to be thrown away idly. He therefore reserved his fire, and walked on.

Nothing appeared to be about the edge of the lake; and after going a short distance he turned off from the water and headed the direction of the cliffs. He hoped to find the herd of yaks among the rocks—for Karl, who knew something of the natural history of these animals, had told him that they frequented steep rocky places in preference to level ground.

Caspar's path now led him through a belt of timber, and then appeared a little opening on which there was a good deal of tall grass, and here and there a low copse or belt of shrubbery.

Of course he went cautiously along—as a hunter should do—at every fresh vista looking ahead for his game.

While passing through the open ground his attention was attracted to a noise that appeared to be very near him. It exactly resembled the barking of a fox—a sound with which Caspar was familiar, having often heard foxes bark in his native country. The bark, however, appeared to him to be louder and more distinct than that of a common fox.

"Perhaps," said he to himself, "the foxes of these mountains are bigger than our German reynards, and can therefore bark louder. Let me see if it be a fox. I'm not going to waste a bullet on him either; but I should like just to have a look at a Himalaya fox."

With these reflections Caspar stole softly through the grass in the direction whence issued the sounds.

He had not advanced many paces when he came in sight of an animal differing altogether from a fox; but the very one that was making the noise. This was certain, for while he stood regarding it, he perceived it in the very act of uttering that noise, or *barking*, as we already called it.

Caspar felt very much inclined to laugh aloud, on perceiving that the barking animal was neither fox, nor dog, nor yet a wolf, nor any other creature that is known to bark, but on the contrary an animal of a far different nature—a deer. Yes, it was really a deer that was giving utterance to those canine accents.

It was a small, slightly-made creature, standing about two feet in height, with horns seven or eight inches long. It might have passed for an antelope; but Caspar observed that on each horn there was an antler—a very little one, only an inch or so in length—and that decided him that it must be an animal of the deer family. Its color was light red, its coat short and smooth, and, on a closer view, Caspar saw that it had a tusk in each jaw, projecting outside the mouth, something like the tushes of the musk-deer. It was, in fact, a closely-allied species. It was the "kakur," or "barking-deer;" so called from its barking habit, which had drawn the attention of the hunter upon it.

Of the barking-deer, like most other deer of India, there are several varieties very little known to naturalists; and the species called the "muntjak" (*Cervus vaginalis*) is one of these. It also has the protruding tushes, and the solitary antler upon its horns.

The "barking-deer is common on the lower hills of the Himalaya Mountains, as high as seven or eight thousand feet ; but they sometimes wander up the courses of rivers, or valley gorges, to a much higher elevation ; and the one now observed by Caspar had possibly strayed up the glacier valley in midsummer, guided by curiosity, or some instinct, that carried it into the beautiful valley that lay beyond. Poor little fellow ! it never found its way back again ; for Caspar bored its body through and through with a bullet from his right-hand barrel, and hung its bleeding carcass on the branch of a tree.

He did not shoot it upon sight, however. He hesitated for some time whether it would be prudent to waste a shot upon so tiny a morsel, and had even permitted it to run away.

As it went off, he was surprised at a singular noise which it made in running, not unlike the rattling of two pieces of loose bone knocked sharply together ; in fact, a pair of castanets. This he could hear after it had got fifty yards from him, and, perhaps, farther ; but there the creature suddenly stopped, turned its head round, and stood barking as before.

Caspar could not make out the cause of such a strange noise, nor, indeed, has any naturalist yet offered an explanation of this phenomenon. Perhaps it is the cracking of the hoofs against each other, or, more likely, the two divisions of each hoof coming sharply together, when raised suddenly from the ground. It is well known that a similar, only much louder noise, is made by the long hoofs of the great moose-deer ; and the little kakur probably exhibits the same phenomenon on a smaller scale.

Caspar did not speculate long about the cause. The

9

creature, as it stood right before the muzzle of his gun, now offered too tempting a' shot, and the right-hand barrel put an end to its barking.

" You're not what I came after," soliloquized Caspar; " but the old stag's no great eating, he's too tough for me.   You, my little fellow, look more tender, and, I dare say, will make capital venison.   Hang there, then, till I return for you ! "

So saying, Caspar, having already strung the kakur's legs, lifted the carcass, and hung it to the branch of a . tree.

Then, reloading his right-hand barrel with a fresh bullet, he continued on in search of the herd of yaks.

CHAPTER XXXIV.

THE ARGUS PHEASANT.

CASPAR proceeded with increased caution. His design was to *stalk* the wild oxen; and he had left Fritz at the hut, as the dog could be of no use in that sort of hunting.

He intended to stalk the animals with more than ordinary caution, for two reasons. The first was, of course, in order to get a shot at them; but there was another reason why he should be careful, and that was, the fierce and dangerous nature of the game. He had not forgotten the way in which the old bull had behaved at their last interview; and Karl had particularly cautioned him, before setting out, to act prudently, and to keep out of the way of the bull's horns. He was not to fire at the yaks, unless there was a tree near, or some other shelter, to which he could retreat if pursued by the bull.

The necessity, therefore, of choosing such a point of attack, would make his stalk all the more difficult.

He walked silently on, sometimes through spots of open ground; at others, traversing belts of woodland, or tracts of thickety jungle. Wherever there was a reach, or open space, he stopped before going out of

the cover, and looked well before him. He had no
wish to come plump on the game he was in search of,
lest he might get too close to the old bull. Fifty or
sixty yards was the distance he desired ; and, with the
large bullets his gun carried, he would have been near
enough at that. .

Several kinds of large birds flew up from his path,
as he advanced ; among others, the beautiful argus-
pheasant, that almost rivals the peacock in the splendor
of its plumage. These rare creatures would whirr
upward, and alight among the branches of the trees
overhead ; and, strange to say, although nearly as large
as peacocks, and of a most striking and singular form,
Caspar could never get his eyes upon them after they
had once perched.

It is the habit of these birds, when aware of the
presence of the hunter, to remain perfectly silent and
motionless, and it requires the keenest eyes to make
them out among the leaves. In fact, the very beauty
of their singular plumage, which makes the argus-
pheasant so marked and attractive an object when side
by side with other birds, is the very thing which, amid
the foliage of trees, renders it so difficult to be seen.
Ocellated as the bird is all over its body, wings, and
tail, the general effect is such as rather to conceal it.
A disk of the same size of an unbroken color, even
though the tints be less brilliant, is far more likely to
arrest the eye-glance. Besides, the collected foliage of
the trees, when gazed at from beneath, presents a species of ocellation, to which that of the argus-pheasant is
in some way assimilated. This may be a provision of
nature, for the protection of this beautiful and otherwise

helpless bird; for it is no great creature at a flight, with all its fine plumes; and, but for its power of thus concealing itself, would easily fall a prey to the sportsman.

Naturalists often, and, perhaps, oftener hunters, have noted this adaptation of the color of wild animals to their haunts and habits. The jaguars, the leopards, and panthers, whose bright, yellow skins, beautifully spotted as they are, would seem to render them most conspicuous objects, are, in reality, the most difficult to be perceived amid the haunts which they inhabit. An animal of equal size, and of the dullest coloring, provided it were uniform, would be more easily seen than they. Their very beauty renders them invisible; since their numerous spots, interrupting the uniformity of color, breaks up the large disk of their bodies into a hundred small ones, and even destroys, to the superficial glance, the form which would otherwise betray their presence.

For some such reason then the argus-pheasant is most difficult to be seen, when once settled on his perch among the leaves and twigs of the trees. But though himself not observed, he sees all that passes below. He is well named. Although the eyes all over his body be blind, he carries a pair in his head, that rival those of the famed watchman from whom he borrows his surname. He keeps the sportsman well in sight; and should the latter succeed in espying him, the argus knows well when he is discovered, and the moment a cock clicks or a barrel is poised upward, he is off with a loud whirr that causes the woods to ring.

But, as already stated, he is no great flyer. The smallness of the primary quills of his wing—as well as

the unwieldy size of the secondaries, forms an impedi
ment to his progress through the air, and his flight is
short and heavy. He is a good runner, however, like
all birds of his kind; and he passes rapidly over the
ground, using his wings in running like the wild tur-
key, to which bird he is kindred. When the argus-
pheasant is at rest or unexcited, his plumage is neither
so bright nor beautiful. It is when showing himself
off in the presence of his females that he appears to
best advantage. Then he expands his spotted wings,
and trails them on the ground in the same manner as
the peacock. His tail, too, becomes spread and raised
erect, whereas at other times it is carried in a line with
the body with the two long feathers folded over each
other.

The argus-pheasant (which closet-naturalists now say
is not a pheasant, but an *argus!*) is peculiar to the
southern parts of Asia, though the limits of its range
are not well understood. It is found in all parts of
India, and also, as is supposed, in China, even in the
northern provinces of that country.

But the argus is not the only beautiful pheasant of
these regions. India, or rather southern Asia, is the
true home of the pheasant tribe. Already nearly a
dozen species of these birds, some of them far more
beautiful than the birds of paradise, are known to
naturalists; and when the ornithology of the Indian
Islands has been thoroughly investigated, a still greater
number will be found to exist there.

The Impeyan pheasant, larger than the common
fowl, rivals the crested peacock in the brilliancy of its
hues. No words can give any adequate idea of the

splendour of this bird. Nearly the whole surface of its plumage is resplendent—dazzling with changing hues of green and steel-blue, of violet and gold. It looks as if its body was clothed in a scale armor of bright shining metal, while the plumage is soft and velvety to the touch. This magnificent bird is a native of the Himalaya Mountains; where is also found another splendid species, the peacock-pheasant of Thibet, the latter closely alied to a still more gorgeous bird, the crested polyplectron of the Moluccas.

One cannot look upon these lovely winged creatures without a, feeling of gratitude to Him who sent them to adorn the earth, and give pleasure to all who may behold them.

CHAPTER XXXV.

STALKING THE YAKS.

CASPAR was not out pheasant-shooting, and there fore these beautiful birds were permitted to fly off unscathed.   Caspar's game was the grunting bull.

Where could the herd be?   He had already traversed half the extent of the valley without finding the yaks; but there was nothing singular in this.   There was plenty of covert among the rocks and woods; and wild animals, however large, have an instinct or a faculty of concealing themselves that often surprises the hunter.   Even the gigantic elephant will get out of sight amidst thin jungle, where you might suppose his huge body could hardly be hidden; and the great black buffalo often springs unexpectedly out of a bushy covert not much bigger than his own body.   Just as partridges can squat unseen in the shortest stubble, or squirrels lie hid along the slenderest branch, so have the larger wild animals the faculty of concealing themselves in a covert proportionately scanty.

The young hunter was aware of this fact; and therefore was not so much surprised that he did not at once come in sight of the yaks.   The former attack upon them, resulting in the loss of two of their number, had rendered them wary; and the noises made in building the hut had, no doubt, driven them to the most secluded corner of the valley. Thither Caspar was bending his steps.

He was calculating that they would be found in some cover, and was beginning to regret that he had not brought Fritz, instead of trying to stalk them, when all at once the herd came under his eyes. They were quietly browsing out in a stretch of open ground—the young calves, as on the former occasion, playing with each other, tearing about over the ground, biting one another, and uttering their tiny grunts, like so many young porkers. The cows and yearlings were feeding unconcernedly—occasionally raising their heads and looking around, but not with any signs of uneasiness or fear. The bull was not in sight!

"Where can *he* be?" inquired Caspar of himself. "Perhaps these may be a different herd; 'one, two, three;'" and Caspar went on to tell over the individuals of the flock.

"Yes," he continued, muttering to himself, "they are the same, I fancy: three cows—four yearlings—the calves—exactly the number—all except the bull.— Where can the old rascal have concealed himself?"

And with his eyes Caspar swept the whole of the open space, and looked narrowly along the selvidge of the timber which grew around it. No bull, however, was to be seen.

"Now where can the old grunter have gone to?" again inquired Caspar of himself. "Is he off by himself, or along with some other herd? Surely there is but the one family in this valley. Yaks are gregarious animals: Karl says so. If there were more of them,

9 *

they would be all together. The bull must be ranging abroad by himself, on some business of his own. After all, I suspect he's not far off. I dare say he's in yonder thicket. I'd wager a trifle the knowing old fellow has a trick in his head. He's keeping sentry over the flock, while he himself remains unseen. In that way he has the advantage of any enemy who may assail them. A wolf, or bear, or any preying beast that should want to attack the calves where they now are, would be certain to approach them by that very thicket. Indeed, I should have done so myself, if I didn't know that there *was* a bull. I should have crouched round the timber and got under cover of the bushes, which would have brought me nicely within range. But now I shall do no such thing; for I suspect strongly the old boy's in the bushes. He would be on me with a rush if I went that way, and in the thicket there's not a tree big enough to shelter a chased cat. It's all brush and thorn bushes. It won't do; I shan't stalk them from that direction; but how else can I approach them? There's no other cover. Ha! yonder rock will serve my purpose!"

Caspar was not half the time in going through this soliloquy that you have been in reading it. It was a mental process entirely, and, of course, carried on with the usual rapidity of thought. The interjection which ended it, and the allusion to a rock, were caused by his perceiving that a certain rock might afford him the necessary cover for approaching the game.

This rock he had observed long before—in fact, the moment he had seen the herd. He could not have failed to observe it, for it lay right in the middle of the open ground, neither tree nor bush being near to hide it. It was of enormous size, too—nearly as big as a hovel, square-sided and apparently flat-topped. Of course, he had noticed it at the first glance, but had not thought of making it a stalking-horse—the thicket seeming to offer him a better advantage.

Now, however, when he dared not enter the thicket—lest he might there encounter the bull—he turned his attention to the rock.

By keeping the boulder between him and the yaks, he could approach behind it, and that would bring him within distance of the one or two of the herd that were nearest. Indeed, the whole flock appeared to be inclining towards the rock; and he calculated, that by the time he could get there himself they would all be near enough, and he might make choice of the biggest.

Up to this time he had remained under cover of the timber, at the point where he first came in sight of the yaks. Still keeping in the bushes, he made a circuit, until the rock was put between him and the herd. Big as the boulder was, it hardly covered the whole flock; and much caution would be required to get up to it without alarming them. He saw that if he could once pass over the first one hundred yards, the rock, then subtending a larger angle of vision, would shield him from their sight, and he might walk fearlessly forward. But the first hundred yards would be awkward stalking. Crawling flat upon his breast appeared to be his only chance. But Caspar had often stalked chamois on his native hills; and many a crawl had he made, over rocks and gravel, and ice and snow. He thought nothing, therefore, of progression in this way, and a hundred yards would be a mere bagatelle.

Without farther hesitation, therefore, he dropped to his marrow-bones, and then flat upon his breast, and in this attitude commenced wriggling and shuffling along like a gigantic salamander.   Fortunately the grass grew a foot or more in height, and that concealed him from the view of the yaks.   On he went, pushing his gun before him, and every now and then raising his eyes cautiously above the sward to note the position of the herd.   When it changed, he also deflected slightly from his course—so as always to keep the centre of the rock aligned upon the bodies of the animals.

After about ten minutes of this horizontal travelling, the hunter found himself within thirty paces of the great boulder.   Its broad sides now appeared sufficient to cover the whole flock ; and as crawling along the ground was by no means pleasant, Caspar was fain to give it up, and take once more to his feet.   He rose erect, therefore ; and running nimbly forward, in another moment he stood behind the rock.

CHAPTER XXXVI.

CASPAR RETREATS TO THE ROCK.

CASPAR now perceived that the rock was not all in one piece. In other words, there were two rocks—both of them immense boulders, but of very unequal size. The largest, as already observed, was of the size of a small house, or it might be compared to a load of hay; while the smaller was not much bigger than the wagon. They lay almost contiguous to each other, with a narrow space, about a foot in width, forming a sort of alley between them. This space resembled a cleft, as if the two blocks had once been united, and some terrible force had cloven them asunder.

Caspar only glanced at these peculiarities as he came up—his eye mechanically searching for the best point of the rock to shelter him from the game, while it afforded him an opportunity of aiming at them. It was altogether a very awkward cover—the rock was square-sided as a wall, with no jutting point that he could crawl behind and rest his gun over. In fact, at the corners it rather hung over, resting on a base narrower than its diameter. There was no bush near to it—not even long grass to accommodate him. The ground was quite bare, and had the appearance of being much trampled, as if it was a favorite resort—in fact, a "rubbing-stone" for the yaks. It was their tracks Caspar saw around it—some of them quite fresh—and conspicuous among the rest were some that by their size must have been made by the hoofs of the bull.

The sight of these large fresh tracks conducted Caspar, and very suddenly too, into a train of reflections that were anything but agreeable.

"The bull's tracks!" muttered he to himself. "Quite fresh, by thunder! Why he must have been here but a minute ago! What if"——

Here Caspar's heart thumped so violently against his ribs, that he could scarce finish the interrogation.

—"*What if he be on the other side of the rock?*"

The hunter was in a dilemma. Up to that moment he had never thought of the probability of the bull being behind the rock. He had taken it into his fancy, that the thicket must be the place of his concealment, but without any very good reason did he fancy this. It was assigning more cunning to the animal than was natural; and now on second thoughts Caspar perceived that it was far more probable the bull should be sunning himself on the other side of the great boulder! There he would be near to the herd,—and likely enough there he *was*.

"By thunder!" mentally exclaimed Caspar, "if he be there, the sooner I get back to the timber the better for my health. I never thought of it. He could run me down in half a minute. There's no place to escape to. Ha!—what!—good!"

These ejaculations escaped from the hunter as he cast his eyes upward. It was a peculiarity in the form of the rocks that had caused him to utter them. He noticed that the lesser one had a sloping ridge that could be easily ascended; and from its highest point the top of the larger might also be reached by a little active climbing.

"·Good!" repeated he to himself; "I'll be safe enough there, and I can easily get up if I'm chased. The top of the rock's equal to any tree. It'll do if I am put to the pinch; so here goes for a shot, bull or no bull!"

Saying this, he once more looked to his gun; and kneeling down close in to the great rock, he commenced shuffling round one of its impending corners, in order to get within view of the herd.

He did not move one inch forward without looking well before him into the plain where the yaks were feeding, but quite as anxiously did he bend his eyes around the edge of the boulder, where he surmised the bull might be. He even listened at intervals, expecting to hear the latter breathing or giving a grunt, or some other sign, by which his presence might be made known.

If behind the rock at all he must be very near, thought Caspar—near enough for his breathing to be heard; and once Caspar fancied that he actually heard a grunt, which did not proceed from any of the herd.

The hunter, however, had less fear now, as he believed he could retreat to the rock before even the swiftest animal could overtake him. He therefore moved on with sufficient confidence.

You are not to suppose that all these thoughts and movements occupied much time. There were not five minutes consumed from the time Caspar arrived at the rocks, until he had taken all his measures; and another minute or two were occupied in creeping round within view of the herd—where at length Caspar arrived.

As yet no bull was seen. He might still be there, but if so, he was farther round the corner of the rock; and the sight of the others now fair before the muzzle of Caspar's gun drove all thoughts of the bull out of his mind. He resolved to fire at the nearest.

Quick as thought the gun was to his shoulder, his finger touched the trigger, and the loud report echoed from the distant cliffs. The ball told, and a cow was bowled over, and lay sprawling on the plain. Bang went the second barrel, and a young bull with a broken leg went hobbling off toward the thicket. The rest of the herd tore away at top speed, and were soon lost sight of in the bushes.

A little calf alone remained by the cow that had fallen. It ran frisking around, uttering its singular cries, and seemingly astonished and unable to comprehend the catastrophe that had befallen its mother!

Under other circumstances Caspar would have pitied that calf—for though a hunter, he was not hard-hearted. But just then he had something else to do than give way to pity.

He had scarce aimed his second shot—even while his finger was still resting on the trigger—when a sound reached his ears that made his heart leap. It spoiled his aim in fact, or the yearling would have had it between his ribs instead of in his hind-leg. That sound could be nothing else than the grunt of the old bull himself; and so close to Caspar did it appear that the hunter suddenly dropped the muzzle of his gun, and looked around thinking the animal was right by him !

He did not see the bull on looking around; but he knew the latter could not be many feet off, just behind the angle of the boulder. Under this impression Caspar sprang to his feet, and ran with lightning speed to ascend the rock.

CHAPTER XXXVII.

FACE TO FACE WITH A FIERCE BULL.

CASPAR leaped on to the lower one, and scrambled up its sloping ridge.   His eyes were turned more behind than before him, for he expected every moment to see the bull at his skirts.   To his astonishment no bull had yet appeared, although as he was running around the rock twice or thrice had he heard his terrific grunting.

He now faced toward the summit, determined to climb up to the safest place.   From the top he would be able to see all around, and could there watch the movements of the bull, as he fancied, in perfect security. He laid his hand on the edge of the rock and drew himself over it.   It was as much as he could do.   The parapet was chin high, and it required all his strength to raise himself up.

His attention was so occupied in the endeavor, that he was fairly upon the top ere he thought of looking before him; and when he did look, he saw, to his amazement and terror, that he was not alone.   *The bull was there too !*

Yes ! the bull was there, and had been there all the while.   The top of the boulder was a flat table, several

yards in length and breadth, and upon this the old bull
had been quietly reclining, basking himself in the sun,
and watching his wives and children as they browsed
on the plain below. As he had been lying down, and
close to that edge of the table which was most distant
from Caspar, the latter could not have perceived him
while approaching the rock. He did not even think of
turning his eyes in that direction, as he would as soon
have thought of looking for the old bull in the top of one
of the trees.   Caspar had quite forgotten what Karl had
told him,—that the summits of rocks and isolated boulders are the favorite haunts of the yaks,—else he might
have kept out of the scrape he had now fairly got into.

On perceiving his dilemma, the young hunter was
quite paralysed; and for some moments stood aghast,
not knowing how to act.

Fortunately for him the bull had been standing at
the farthest extremity of the table, looking out over the
plain. The trouble he was in about his family occupied
all his attention, and he stood loudly grunting to them
as if calling them back. He was unable to comprehend
what had caused such a rout among them; although he
had already experienced the dire effect of those loud
detonations.   He was "craning" forward over the
edge, as if half determined to leap from the summit, instead of turning to the easier descent by which he had
got up.

As Caspar scrambled up to the ledge, the rattle of
his accoutrements on the rock reached the ears of the
bull; and just as the former had got to his feet the
latter wheeled round, and the two were now face to
face !

There was a moment's pause. Caspar stood in terror; his antagonist, perhaps, also surprised at the unexpected rencontre. It was a very short pause, indeed. Almost in the next instant the fierce yak, uttering his terrific cry, charged forward.

There was no chance to evade the shock by springing to one side or the other. The space was too circumscribed for such a manœuvre, and the most adroit matador could not have executed it where Caspar stood. He was too near the edge of the rock to make the experiment. His only hope lay in bounding back as he had come ; which he did almost mechanically upon the instant.

The impetus of the leap, and the slanting surface of the lower boulder, carried him onward to the bottom ; and, unable any longer to retain his feet, he fell forward upon his face. He heard the rattle of the bull's hoofs upon the rock behind him ; and before he could recover his feet again he felt the brute trampling over him.

Fortunately he was not hurt, and fortunately the same impetus that had flung him upon his face also carried his antagonist far beyond him ; and before the latter could turn from his headlong charge, the young hunter again stood erect.

But whither was he to run ? The trees were too far off ;—oh ! he could never reach them. The fierce beast would be on him ere he could half cross the open ground, and would drive those terrible horns into his back. Whither ?—whither ?

Confused and irresolute,. he turned and rushed back up the rock.

This time he scaled the slope more nimbly ; more lightly did he leap upon the ledge, but without any feeling of hope.   It was but the quick rush of despair,— the mechanical effort of terror.

The manœuvre did not yield him a minute's respite. His fierce antagonist saw it all, and went charging after.

Lightly the huge brute bounded up the slope, and then leaped upon the table, as if he had been a chamois or a goat.   No pause made he, but rushed straight on with foaming tongue and flaming eye-balls.

Now, indeed, did Caspar believe his last moment had come.   He had rushed across the table of granite, and stood upon its extremest end.   There was no chance to get back to the place where he had ascended.   His vengeful antagonist was in the track, and he could not pass him.   He must either spring down from where he stood, or be tossed from the spot upon the horns of the fierce bull.   Dizzy was the height,—over twenty feet, —but there was no alternative but take the leap.   He launched himself into the air.

He came down feet foremost, but the terrible shock stunned him, and he fell upon his side.   The sky was darkened above him.   It was the huge body of the bull that had bounded after, and the next moment he heard the heavy sound of the animal's hoofs as they came in contact with the plain.

The hunter struggled to regain his feet.   He rose and fell again.   One of his limbs refused to perform its functions.   He felt there was something wrong ; he believed that his leg was broken !

Even this fearful thought did not cause the brave

youth to yield. He saw that the bull had recovered himself, and was once more approaching him. He scrambled towards the rock, dragging the useless limb behind him.

You will suppose that there was no longer a hope for him, and that the wild ox rushing upon him must certainly gore him to death. And so he would have done, had not Caspar been in the hands of Providence, who gave him a stout heart, and enabled him to make still another effort for his safety.

As he turned toward the boulder, an object came before his eyes that filled him with fresh hopes. That object was the cleft between the rocks. It was, as already described, about a foot in width, and separated the two boulders at all points,—except along the top, where they rested against each other.

Caspar's quick mind at once perceived the advantage. If he could only reach this crevice, and crawl into it in time, he might still be saved. It was big enough for his body; it would be too narrow to admit that of his huge antagonist.

On hands and knees he glided along with desperate speed. He reached the entrance of the crevice. He clutched the angle of rock, and drew himself far inward. He had not a moment to spare. He heard the horns of the bull crash against the cheeks of the chasm; but the charge was followed by a grunt of disappointment uttered by the furious animal.

A cry of joy involuntarily escaped from the lips of the hunter,—who felt that he was saved-!

CHAPTER XXXVIII.

CASPAR IN THE CLEFT.

CASPAR breathed freely. He had need; for the peril he had passed, and the rushing backward and forward, and springing over the rocks, had quite taken away his breath. He could not have lasted another minute.

The bull, thus balked of his revenge, seemed to become more furious than ever. He rushed to and fro, uttering savage grunts, and at intervals dashing his horns against the rocks, as if he hoped to break them to pieces, and open a passage to his intended victim. Once he charged with such fury that his head entered the cleft till his steaming snout almost touched Caspar where he lay. Fortunately, the thick hairy shoulders of the bull hindered him from advancing farther; and in drawing back his head, he found that he had wedged himself; and it was with some difficulty that he succeeded in detaching his horns from the rock !

Caspar took advantage of his struggles; and seizing a stone that lay near at hand, he mauled the bull so severely about the snout, that the brute was fain to get his head clear again ; and although he still stood madly pawing by the outside of the cleft, he took care not to repeat his rude assault.

Caspar now seeing that he was safe from any imme-
diate danger, began to feel uneasiness about his broken
limb. He knew not how long he might be detained
there—for it was evident that the yak was implacable,
and would not leave him while he could keep his eyes
upon him. It is the nature of these animals to hold
their resentment so long as the object of their vengeance is in sight. Only when that is hidden from
them, do they seem to *forget*—for it is probable they
never *forgive*.

The bull showed no signs of leaving the ground. On
the contrary, he paced backward and forward, grunting
as fiercely as ever, and at intervals making a rush
towards the entrance as if he still had hopes of reaching his victim.

Caspar now regarded these demonstrations with in-
difference. He was far more concerned about his limb;
and as soon as he could turn himself into a proper position, he began to examine it.

He felt the bone carefully from the knee downward.
He knew the thigh was safe enough. It was his ankle-
joint, he feared, was broken. The ankle was already
swollen and black—badly swollen, but Caspar could
detect no evidence of a fracture of the bones.

"After all," soliloquized he, "it may be only sprained.
If so, it will be all right yet."

He continued to examine it, until he at length arrived
at the conviction that it was "only a sprain."

This brought him into good spirits again, though the
leg was very painful; but Caspar was a boy who could
bear pain very stoically.

He now began to ponder upon his situation. How

was he to be rescued from his fierce besieger ? Would
Karl and Ossaroo hear him if he were to shout ? That
was doubtful enough. He could not be much less than
a mile from them ; and there were woods and rough
ground between him and them. They might be chopping, too, and would not hear his calls. Still, they would
not always be chopping, and he could keep up a constant shouting till they did hear him. He had already
noticed that in the valley, shut in on all sides as it was
by cliffs, sounds were transmitted to a great distance—
in fact, the cliffs seem to act as conductors somewhat
after the manner of a whispering-gallery. No doubt,
then, Karl and Ossaroo would hear him—especially if
he gave one of his shrill whistles ; for Caspar knew
how to whistle very loudly, and he had often made the
Bavarian hills ring again.

He was about to make the Himalayas ring, and
had already placed his fingers to his lips, when the
thought occurred to him that it would be wrong to do
so.

" No," said he, after reflecting a moment, " I shall
not call them. My whistle would bring Karl, I know.
He would come running at the signal. I might not be
able to stop him till he had got quite up to the rocks
here, and then the bull ! No—Karl's life might be
sacrificed instead of mine. I shall not whistle."

With these reflections, he removed his fingers from
his lips, and remained silent.

" If I only had my gun," thought he, after a pause,—
" if I only had my gun, I'd soon settle matters with you,
you ugly brute ! You may thank your stars I have
dropped it."

10

The gun had escaped from Caspar's hands as he fell upon his face on first rushing down from the rock. It was no doubt lying near the spot where he had fallen, but he was not sure where it had been flung to.

"If it was not for this ankle," he continued, "I'd chance a rush for it yet. Oh! if I could only get the gun here; how I'd fix the old grunter off, before he could whisk that tail of his twice—that I would."

"Stay!" continued the hunter, after some minutes' pause, "my foot seems to get well. It's badly swollen, but the pain's not much. It's only a sprain! Hurrah!—it's only a sprain! By thunder! I'll try to get the gun."

. With this resolve, Caspar raised himself to a standing attitude, holding by the rocks on both sides.

The lane between them just gave him room enough to move his body along; and the cleft being of a uniform width from side to side, he could get out on either side he might choose.

But, strange to relate, the old bull, whenever he saw the hunter move towards the opposite side, rushed round to the same, and stood prepared to receive him upon his horns!

This piece of cunning, on the part of his antagonist, was quite unexpected by Caspar. He had hoped he would be able to make a sally from one side of the rock while his adversary guarded the other; but he now saw that the animal was as cunning as himself. It was but a few yards round from one side to the other, and it would be easy for the bull to overtake him, if he only ventured six feet from the entrance.

He made one attempt as a sort of feint or trial; but

was driven back again into the crevice almost at the point of his antagonist's horns.

The result was, that the yak, now suspecting some design, watched his victim more closely, never for a moment taking his eyes off him.

But withal Caspar had gained one advantage from the little sally he had made. He had seen the gun where it lay, and had calculated the distance it was off. Could he only obtain thirty seconds of time, he felt certain he might secure the weapon ; and his thoughts were now bent on some plan to gain this time.

All at once a plan was suggested to him, and he resolved to make trial of it.

The yak habitually stood with his head close up to the crevice—the froth dropping from his mouth, his eyes rolling fiercely, and his head lowered almost to the earth.

Caspar could have thrust his head with a spear—if he had been armed with one—or he could even have belabored it with a cudgel.

" Is there no way," thought he, " that I can blind the brute ? Ha ! By thunder, I have it ! " exclaimed he, hitting upon an idea that seemed to promise the desired result.

As quick as thought he lifted over his head his powder-horn and belt ; and, then stripping off his jacket, took the latter in both hands, held it spread out as wide as the space would permit. He now approached the edge of the cleft in hopes of being able to fling the jacket over the horns of the bull, and, by thus blinding him, get time to make a rush for his gun.

The idea was a good one ; but, alas ! it failed in the

execution. Caspar's arms were confined between the
boulders, and he was unable to fling the jacket adroitly.
It reached the frontlet of the bull; but the latter, with
a disdainful toss of his head, flung it to one side, and
stood fronting his adversary, as watchful of his movements as ever.

Caspar's heart sunk at the failure of his scheme, and
he retreated despairingly back into the cleft.

"I shall have to call Karl and Ossaroo in the end,"
thought he. "No! not yet!—not yet! Another plan!
I'll manage it yet, by thunder!"

What was Caspar's new plan? We shall soon see.
He was not long in putting it to the test. A youth
quick in action was Caspar.

He seized his huge powder-horn, and took out the
stopper. Once more he crept forward towards the bull,
and as near the snout of the latter as it was safe for him
to go. Holding the horn by its thick end, and reaching far out, he poured upon the levellest and driest spot
a large quantity of powder; and, then drawing the horn
gradually nearer, he laid a train for several feet inward.

Little did the grunting yak know the surprise that
awaited him.

Caspar now took out his flint, steel, and touchpaper,
and in a moment more struck a fire, and touched off
the train.

As he had calculated, the exploding powder flashed
outward and upward, taking the bull by surprise with the
sudden shock, at the same time that it enveloped him
in its thick sulphury smoke. The animal was heard rout-
ing and plunging about, not knowing which way to run.

This was the moment for Caspar; who, having already prepared himself for the rush, sprang suddenly forth, and ran towards his gun.

With eagerness he grasped the weapon; and, forgetting all about his sprained ankle, ran back with the speed of a deer. Even then, he was not a moment too soon in reaching his retreat; for the bull, having recovered from his surprise, saw and pursued him, and once more sent his horns crashing against the rocks.

" Now," said Caspar, addressing his fierce besieger, and speaking with a confidence he had not hitherto felt, " that time you were more scared than hurt; but the next time I burn powder, the case will be rather different, I fancy. Stand where you are, old boy. Another minute allow me! and I'll raise this siege, without giving you either terms or quarter."

As Caspar continued to talk in this way, he busied himself in loading his gun. He loaded both barrels— though one would have been sufficient; for the first shot did the business clear as a whistle. It tumbled the old bull off his legs, and put an end to his grunting at once and for ever!

Caspar now came forth from the cleft; and, placing his fingers to his lips, caused the valley to ring with his loud whistle. A similar whistle came pealing back through the woods; and, in fifteen minutes' time, Karl and Ossaroo were seen running forward to the spot; and soon after had heard the particulars of Caspar's adventure, and were congratulating him on his escape.

The yaks were skinned and quartered, and then carried home to the hut. The young bull, that had been wounded, also turned up close at hand; and was finished by the spear of Ossaroo. Of course, he too was skinned and quartered, and carried home; but all this labor was performed by Karl and Ossaroo; for Caspar's ankle had got so much worse, that he had himself to be carried to the hut on the backs of Ossaroo and his brother.

CHAPTER XXXIX.

THE SEROW.

KARL and Ossaroo had their adventure, though it was not of so dangerous a character as that of Caspar. They were spectators rather than actors in it. Fritz was the real actor, and Fritz had come off only second best, as a huge gash in his side testified.

They had chosen a pine, and were busy hacking away at it, when a confused noise—a mixture of yelping and barking—fell upon their ears, and caused them to hold their hands, and listen. It was a thin piece of woods, where they were—composed principally of straggling pine-trees without underwood, and they could see to a distance of several hundred yards around them.

As they stood looking out, a large animal, evidently in flight, came dashing past the spot. He did not appear to be a fast runner, and they had a good view of him. He was nearly as large as a jackass, and had something of the appearance of one, but a pair of stout horns, twelve inches in length, and very sharp-pointed, showed that he was a cloven-hoofed animal. His hair was coarse and rough; dark brown on the upper parts of his body, reddish on the sides, and whitish under neath. Along the back of the neck he was maned like a jackass, and the neck itself was thick with rather a large head to it. The horns curved backwards so as to lie close along the neck; the legs of the animal were thick and stout, and he appeared to be altogether a stupid creature, and ran with a clumsy ungainly gait.

Neither Karl nor Ossaroo had ever seen such an animal before, but they guessed it to be the "thar," or "serow,"—one of the tribe of antelopes, known as the *goat-like* antelopes,—of which there are several species in the East Indies.

They guessed aright. It was the serow, (*Capricornis bubalina.*)

But the creature was not alone. Although we have said he was not running very swiftly, he was going as fast as his thick legs would carry him. And he had good reason too, for, close upon his heels, came a pack of what Karl supposed to be red wolves, but which Ossaroo recognized as the wild dogs of India. There were about a dozen of these, each nearly as large as a wolf, with long necks and bodies, somewhat long muzzles, and high, erect, round-tipped ears. Their general color was red, turning to reddish white underneath. The tops of their long bushy tails were black, and there was a brown patch between the orbits of their eyes, which added to the fierce wolf-like expression that characterized them. It was from them that the howling and yelping had proceeded. They were in full cry after the serow.

Fritz, on hearing the music, would have bounded forth and joined them; but to keep him out of harm's way, Karl had tied him to a tree before commencing work, and Fritz, *nolens volens*, was compelled to keep his place.

The chase swept by, and both dogs and antelope were soon lost to the sight, though their howling could still be heard through the trees.

After a time it grew louder, and the wood-cutters, perceiving that the chase was again coming in their direction, stood watching and listening. A second time the serow appeared crossing the open tract, and the dogs, as before, close at his heels.

Once more all disappeared, and then, after a short interval, "hark back" was the cry; and, to their surprise, Karl and the shikarree again saw the wild dogs pressing the serow through the woods.

Now it appeared to both that the dogs might easily have overtaken the antelope at any moment; for they were close up to his heels, and a single spring, which any of them might have given, would have launched them upon its flanks. Indeed, it appeared as if they were running it only for their amusement, and at any moment could have overtaken it !

This observation of our wood-cutters was partially true. The wild dogs could at any moment have overtaken the antelope, for they had done so already; having turned it more than once. But for all that, they were not running it out of mere sport. They were thus chasing the game back and forward in order to *guide it to their breeding-place, and save themselves the trouble of carrying its carcass thither !* This was in reality what the wild dogs were about, and this accounted for their odd behavior. Ossaroo, who knew the wild dogs well, assured the Sahib Karl, that such is their practice,

that—whenever they have young ones—they hunt the
larger animals from point to point until they get them
close to their common burrowing place ; that then they
all spring upon the victim, and worry it to death, leaving the puppies to approach the carcass and mangle it
at their pleasure !

The plant-hunter had already heard of this singular
practice having been observed in the " wild honden," or
hunting-dogs of the Cape, and was therefore less surprised at Ossaroo's account.

Of course it was not then that Karl and Ossaroo
conversed upon these topics. They were too busy in
watching the chase, which once more passed within
twenty yards of the spot where they were standing.

The serow seemed now to be quite done up, and it
appeared as if his pursuers might at any moment have
pulled him down. But this they evidently did not wish
to do. They wanted to drive him a little farther.

The creature, however, was not going to accommodate them. He had run enough. A very large tree
stood in his way. Its trunk was many feet in diameter,
and great broad buttresses stood out from its flanks,
enclosing angular spaces between them, any of which
would have made a stall for a horse. It was just the
sort of place which the serow was looking out for ; and
making a sharp rush for the tree, he entered one of
these divisions, and wheeling around, buttocks to the
stump, stood firmly to bay.

This sudden manœuvre evidently disconcerted his
fierce pursuers. There were many of them that knew
the serow well, and trembled at the sight of his horns
when brought too close to them. They knew his tactics

too, and were well aware that once in a position, like that he had now taken up, he became a dangerous customer to deal with.

Knowing this, most of the old dogs held back. But there were several young ones in the pack, rash, hot-blooded fellows, who, vain of their prowess, were ashamed to hang their tails at this crisis ; and these, without more ado, rushed in upon the antelope. Then ensued a scene that caused Ossaroo to clap his hands and shake his sides with laughter. A desperate struggle was carried on. Right and left pitched the wild dogs, some yelping, some skulking back, crippled and limping ; while one or two soon lay stretched out dead ; transfixed as they had been by the pointed horns of the antelope. Ossaroo enjoyed this scene, for the shikarree had a great dislike to these wild dogs, as they had often interfered with his stalking.

How the battle would have ended, or whether the bold buck would have beaten off his numerous enemies, will never be known ; for while the contest was raging, the great boar-hound, Fritz, contrived somehow or other to slip his fastening, and the next moment he was seen -rushing like a streak of fire towards the *mêlée*. The wild dogs were as much terrified by his sudden appearance in their midst as the quarry itself could have been, and, without staying to examine the interloper, one and all of them took to their heels, and soon disappeared behind the trees.

Fritz had never seen a serow before, but taking it for granted it was fair game, he sprang at the creature on sight. Better for Fritz had it been a Saxon boar, for it cost him several sharp rips, and a long struggle before he became master of the field ; and it is doubtful whether he would not have suffered still worse, had not a pea of lead from the rifle of his master aided in bringing the strife to an end.

The game, but for its hide, was hardly worth taking home ; as the flesh of the serow is very coarse, and poor eating. For all that, the animal is eagerly hunted by the natives of the Himalayas ; partly because it is not difficult to come up with, and partly that these poor people are not very epicurean in their appetites.

CHAPTER XL.

OSSAROO CHASED BY WILD DOGS.

IF Ossaroo hated any living creature more than another, the wild dogs, as already hinted at, were his particular aversion. They had often spoiled a stalk upon him, when he was in the act of bringing down an axis or an antelope with his arrows, and they themselves were not worth bending a bow upon. Their flesh was not fit to be eaten, and their skins were quite unsalable.   In fact, Ossaroo regarded them as no better than filthy vermin, to be destroyed only for the sake of exterminating them.

Hence it was that the shikarree was so delighted, when he saw the old serow dealing death among his canine antagonists.

But it was written in the book of fate, that Ossaroo should not sleep that night until he had done penance for this exultation.

Another adventure was in store for him, which we shall now relate.

From the place where the yaks had been killed to the hut was a very long distance—full three quarters of a mile; and, of course, transporting the skins and meat thither required Karl and Ossaroo to make many journeys backward and forward.   Caspar was laid up

with his sprained ankle, and could give them no assistance.   As we have said, they had to carry *him* home
as well as the meat.

The work occupied them all the rest of the day, and,
when twilight arrived, there was still one joint to be
got home.   For this joint Ossaroo started alone, leaving
the others at the hut to cook the supper.

On cutting up the meat, they had taken the precaution
to hang the pieces upon high branches, out of the reach
of beasts of prey.   Experience had taught them, that
there were many of these in the place, ravenous enough
to devour a whole carcass in a few minutes.   What
kind of wild beast had carried off the flesh of the cow-
yak, they knew not.   Karl and Caspar believed they
were wolves, for the wolf, in some form or other, is
found in every quarter of the globe; and in India
there are two or three distinct species—as the "land-
gah," or Nepaul wolf, (*Canis pallipes*,) and the "be-
riah," another Indian wolf, of a yellow color, slenderly
made, and about the size of a greyhound, with long,
erect ears, like the jackal.   The jackal, too, which is
only a smaller wolf, and the common or brindled hyena,
inhabit these countries; so that it was difficult to say
which of all these ravenous creatures had committed
the depredation.   Ossaroo's opinion was, that it was
done by *dogs*, not . wolves; and, perhaps, by the very
pack that had that day been seen in pursuit of the antelope.   It made no great difference, as far as that went;
for these same wild dogs are in reality more wolf than
dog, and in habits quite as ferocious and destructive as
the wolves themselves.   But to return to Ossaroo and
his adventure.

When the shikarree arrived on the ground where the meat had been left, he was not much surprised to see a number of wild dogs skulking about. Half a dozen of them were standing under the joint, where it hung from the branch; some of them in the act of springing upward, and all of them regarding the tempting morsel with fierce, hungry looks. The offal and " giblets " they had already disposed of, so that not the smallest fragment could be seen lying about. What Ossaroo regretted most was, that he had brought with him neither bow nor arrow nor spear, nor, in short, any thing in the shape of a weapon. Even his long knife he had left behind, in order that he might carry the large joint with greater ease.

On seeing the hated dogs, however, he could not resist the temptation of having a shy at them; and, gathering up a handful of bulky stones, he rushed into their midst, and pelted at them right and left.

The dogs, startled by this sudden onslaught, took to their heels, but Ossaroo could not help observing that they did not appear to be so badly frightened; and, some of them that left the ground sulky and growling, stopped at no great distance from the spot, and appeared half inclined to come back again !

It was the first time in his life that Ossaroo felt something like fear of the wild dogs. He had been in the habit of chasing them on sight, and they had always scampered off at the sound of his voice. These, however, seemed to be larger and fiercer than any he had before encountered, and it was evident there was fight in them. It was nearly dark, and at night such animals are much bolder than during the daylight. Night is,

in fact, their true time for rapine and desperate deeds.
Ossaroo reflected, moreover, that these dogs had, in all
probability, never before encountered man, and were,
therefore, less inclined to fear or flee from him.

It was not without some misgiving, therefore, that
he found himself in their presence, thus unarmed and
alone.

When his armful of stones was exhausted, some of
the dogs still remained within sight, looking in the gray
twilight much larger than they actually were.

Ossaroo reflected for a moment whether he would
gather some more rocks, and give them a fresh pelting.
On second thoughts, he concluded it would be more
prudent to let them alone. They were already almost
at bay, and any farther demonstration on his part might
provoke them to turn upon him in earnest. He determined, therefore, to leave them as they stood, and hurry
off with his load.

Without more ado, he took down the quarter of yak-
beef, and, placing it upon his shoulders, turned home-
ward toward the hut.

He had not gone very far when he began to suspect
that the dogs were after him. In fact, he more than
suspected it, for the pattering of feet upon the dead
leaves, and an occasional low growl that reached his
ears, convinced him they *were* after him. The heavy
burden upon his shoulders, pressing his head forward
and downward, prevented him from seeing either to
one side or the other, and to look behind, it would be
necessary for him to turn quite round.

But the pattering of the feet sounded nearer, and the
short half-bark, half-growl, became more frequent, until

Ossaroo found himself at length constrained to turn, from sheer apprehension of being attacked in the rear.

The sight that met his eyes was enough to have terrified the stoutest heart. Instead of half a dozen of the wild dogs which he expected to see following him, there were far above a score of them, and they appeared to be of every age, sex, and size. In fact, all the dogs of the valley were trooping at his heels, as if they had been all summoned to join in the attack.

But the stout shikarree was not yet dismayed. He had been accustomed to hold the wild dogs in too great contempt to be so easily frightened, even by such numbers of them, and he resolved to make another attempt to drive them off.

Leaning the beef, therefore, against a tree, he stooped down and groped the ground, until he had again armed himself with pebbles as big as paving-stones; and rushing some paces backward, he flung them with all his might in the teeth of his tormentors. Several of the pebbles happened to hit in the right place, and more than one of the dogs ran howling away; but the fiercer and older ones scarce yielded their ground, and only answered the assault by a fierce grinning and jabbering, while their white teeth could be distinguished under the moonlight set in angry menace.

Upon the whole, Ossaroo gained but little by this new demonstration; and as he reshouldered his load, he saw the dogs gathering thick as ever behind him.

Perhaps he would not have taken up his burden again, but an idea had suddenly entered his mind; he had conceived a plan of getting rid of his ugly followers.

He knew that he was near the edge of the lake. He remembered that between him and the hut there lay a long reach of water, where the lake ran up into a sort of branch or bay. He knew that this bay, even at its neck, was quite shallow and fordable. He had, in fact, waded across it that very day in order to shorten the path. He was just then within a hundred yards of the fording-place; and if the dogs contemplated attacking him, he would be able to reach the water before they were likely to begin their attack. He would take to the water, and that would throw them off. With all their fierceness, they surely would not follow him into it?

Acting under this impression, he reshouldered his load and hurried forward. He did not waste time to look about. He need not have looked around to convince himself that he was still followed, for the thick pattering of the feet, the snarling, and chattering, were behind him as before. Every moment it sounded nearer and nearer, and at length when Ossaroo arrived by the water's edge he fancied he could hear the breathing of the brutes close to his very ankles.

He made no halt, but dashed at once into the lake, and plunged wildly across. The noise made by himself in wading knee-deep prevented him from hearing other sounds; and he did not look to see whether he was followed until he had climbed out on the opposite shore of the bay. Then he paused and turned around. To his chagrin the whole pack were in the water, crossing like hounds after a stag! Already they were half over. They had no doubt hesitated a moment before taking to the water, and this gave Ossaroo some advantage, else they would have landed as soon as he. As it was, they would soon take up the distance.

Ossaroo hesitated a moment as to whether he should abandon his burden, and retreat towards the hut; but the thought of yielding to a pack of wild dogs was too much for his hunter pride; and, wheeling suddenly into the path, he hurried onward with his load. It was now but a short distance to the hut. He had still hopes that he might reach it before his pursuers would make up their minds to assail him.

On he hastened, making his limbs do their best. Once more came the pattering feet; once more the growling, and yelping, and jibbering of the wild dogs from behind; once more their hot breathing seemed to be felt close to his heels; and then, all at once, the quarter of yak-beef appeared to increase in weight, and grow heavier and heavier, until it came suddenly to the ground, pulling Ossaroo upon his back. Several of the ravenous brutes had seized upon and dragged both burden and bearer to the earth!

But Ossaroo soon recovered his feet; and, seizing a large pole, that fortunately lay near, commenced laying around him right and left, at the same time making the woods echo with his yells.

A terrible *mêlée* ensued, the dogs showing fight, seizing the pole in their teeth, and springing forward upon the hunter whenever an opportunity offered. The latter, however, handled his *improvised* weapon so well, that for a long time he kept the whole pack at bay.

He was growing very tired, and no doubt in a few minutes more would have been obliged to succumb, when he, as well as the joint of yak-beef, would soon

have disappeared from the world; but, before this ter
rible event could happen, the large spotted body of
Fritz was seen rushing into the midst of the crowd.
Fritz was followed by his master, Karl, armed with the
double-barrelled gun, which soon opened fire, scatter-
ing the wild pack like a flock of sheep, and laying out
more than one of their number at the feet of Ossaroo.

The scene was soon over after the arrival of Karl
and Fritz, and Ossaroo was delivered from his peril;
but if ever a follower of Brahma swore vengeance
against any living creature, Ossaroo did that very
thing against the wild dogs

CHAPTER XLI.

OSSAROO'S REVENGE.

So indignant was Ossaroo with these animals that he vowed he would not lie down till he had taken wholesale revenge, and Karl and Caspar were curious to know how he intended to take it. They knew the dogs would be like enough to come round the hut during the night. Indeed, they heard them yelping not far off at the moment; but for all that how were they to be killed, for that was the sort of revenge the shikarree meditated taking? It would never do to expend powder and shot on such worthless animals; besides firing at them in the darkness would be a very uncertain mode of killing even a single one of them.

Did Ossaroo intend to sit up all night and shoot at them with his arrows? The chances were he should not hit one; and from the way Ossaroo talked he had made up his mind to a whole hetacomb! Certainly he could not do it with his bow and arrows. How then was he going to take the wholesale vengeance he had vowed?

They knew of no sort of trap that could be arranged, whereby more than a single dog might be captured; and it would take some time with such weapons as they had to construct the rudest kind of trap. True, there was the " dead-fall " that might be rigged up in a few minutes from logs that lay near; but that could only fall once, crushing one victim, unless Ossaroo sat up to rearrange it. Besides, the cunning dogs might not go under it again, after one of their number had been immolated before their eyes.

Karl and Caspar could not conceive what plan Ossaroo intended to pursue; but from experience they knew he had some one; and therefore they asked him no questions, but watched his proceedings in silence.

The first thing that Ossaroo did was to collect from the antelope all the tendons or sinews that he could lay his fingers on. Some, also, he obtained from the barking deer, which Caspar had killed in the morning; and others he took from the limbs of the yaks that had been brought home in their skins. In a short while he had a goodly bunch of these tough strings; which he first dried before the fire, and then twisted after his own fashion into slender cords. In all he made more than a score of them—Karl and Caspar of course acting under his directions, and lending him all necessary help during the operation. These cords, neatly twined and dried by the heat, now resembled strings of coarse catgut; and it only remained for Ossaroo to knot and loop them, and form them into snares.

Of course Karl and Caspar now knew what Ossaroo purposed—to snare the dogs of course. Yet how the snares were to be set, or how a wild dog could be captured with a piece of catgut, was more than they could comprehend. Surely, thought they, the dogs will gnaw such a string to pieces in half a minute, and set themselves free again? So it would have appeared, and so they would doubtless have done had the snares been set for them in the ordinary manner. But Ossaroo had a plan of his own for setting snares, and it was by this plan he intended to succeed in capturing the dogs.

The next thing Ossaroo did was to provide himself with an equal number of stoutish thongs, which his knife and the numerous raw hides that lay about soon enabled him to do. · When these were all prepared, about twenty small skewer-like rods were obtained from the bushes and sharpened at one end. Then a like number of "griskins" were cut from the antelope venison—it being esteemed of least value; and thus provided, Ossaroo started forth to set his snares.

Karl and Caspar of course accompanied him, the latter limping on one leg, and carrying a large pine-torch —for as the moon had gone down, and it was now quite dark, they required a light to do the work. Karl was loaded with the thongs, skewers, and griskins, while Ossaroo himself was in charge of the snares.

Now it so happened that not far from the hut, and all around it, there grew numbers of low trees, with long branches that extended horizontally outward. They were a species of the *pyrus,* or mountain-ash, sometimes known as "witch hazel." The branches, though long, were thin, tough, and elastic, and not much burdened with either branchlets or leaves. They were the very things for Ossaroo's purpose, and he had observed this before it had become quite dark, and while he was meditating upon some plan to get square with the wild dogs. Upon these branches he was now to operate.

Reaching up he caught one of them in his hand,

drew it downwards, and then suddenly let it go again, in order to try the "spring" of it. It appeared to satisfy him; and, once more laying hold of it, he stripped off its leaves and twigs, and then tied the raw-hide thong to its upper end. To the other end of the string was next adjusted the skewer-like rod, and this last was fastened in the ground in such a way as to hold the branch bent downward with considerable force, while a very slight jerk upon the pin itself would set the former free. The shikarree now arranged his piece of venison for a bait, fixing it so that it could not possibly be dragged away or even slightly tugged without setting free the rod-trigger, and consequently the bent branch. Last of all, was arranged the snare, and this was placed in such a position with regard to the bait, that any animal attempting to seize the latter must necessarily have the whole or part of its body encircled by the ready running noose.

When all these matters were arranged to his satisfaction, Ossaroo proceeded to another tree, and went through a similar process of snare-setting; and then to another, and so on till the whole of his snares were disposed of, when the party returned to the hut.

They sat for half-an-hour longer, listening in hopes that before retiring they might enjoy the sport of seeing a wild dog snared. Whether it was that the torchlight had frightened them off for a while, or from some other cause, neither yelp, nor growl, nor noise of any kind, gratified the ears of the listeners; so they gave it up, and, shutting the rude door of the hut, one and all of them went soundly to sleep.

The fact is, the day's work had been one of the hardest of their lives. All were as tired as hod-carriers; and they were glad to stretch themselves once more on the fragrant leaves of the rhododendrons.

Had they not slept so soundly, they might have heard a considerable confusion of noises throughout the night. What with barking and growling, and yelping and howling, and snapping and snarling, and the creaking of branches and the rattling of twigs,. there was a constant medley, that ought to have awakened the three sleepers long before daylight. It did awake them, however, at last; and as the light streamed through the apertures of the hut, all three sprang to their feet and rushed out into the open air. It was still only gray light; but as soon as they had rubbed their eyes clear of sleep, a sight was before them that caused Karl and Caspar to break out into loud laughter, while Ossaroo jumped about vociferating his delight in wild yells of triumph. Nearly every snare they had set had caught its victim —nearly every tree around the hut carried a dog swinging to its branches—some by the neck hanged quite dead—some round the body alive and struggling—while there were others suspended by a single leg, their snouts almost touching the earth, and their tongues hanging from their frothy jaws!

It was the strangest of all scenes; and Ossaroo had, as he had vowed, a full measure of vengeance—which he now carried to its completion, by seizing his long spear, and putting an end to the struggles of the hideous brutes.

11

CHAPTER XLII.

THE CREVASSE BRIDGED.

YOUNG reader, I shall not weary you by relating every little circumstance which occurred during the time that the bridge was being constructed. Suffice it to say, that all hands were busy,—both night and day, I might almost say,—until it was finished. Although they were in no want of any thing, and might have lived their lives out in this place, yet the thought that they were imprisoned—cut off from all fellowship with mankind—weighed heavily upon their spirits, and not an hour was wasted in idle amusement. The whole of their time was given up to that which engrossed all their thoughts—the construction of the bridge—that link, which was wanting to unite them once more with the world, and free them from their lonely captivity.

They were a whole month in getting their bridge ready; which, after all, consisted only of a single pole of about six inches in diameter, and better than a hundred feet in length. It was nothing more than two slender pine-trees spliced together by means of raw-hide thongs. But then these trees had to be shaved down to a nearly uniform thickness, and this had to be done with the small hatchet and knives; and the wood had to be charred by fire until it was quite dry and light; and the splicing had to be made with the greatest neatness and strength, so that there would be no danger of its yielding under a weight; and, moreover, a great many ropes had to be twisted, and many animals had to be captured and killed, to obtain the materials for these ropes; and other apparatus had to be made—so that the getting that bridge ready was a good month's work for all hands.

At the end of a month it *was* ready; and now behold it in the gorge of the glacier, and lying along the snowy surface of the ice, one end of it within a few feet of the crevasse! Thither they have transported it, and are just preparing to put it in its place.

The first thought that will strike you, will be how that piece of timber is to be placed across that yawning chasm. It is quite long enough to reach across—for they calculated that before making it—and there are several feet to lap over at each end; but how on earth is it to be extended across? If any one of the party was upon the opposite side, and had a rope attached to the end of the pole, then it would be easy enough to manage it. But as there could be nothing of this kind, how did they intend acting? It is evident they could not push it across before them; the end of such a long pole would naturally sink below the horizontal line before reaching the opposite side; and how was it to be raised up? In fact, as soon as they should push it a little more than half its length outward, its own weight would overbalance their united strength, and it would be likely to escape from their hands and drop to the bottom of the cleft—whence, of course, they could not

recover it. This would be a sad result, after the trouble they had had in constructing that well-balanced
piece of timber.

Ah ! they were not such simpletons as to have worked
a whole month without first having settled all these
matters. Karl was too good an engineer to have gone
on thus far, without a proper design of how his bridge
was to be thrown across. If you look at the objects
lying around, you will perceive the evidence of that
design. You will understand how the difficulty is to be
got over.

You will see there a ladder nearly fifty feet in length
—several days were expended in the making of this ;
you will see a strong pulley, with block-wheels and
shears—this cost no little time in the construction ; and
you will see several coils of stout raw-hide rope. No
wonder a month was expended in the preparation of the
bridge !

And now to throw it across the chasm ! For that
purpose they were upon the ground, and all their apparatus with them. Without farther delay the work
commenced.

The ladder was placed against the cliff, with its lower
end resting upon the glacier, and as close to the edge
of the crevasse as was reckoned safe.

We have said that the ladder was fifty feet in length ,
and consequently it reached to a point on the face of
the cliff nearly fifty feet above the surface of the glacier.
At this height there chanced to be a slight flaw in the
rock—a sort of seam in the granite—where a hole could
easily be pierced with an iron instrument.

To make this hole a foot or more in depth was the

work of an hour. It was done by means of the hatchet, and the iron point of Ossaroo's boar-spear.

A strong wooden stake was next inserted into this hole, fitting it as nearly as possible; but, in order to make it perfectly tight and firm, hard wooden wedges were hammered in all around it.

When driven home, the end of this stake protruded a foot or more from the wall of the cliff; and, by means of notches cut in the wood, and raw-hide thongs, the pulley was securely rigged on to it.

The pulley had been made with two wheels; each of them with axles strong enough to bear the weight of several hundreds. Both had been well tested before this time.

Another stake was now inserted into the cliff, within a few feet of the surface of the glacier. This was simply to be used as a belaying-pin, to which the ends of the pulley-ropes could be fastened at a moment's notice.

The next operation was the reeving of the ropes over the wheels of the pulley. This was the work of but a few minutes, as the ropes had already been carefully twisted, and had been made of just the thickness to fit the grooves of the wheels.

The ropes—or cables, as the boys called them—were now attached at one end to the great pole which was to form the bridge. One to its end, and the other to its middle, exactly around the place where it was joined.

The greatest pains was taken in adjusting these knots, particularly the one in the middle; for the duty which this cable was called upon to perform was, indeed, of a most important character.

It was to act as the main pier or support of the

bridge—not only to prevent the long pole from " swag-ging " downward, but in fact to keep it from breaking altogether. But for Karl's ingenuity in devising this support, a slender pole, such as that they had prepared, would never have sustained the weight of one of them ; and had they made it of heavier scantling, they could not have thrown it across the chasm. The centre sup-port, therefore, was the chief object of their solicitude; and this cable, as well as the pulley-wheel over which it passed, were made much stronger than the other. The second rope was intended to hold up the end of the pole, so that, on approaching the opposite side of the chasm, it could be kept high enough to be raised above the ice.

The ropes being now completely rigged, each man took his place. Ossaroo, who was the strongest of the party, was to push the bridge forward ; while Karl and Caspar attended to the pulley and the ropes. Rollers had already been laid under the poles ; for, although but six inches in diameter, its great length rendered it no easy matter to slide it forward, even with the advan-tage of the slippery surface of frozen snow.

The word was given by Karl, and the pole com-menced moving. Soon its end passed over the brink of the chasm, close by the edge of the black rock. Slowly and gradually it moved forward, and not one of them uttered a word. They were all too much ab-sorbed in attending to their various duties to speak a sentence.

Slowly and gradually it moved onward, creeping along the cliff, like some huge monster, and protruding its muzzled snout far over the deep chasm.

At length the nearest roller approached the brink, and it became necessary to stop the motion till these could be rearranged.

This was easily done. A few turns of the cables around the belaying-pin, and all stood fast. The pulley-wheels worked admirably, and the cables glided smoothly over the grooved blocks.

The rollers were soon readjusted—the cables again freed from the pin, and the bridge moved on.

Slowly and gradually—slowly but smoothly and surely, it moved, until its farther end rested upon the opposite cheek of the crevasse, lapping the hard ice by several feet. Then the cables were held taut, and securely fastened to the belaying-pin. The nearer end of the pole was tied with other ropes—so that it could not possibly shift from its place—and the yawning abyss was now spanned by a bridge!

Not till then did the builders rest to look upon their work; and, as they stood gazing upon the singular structure that was to restore them to liberty and home, they could not restrain themselves, but gave vent to their triumphant feelings in a loud huzzah!

CHAPTER XLIII.

THE PASSAGE OF THE CREVASSE.

I KNOW you are smiling at this very poor substitute for a bridge, and wondering how they who built it were going to cross upon it. Climbing a Maypole would be nothing to such a feat. It may seem easy enough to cling to a pole six inches in diameter, and even to " swarm " along it for some yards, but when you come to talk of a hundred feet of such progression, and that over a yawning chasm, the very sight of which is enough to make the head giddy and the heart faint, then the thing becomes a feat indeed. Had there been no other mode of getting over, like enough our heroes would have endeavored to cross in that way.

Ossaroo, who had " swarmed " up the stem of many a bamboo and tall palm-tree, would have thought nothing of it; but for Karl and Caspar, who were not such climbers, it would have been rather perilous. They had, therefore, designed a safer plan.

Each was provided with a sort of yoke, formed out of a tough sapling that had been sweated in the fire and then bent into a triangular shape. It was a rude isosceles triangle, tied tightly at the apex with raw-hide thongs; and thereto was attached a piece of well-twisted

rope, the object of which was to form a knot or loop over the pole, to act as a runner. The feet of the passenger were to rest on the base of the yoke, which would serve as a stirrup to support the body, while one arm would hug the pole, leaving the other free to push forward the runner by short gradations. In this way each was to work himself across. Their guns, and the few other things, were to be tightly strapped to their backs They had only those that were worth bringing along, As for Fritz, he was not to be left behind, although the transporting him across had offered for some time a serious difficulty. Ossaroo, however, had removed the difficulty by proposing to tie the dog up in a skin and strap him on his (Ossaroo's) own back, and thus carry him over. It would be nothing to Ossaroo.

In less than half-an-hour after the bridge was in its place, the three were ready to cross. There they stood, each holding the odd-looking stirrup in his hand, with his *impedimenta* strapped securely on his back. The head of Fritz, just showing above the shoulder of the shikarree, while his body was shrouded in a piece of shaggy yak-skin, presented a very ludicrous spectacle, and his countenance wore quite a serio-comical expression. He seemed quite puzzled as to what was going to be done with him.

Ossaroo proposed crossing first; and then Caspar, brave as a lion, said that he was the *lightest,* and *ought* to go *first.* Karl would not listen to either of them. Karl alleged that, as he was the builder of the bridge, by all usage it was his place to make trial of it. Karl being the Sahib of the party, and, of course, the man of most authority, carried his point.

11 *

Stepping cautiously to the point where the pole rested on the ice, he looped the hide-rope over it, and then suffered the yoke to drop down. He then grasped the pole tightly in his arms, and placed his feet firmly in the stirrup. For a moment or two, he pressed heavily upon the latter, so as to test its strength, while he held on by the beam above; and then, disengaging his left arm, he pushed the runner forward upon the pole, to the distance of a foot or more. This, of course, carried the stirrup along with it, as well as his feet; and then, throwing forward the upper part of his body, he swung himself out above the abyss.

It was a fearful sight, even to those who watched him, and would have been too perilous a feat for idle play; but the very nature of their circumstances had hardened them to undergo the danger.

After a time, Karl was far out from the ice, and seemed to hang upon a thread between heaven and earth!

Had the pole slipped at either end, it would have precipitated the adventurous Karl into the chasm; but they had taken every precaution against this. At the nearer end, they had rendered it secure by rolling immense rocks upon it; while, on the opposite side, it was held in its place by the cable, that had been drawn as tight as the pulley could make it.

Notwithstanding the mainstay in the middle, it sank considerably under the weight of Karl's body; and it was plain that, but for this contrivance, they could never have crossed. When half-way to the point where this stay was attached, the pole bent far below the level of the glacier, and Karl now found it up-hill work to force the runner along. He succeeded, however, in reaching the stay-rope in safety.

Now he had arrived at one of the "knottiest" points of the whole performance. Of course, the runner could go no farther, as it was intercepted by the stay. It was necessary, therefore, to detàch it altogether from the pole, and then readjust it on the other side of the cable.

Karl had not come thus far to be stopped by a difficulty of so trifling a kind. He had already considered how he should act at this crisis, and he delayed only a moment to rest himself. Aided by the mainstay itself, which served him for a hand-rope, he mounted cross-legs upon the timber, and then, without much trouble, shifted his runner to the opposite side. This done, he once more "sprang to his stirrup," and continued onward.

As he approached the opposite edge of the chasm, he again encountered the up-hill difficulty ; but a little patience and some extra exertion brought him nearer and nearer, and still nearer, until at last his feet kicked against the icy wall.

With a slight effort, he drew himself upon the glacier ; and, stepping a pace from the brink, he pulled off his cap, and waved it in the air. A huzza from the opposite side answered his own shout of triumph. But louder still was the cheer, and far more heartfelt and joyous, when, half-an-hour afterwards, all three stood side by side, and, safe over, looked back upon the yawning gulf they had crossed !

Only they who have escaped from some terrible doom —a dungeon, or death itself—can understand the full, deep emotions of joy, that at that moment thrilled within the hearts of Karl, Caspar, and Ossaroo.

*   \`   *   *   *   *

Alas! alas! it was a short-lived joy,—a moment of happiness to be succeeded by the most poignant misery,—a gleam of light followed by the darkest of clouds!

Ten minutes had scarce elapsed. They had freed Fritz from his yak-skin envelope, and had started down the glacier, impatient to get out of that gloomy defile. Scarce five hundred steps had they taken, when a sight came under their eyes that caused them suddenly to halt, and turn to each other with blanched cheeks and looks of dread import. Not one of them spoke a word, but all stood pointing significantly down the ravine. Words were not needed. The thing spoke for itself.

Another crevasse, far wider than the one they had just crossed, yawned before them! It stretched from side to side of the icy mass; like the former, impinging on either cliff. It was full two hundred feet in width, and how deep. Ugh! they dared hardly look into its awful chasm! It was clearly impassable. Even the dog appeared to be aware of this; for he had stopped upon its edge, and stood in an attitude of fear, now and then uttering a melancholy howl!

Yes, it was impassable. A glance was sufficient to tell that; but they were not satisfied with a glance. They stood upon its brink, and regarded it for a long while, and with many a wistful gaze; then, with slow steps and heavy hearts, they turned mechanically away.

I shall not repeat their mournful conversation. I

shall not detail the incidents of their backward journey to the valley.   I need not describe the recrossing of the crevasse—the different feelings with which they now accomplished this perilous feat.   All these may be easily imagined.

It was near night when, wearied in body and limb—downcast in mien and sick at heart—they reached the hut, and flung themselves despairingly upon the floor.

"My God ! my God !" exclaimed Karl, in the agony of his soul, "how long is this hovel to be our home ?"

CHAPTER XLIV.

NEW HOPES.

THAT night was passed without much sleep. Painful reflections filled the minds of all and kept them awake— the thoughts that follow disappointed hopes. When they did sleep it was more painful than waking. Their dreams were fearful. They dreamt of yawning gulfs and steep precipices—of being suspended in the air, and every moment about to fall into vast depths where they would be crushed to atoms. Their dreams, that were only distorted pictures of the day's experience, had all the vividness of reality, and far more vivid in their horror. Often when one or other of them was awakened by the approaching climax of the dream, he endeavored to keep awake rather than go through even in a vision such horrible scenes.

Even the dog Fritz was not free from similar sufferings. His mournful whimpering told that his sleep like theirs was troubled and uneasy.

A bright sunshiny morning had its beneficial effect upon all of them. It aided the reaction—consequent on a night of such a dismal character—and as they ate their breakfasts of broiled meat they were again almost cheerful. The buoyancy of Caspar's spirits had wellnigh returned, and his fine appetite showed itself in full vigor. Indeed all of them ate heartily, for on the preceding day they had scarce allowed themselves time to taste food.

"If we must remain here always," said Caspar, "I see no reason why we need starve ourselves! There's plenty to eat, and a variety of it, I can say. I don't see why we shouldn't have some fish. I am sure I have seen trout leap in the lake. Let us try a fly to-day. What say you, Karl?"

Caspar said this with the intention of cheering his brother.

· "I see no harm in it," answered the quiet botanist. "I think there are fish in the lake. I have heard there is a very eatable kind of fish in all the rivers of the Himalayas, known as the 'Himalayan trout'— though it is misnamed, for it is not a trout but a species of carp. It may be found here, I dare say; although it is difficult to imagine how fish could get into this sequestered lake."

"Well," rejoined Caspar, "we must think of some plan to get them *out* of it. We have neither nets, rods, hooks, nor lines. What's to be done? Can you think of any way of taking the fish, Ossaroo?"

"Ah! Sahib," replied the shikarree, "give me bamboo, me soon make net to takee fish—no bamboo—no net—no matter for net—Ossaroo poison the water—get all da fish."

"What! poison the water? how would you do that? Where is the poison?"

"Me soon find poison—bikh poison do."

"'Bikh' poison—what is that?"

" Come, Sahib ! me show you bikh plant—plenty grow here."

Both Karl and Caspar rose and followed the shik-arree.

They had not gone many paces when their guide stooped and pointed to a plant that grew in plenty about the place. It was an herbaceous plant, having a stem nearly six feet high, and rather broad digitate leaves, with a loose spike of showy yellow flowers at the top.

Caspar rather hastily took hold of one of the plants ; and, plucking off the spike, held it to his nose, to see whether the flowers had any perfume. But Caspar dropped the nosegay as hastily as he had seized it, and with an exclamation of terror turned towards his brother, into whose arms he staggered half swooning! Fortunately he had taken but a very slight " sniff" of that dangerous perfume, else he might have been laid up for days. As it was he felt giddy for hours after.

Now this singular plant the botanist Karl recognized at a glance. It was a species of aconite, or wolf's-bane, and very similar to the kindred species, *Aconitum napellus,* or " monk's hood," of Europe, whose roots furnish the most potent of poisons.

The whole plant—leaves, flowers, and stem—is of a poisonous nature, but the roots, which resemble small turnips, contain the essence of the poison. There are many species of the plant found in different parts of the world, and nearly a dozen kinds in the Himalaya Mountains themselves ; but the one pointed out by Ossaroo was the *Aconitum ferox* of botanists, the species from which the celebrated " bikh " poison of the Hindoos is obtained.

Ossaroo then proposed to poison the fish by throwing a sufficient quantity of the roots and stems of the plant into the lake.

This proposal, however, was rejected by Karl, who very properly observed, that although by that means they might obtain a plentiful supply of fish, they would destroy more than they could use at the time, and perhaps leave none for the future. Karl had already begun to talk about a "future" to be spent on the shores of this lovely lake. The belief that they might never go out of the valley was already taking shape in the minds of all three, though they did not care to give expression to such sad imaginings.

Karl tried to be cheerful, as he saw that Caspar was gay.

" Come," said he, " let us not mind the fish to-day. I own that fish is usually the first course, but go along with me. Let us see what kind of vegetables our garden has got. I am sure we may live better if we only try. For my part I am getting tired of broiled meat, and neither bread nor vegetables to eat along with it. Here I dare say we shall find both; for whether it be due to the birds, or its peculiar climate—or a little to both most likely—our valley has a flora such as you can only meet with in a botanic garden. Come then! let us see what we can find for the pot."

So saying Karl led the way, followed by Caspar, Ossaroo, and the faithful Fritz.

" Look up there ! " said the botanist, pointing to a tall pine that grew near. " See those large cones. Inside them we shall obtain seeds, as large as pistachio-nuts, and very good to eat. By roasting them, we can make an excellent substitute for bread."

"Ha, indeed!" exclaimed Caspar, "that is a pine-tree. What large cones! They are as big as artichokes. What sort of pine is it, brother?"

"It is one of the kind known as the 'edible pines,' because their seeds are fit for food. It is the species called by botanists *Pinus Gerardiana*, or the 'neosa' pine. There are pines whose seeds are eatable in other parts of the world, as well as in the Himalaya Mountains,—for instance, the *Pinus cembra* of Europe, the 'ghik' of Japan, the 'Lambert' pine of California, and several species in New Mexico, known among the people as 'piñon' trees. So you perceive that besides their valuable timber—to say nothing of their pitch, turpentine, and resin—the family of the pines also furnishes food to the human race. We shall get some bread from those cones whenever we desire it!"

So saying, Karl continued on in the direction of the lake.

"There again!" said he, pointing to a gigantic herbaceous plant, " rhubarb, you see!"

It was, in fact, the true rhubarb, which grows wild among the Himalaya Mountains, and whose great broad red-edged leaves, contrasting with its tall pyramid of yellow bracts, render it one of the most striking and beautiful of herbaceous plants. Its large acid stems—which are hollow and full of pure water—are eaten by the natives of the Himalayas, both raw and boiled, and its leaves when dried are smoked as tobacco. But there was a smaller species that grew near, which Ossaroo said produced much better tobacco; and Ossaroo was good authority, since he had already dried some of the leaves, and had been smoking them ever since their arrival in the valley. In fact, Ossaroo was quite out of betel-nut, and suffered so much from the want of his favorite stimulant, that he was glad to get any thing to smoke ; and the " chula," or wild rhubarb-leaves, answered his purpose well. Ossaroo's pipe was an original one certainly ; and he could construct one in a few minutes. His plan was to thrust a piece of stick into the ground, passing it underneath the surface—horizontally for a few inches, and then out again—so as to form a double orifice to the hole. At one end of this channel he would insert a small joint of reed for his mouth-piece, while the other was filled with the rhubarb tobacco, which was then set on fire. It was literally turning the earth into a tobacco-pipe !

This method of smoking is by no means uncommon among the half-civilized inhabitants of India as well as Africa, and Ossaroo preferred a pipe of this kind to any other.

Karl continued onward, pointing out to his companions several species of edible roots, fruits, and vegetables which the valley contained. There were wild leeks among the number. These would assist them in making soup. There were fruits too,—several species of currants, and cherries, and strawberries, and raspberries, —kinds that had long been introduced to European gardens, and that to Karl and Caspar looked like old acquaintances.

"And there !" continued Karl, "see the very water produces food for us. Look at the lotus, (*Nelumbium speciosum.*) Those large pink and white flowers are the flowers of the famed lotus. Its stalks may be eaten, or, if you will, their hollow tubes will serve us as cups to drink out of. There, too, is the horned water root (*Trapa bicornis*), also excellent eating. Oh! we should be thankful. We are well provided with food."

Yet the heart of Karl was sore while thus endeavoring to talk cheerfully.

CHAPTER XLV.

NEW SURVEY OF THE CLIFF.

YES, the hearts of all three were far from being contented, though they returned to the hut laden with fruits, and roots, and nuts, and vegetables ; out of which they intended to concoct a better dinner than they had been lately accustomed to.

The rest of that day was spent about the hut, and a good deal of it was given up to culinary operations. Not that any of the party cared so much for a good dinner ; but being thus engaged prevented them from reflecting as much as they would otherwise have done upon their painful situation. Besides, they had no other work to do. They had no longer a motive for doing any thing. Up to that moment the preparing the ropes and timbers of the bridge had kept them employed ; and the very work itself, combined with the hope which they then felt, enabled them to pass the time pleasantly enough. Now that these hopes were no more,—that their whole scheme had ended in failure, they felt restless,—and could think of nothing upon which to employ themselves. Preparing their dinner, therefore, out of the new and varied materials that had come into their hands, was, at least, some distraction to their gloomy thoughts.

When dinner was ready, all of them ate heartily, and with a relish. Indeed, they had been so long without vegetables that these tasted to them as fine as any they had ever eaten. Even the wild fruits appeared equal to the best they had ever gathered from an orchard !

It was a little after midday, as they were enjoying this dessert. They were seated in the open air, in front of the hut, and Caspar was doing most part of the talking. He was doing his best to be cheerful, and to make his companions so as well.

"They're the best strawberries I've eaten for a month," said he ; "but I think a trifle of sugar and a drop of cream would be an improvement. What say you, Karl ? "

"It would," he replied, nodding assent.

"We did wrong to kill all our cows," continued Caspar, with a significant look at one of the yak-skins that lay near.

"By-the-bye," said Karl, interrupting him, "I was just thinking of that. If we are to stay here all our lives,——oh ! "

The painful reflection, again crossing Karl's mind, caused him to exclaim as he did. He left his hypothetic sentence unfinished, and relapsed into silence.

Several days after this Karl left the hut, and, without telling his intention to either of his companions, walked off in the direction of the cliffs. Indeed, he had no very definite nor determined aim in so doing ; a sort of hopeless idea had come into his mind of making the circuit of the valley, and once more surveying the precipice all round it.

Neither of the others offered to accompany him, nor

did they question him as to his object in setting out. Both had gone about business of their own. Caspar had become engaged in making a washrod for his gun, and Ossaroo a net to catch the large and beautiful fish that abounded in the lake. Karl, therefore, was permitted to set forth alone.

On reaching the precipice, he turned along its base, and walked slowly forward, stopping every yard or two, and looking upward. Every foot—nay, I might say every inch, of the cliff did he scan with care,—even with more care than he had hitherto done; though that would appear hardly possible, for on the former occasions on which the three had examined it, their reconnoissance had been most particular and minute.

But a new idea had shadowed itself in the mind of Karl; and it was in obedience to this, that he now proceeded with a fresh examination of the precipitous enclosure that imprisoned them. It is true it was but a sort of forlorn hope that he had conceived; but a forlorn hope was better than no hope at all, and therefore Karl was determined to be satisfied.

The thought that had been forming in his mind was, that after all it might be possible for them to *scale the cliff*. That they could not do so by climbing he was already satisfied; as were all three. Of this their former examinations had convinced them. But there were other ways of getting up a precipice, besides merely climbing with one's hands and feet; and one of these ways, as already said, had for some time been shadowing itself in the mind of Karl.

What plan, you will ask, had he now conceived? Did he design to make use of ropes?

Not at all. Ropes could be of no service to him in going up a cliff. They might, had they been fastened at the top; for then both he and his companions would soon have contrived some way of getting up the ropes. They could have made a ladder of a single rope by which they might have ascended, by simply knotting pieces of sticks at short intervals, to serve as rests for their feet, and they knew this well. Such a contrivance would have suited admirably, if they had been required to *descend* a precipice, for then they could have let the rope down, and fastened it at the top themselves. But to go up was altogether a different operation; and it was necessary for at least one to be above to render it at all practicable or possible. Of course, if one could have got to the top by any means, the others could have done so by the same; and then the rope-ladder would not have been needed at all.

No. Such a contrivance could not be used, and indeed they had never thought of it—since to the meanest comprehension it was plainly impossible. Karl therefore was not thinking of a rope-ladder.

Nevertheless it was actually about *a ladder* that he was thinking—not made of ropes, but of timber—of sides and rounds like any other ladder.

"What!" you will exclaim, "a ladder by which to scale the cliff! Why, you have told us that it was three hundred feet in sheer height? The longest ladder in the world would not reach a third of the way up such a precipice. Even a fireman's ladder, that is made to reach to the tops of the highest houses, would be of no use for such a height as that?"

"Quite true! I know all that as well as you," would have been Karl's reply to your objections.

"What, then, Master Karl? Do you design to make a ladder that will be taller than all we have ever seen —tall enough to reach to the top of a precipice three hundred feet high? We know you have both energy and perseverance; and, after witnessing the way that you worked at the building of your bridge, and the skill with which you built it, we are ready to believe that you can accomplish a very great feat in the joiner's line; but that you can make a ladder three hundred feet in length, we are not prepared to believe—not if you had a whole chest of tools and the best timber in the world. We know you might put a ladder together ever so long, but would it hold together? or even if it did, how could you set it up against the cliff? Never. Three of the strongest men could not do it,—nor six neither,—nor a dozen, without machinery to assist them; therefore scaling the cliff by means of a wooden ladder is plainly impracticable; and if that be your idea, you may as well abandon it."

"Quite true, I know all this as well as you," would have been Karl's reply; "but I had no idea of being able to scale the cliff by means of a ladder. It was not of *a ladder*, but of *ladders*, I was thinking."

"Ha! there may be something in that."

Karl knew well enough that no single ladder could be made of sufficient length and strength to have reached from the bottom to the top of that great wall; or if such could be constructed, he knew equally well that it would be impossible to set it up.

But the idea that had been forming in his mind was, that several ladders might effect the purpose—one placed above another, and each one resting upon a *ledge*

12

of the cliff, to which the one next below should enable
them to ascend.

In this idea there was really some shadow of practicability, though, as I have said, it was but a very forlorn
hope. The amount of its practicableness depended
upon the existence of the *ledges;* and it was to ascertain this that Karl had set forth.

If such ledges could be found, the hope would no
longer have been forlorn. Karl believed that with time
and energy the ladders might be constructed, notwithstanding the poor stock of carpenter's tools at their
service ; though he had scarce yet thought of how the
holes were to be made to receive the rounds, or how
the ladders themselves might be set upon the ledges, or
any other detail of the plan. He was too eager to be
satisfied about the first and most important point—
whether there were ledges that would answer the purpose ?

With his eyes, therefore, keenly scanning the face of
the cliff, he kept on along its base, walking slowly, and
in silence.

CHAPTER XLVI.

KARL CLIMBS THE LEDGE.

HE continued on until he had reached that end of the valley most remote from the hut, and along the whole of the cliffs that he passed his reconnoissance had been fruitless. He saw many ledges, and some of considerable width—quite wide enough to rest a ladder upon, and also allow it a proper lean to the wall. Some were higher and some lower; but unfortunately they were not above one another, as Karl desired to find them. On the contrary, they were far apart—so that if one of them could have been reached by means of a ladder, as many of them might, this would in no way facilitate communication with the one that was higher up.

Of course then, for Karl's purpose, these ledges were of no avail; and, after observing their relative situations, he passed on with looks of disappointment.

At the farthest end of the valley—that is, the place farthest from the hut—there was a little bay, or indentation, in the cliffs. As already stated, there were several of these at intervals around the valley, but the one in question was the largest of any. It was very narrow, only a few yards in width, and about a hundred in depth—that is, a hundred yards from the line, which indicated the general outline of the valley, to the apex of the angle where the indentation ended. Its bottom was nearly upon the same level with that of the valley itself, though it was raised a little higher in some places by loose rocks, and other *débris* that had fallen from the impending cliffs.

Karl had entered this bay, and was regarding its cliffs all around with intense eagerness of glance. Any one who could have seen him at that moment would have observed that his countenance was brightening as he gazed; and that pleasant thoughts were springing up within his bosom. Any one who had seen that face but the moment before, and had looked upon it now, could not fail to have noticed the change that had so suddenly come over it,—a perfect contrast in its expression. What had produced this metamorphosis? Something of importance, I warrant; for the young botanist, naturally of a sober turn, but now more than ever so, was not given to sudden transitions of feeling. What, then, was the cause of his joy?

A glance at the cliff will answer these interrogatories.

At the first glance it might be noted that that part of the precipice surrounding the bay—or ravine, as it might more properly be called—was lower than elsewhere,—perhaps not quite three hundred feet in height. It was not this peculiarity, however, at which Karl was rejoicing. A ladder of three hundred feet was not to be thought of any more than one of three thousand. It was that he had just observed upon the face of the cliff a series of ledges that rose, shelf-like, one above the other. The rock had a seamed or stratified appearance, although it was a species of granite; but the strata were not by any means regular, and the ledges were at unequal distances from each other. Some, too, were broader than the rest, and some appeared very narrow indeed; but many of them were evidently of sufficient width to form the stepping-place for a ladder. The lower ones especially appeared as though they might easily be scaled by a series of ladders, each from twenty to thirty feet long,—but with regard to those near the top, Karl had great doubts. The shelves did not seem more distant from each other than those below, but their horizontal breadth appeared less. This might possibly be an optical delusion, caused by the greater distance from which they were viewed; but if so, it would not much mend the matter for the design which Karl had in view—since the deception that would have given him an advantage in the breadth would have been against him in the height, making the latter too great, perhaps, for any ladder that could be got up.

If you have ever stood by the bottom of a great precipice, you may have noticed how difficult it is to judge of the dimensions of an object far up its face. A ledge several feet in width will appear as a mere seam in the rock, and a bird or other creature that may be seen upon it, will, to the eyes of the beholder, be reduced far below its real bulk. Karl was philosopher enough to understand these things. He had studied in an elementary way, the laws of optics, and therefore was not going to come to conclusions too hastily.

In order the better to form judgment about the breadth of the ledges, and the height of the respective intervals between them, he stepped back as far as the ground would permit him.

Unfortunately this was not far, for the cliff on the other side, as already stated, was but a few paces distant. Consequently he was soon stopped by the rocks, and his situation for viewing the upper portion of the cliff was anything but an advantageous one.

He scrambled up one of the highest boulders, and took his survey from its top, but he was still not satisfied with his " point of view." He saw, however, that it was the best he could obtain ; and he remained for a good while upon his perch—with eyes bent upon the opposing precipice, now fixed upon a particular spot, and now wandering in one long sweep from bottom to top, and back again from top to bottom.

During this operation the expression upon his face once more changed to one of deep gloom, for he had discovered an obstacle to his designs that appeared insurmountable. One of the spaces between two of the ledges was too great to be spanned by a ladder, and this, too, was high up the cliff. It could never be scaled !

He noticed that the first ledge from the bottom was about half as high from the ground as this one was from that immediately below it.

Hitherto he had been but guessing at the height; but it now occurred to him that he should throw conjecture aside, and ascertain by actual measurement the distance from the ground to the first ledge. This might be easily accomplished—Karl saw that,—and once done, it would give him a better idea of the distance between the ledges high up.

It has been stated that the measurement could be easily made, and that Karl knew this; but how? The ledge appeared to be full forty feet from the ground, and how was it to be reached by a measuring rule? But Karl had no measuring rule; and it was not in that way he intended to go about it.

You will be conjecturing that he looked out for a tall sapling, of sufficient length to reach the ledge, and then afterwards ascertained the number of feet and inches of the sapling. Certainly this mode would have done well enough, and Karl would very likely have made use of it, had not an easier offered itself—or one that at the moment appeared readier to him. He could have told the height by triangulation, but that would also have involved the procuring of a sapling—and some tedious calculation besides, which would have required time, with not the most certain results either.

Both these plans had occupied his thoughts for a while. The first was rejected on account of the difficulty of obtaining a rod of sufficient length,—the second was set aside by Karl just then perceiving that without much difficulty, he might climb up to the ledge itself. There was a portion of the rock below with a slanting face, and here and there some broken hollows and jutting points that would serve him as foot-holds.

Once upon the ledge, the measurement would be simple enough. It would be only to let down a string with a small stone at the end, like a plumber's line; and then mark how much string it required to reach the ground.

He chanced to have about him a longish piece of raw-hide thong, that would serve admirably, and to

carry out his purpose, he at once determined upon ascending to the ledge.

Drawing the thong from his pocket, and attaching to
one end of it the piece of stone, he approached the cliff,
and commenced scrambling upward.

He found it a more difficult task than it had appeared,
and it was just as much as he could do to reach the
ledge in safety.   Had it been Caspar, the climbing
would have been a mere bagatelle ; used, as the young
hunter had been, to the precipices of the Alps while
following the rock-loving chamois.

But Karl was no great hand at such gymnastic exer-
cises ; and he was all out of breath, and a little bit
frightened at his rashness, before he had placed himself
safely on the shelf.

Stepping along it, therefore, till he reached a point
where the cliff below was vertical, he dropped his stone
and line, and soon completed his measurement.   Alas !
it proved to be far higher than he had conjectured in
viewing it from below.   His spirits fell as he contemplated the result.   He was now certain that the space
higher up could not be spanned by any ladder they
might be able to construct.

With sad heart, he returned to the place where he
had made the ascent, intending to go down again.   But
it is sometimes easier to say go down than to do it ; and
to Karl's great consternation he saw at the first glance
that he could no more go down than fly upward into
the air.   Beyond a doubt he was in a fix ; regularly
"nailed" upon the cliff.

CHAPTER XLVII.

KARL IN A FIX.

It is not difficult to comprehend the reason. Any one who has ever climbed up a steep ascent,—such as a piece of wall, the mast of a ship, or even an ordinary ladder,—will have noticed that the going up, is much easier than the getting down again; and where the ascent is very steep and difficult, it is quite possible that a person may make their way to the top, without being able to get back to the bottom. The difficulty of descending is much greater than that of ascending. In the latter, you can see where you are to set your feet, and also what you are to take hold of with your hands; whereas, in the former you have not this advantage; but must grope your way downward, and are therefore continually exposed to the danger of missing your footing, and being precipitated to the bottom.

This was just the situation in which the plant-hunter found himself. It was as much as he had been able to pull himself up; it was more than he could do to let himself down again; this he perceived at a single glance.

It is true that the rock slanted a little, and he had clearly seen this from below. Now that he looked at it

from above, he could scarcely perceive any slant. It
appeared almost vertical, and it was full forty feet to
the bottom ; a fearful height when viewed from above ;
He wondered how he had been able to climb up at all,
and he was now vexed with himself for having been so
rash and foolish.

But he could not stay there all night. Something
must be done, to free him from his unpleasant situation ; and, gathering resolution, he made an attempt to
descend.

He knelt down upon the ledge, with his face turned
toward the cliff and his back outwards. Then, grasping the rock, in his hands, he allowed his feet to slip
over. He succeeded in finding the uppermost steps,
but then came the difficulty. He dared not let go with
his hands, so as to get another step downward ; and, on
lowering his feet to feel for a fresh foothold, he could
not discover any. Repeatedly he ran his toes over the
face of the rock, groping for a notch or jutting point,
but he could find nothing upon which to rest either foot,
and he was at length obliged to draw them up, and place
himself back upon the ledge.

He now bethought him that there might be a better
place for making the descent; and, rising to his feet,
he proceeded to search for it. He had no difficulty in
passing along the ledge; it was several feet in width,
and he could walk erect upon it without danger. It
extended for nearly fifty yards along the face of the
cliff, and was of nearly equal breadth all the way.

Karl proceeded along it from one end to the other, at
every step or two stopping and looking downward.

But his examination ended in disappointment. There

was no path leading from it, at all practicable for any
other creature than a cat, or some other animal with
crooked claws,—at all events, there was no place where
Karl himself could get down,—and he turned to go back
to the point where he had ascended, with a feeling
of apprehension that he was not going to get down
at all !

On proceeding along the ledge, he had not yet bent
his eyes upon the cliff that rose behind,—his attention
being altogether occupied with the part that lay below ;
on going back, however, his eye ranged more freely,
and he now noticed a dark hole in the rock, a few feet
above the level of the ledge. This hole was about as
big as an ordinary doorway, and upon closer examination, Karl perceived that it was the mouth of a cave.
He noticed, moreover, that it appeared to grow wider
beyond the entrance, and was no doubt a cavern of
large dimensions. He had no further curiosity in relation to it ; only that the reflection crossed his mind that
he might be compelled to pass the night there. This
was probable enough ; unless, indeed, Ossaroo or Caspar should come in search of him before nightfall, and
relieve him from his elevated prison. But it was just
as likely they might not ; for frequently one of the party
was out for hours together, without causing any uneasiness to the rest, and it would be after night before they
would feel any apprehension about his absence. In the
darkness, too, they might go in the wrong direction to
search for him, and might wander about through the
woods a long time before coming near the place where
he was. He was in the very farthest corner of the valley, and shut up in the ravine, with rocks and high

woods between him and them; and thus his shouts could not be heard at any great distance.

These were the reflections that passed through his mind, as he returned along the ledge to the point where he had climbed up. He did not enter the cave to examine it—as he would certainly have done under other circumstances—but his curiosity was now controlled by the apprehension he very naturally felt in the dilemma in which he was placed.

That he could do nothing to free himself from it was clear enough to his mind. He must wait, therefore, until either Caspar came, or Ossaroo, or both; and, summoning all his patience, he sat down upon the ledge and waited.

Of course, he did not wait in silence. He had the sense to know, that if he kept silent they might not find him at all; and therefore, at short intervals, he rose to his feet, and shouted at the top of his voice, causing the cliffs to reverberate in numberless echoes.

The echoes, however, were the only replies he received. Loud as were his cries, they were not heard either by Caspar or Ossaroo.

CHAPTER XLVIII.

THE TIBET BEAR.

FOR full two hours sat Karl, chewing the cud of impatience. As yet the feeling he experienced was only one of impatience, mingled with a considerable amount of chagrin at being in such a scrape, and having got himself into it in so simple a manner. He had no very painful apprehensions about the result—since he made quite sure that his companions would come to his relief in the end. They might not find him that day, or that night, and he might have to remain all night upon the ledge. This, however, would be no great hardship. He might suffer a little from want of his supper, and he might have to sleep in the cave, but what of that to one so inured to hunger, and to sleeping in the open air, as he was? Even had there been no shelter, he could have stretched himself along the ledge, and slept that way without much minding it. Certainly in the morning the others would be after him, his shouts would guide them to the spot, and then it would be all right again.

Such was the reasoning of Karl, and therefore, knowing that he had but little to fear, he was not acutely anxious.

While he was thus comfortably communing with himself, however, his eyes rested upon an object that rendered him anxious enough—nay, more than anxious —badly frightened, would be nearer the words.

His ears first guided him to this new cause of alarm. While sitting on the ledge, and not saying a word, he heard a sound that resembled the snort of a jackass, just as one commences to bray.

There were some bushes growing at no great distance from the bottom of the cliff, and it was from the midst of these bushes the sound appeared to proceed.

After hearing the snort, Karl kept both eyes and ears acutely bent—the former fixed upon the bushes; and in a minute after, the sound was repeated, though he did not see the creature that uttered it. He saw, however, by the motion of the twigs, that something was passing through the thicket; and the loud snapping of dead sticks, and crackling of branches, proved that it was an animal of great weight and dimensions.

Karl was not long in doubt as to the dimensions; for the instant after he beheld the body of a large beast emerging from the thicket, and moving out into the open ground.

It required no skill to tell what sort of animal it was —a bear beyond the probability of a doubt—and yet it was of a species that Karl had never before seen. But there is such a similitude between the members of the Bruin tribe, that he who has ever seen one—and who has not?—will easily recognize all the rest of the family.

The one which now presented itself to the observation of our plant-hunter, was of medium size—that is, less than the great polar bear, or the "grizzly" of the Rocky Mountains, but larger than the Bornean species, or the sun-bear of the Malays. It was scarce so large as the singular sloth-bear, which they had encountered near the foot of the mountains, and with which they had had such a ludicrous adventure. It was but little less, however, than the "sloth," and, like it, was of a deep black color, though its hair was neither so long nor shaggy. Like the latter, too, its under lip was whitish, with a white mark on its throat resembling a Y —the stem of the letter being placed upon the middle of its breast, and the fork passing up in front of the shoulders—for this is a mark which belongs to several species of Southern Asiatic bears. In other respects the bear in question was peculiar. It had a neck remarkably thick; a flattened head, with the forehead and muzzle forming almost a straight line—and on this account distinguishing it from the sloth-bear, in which the forehead rises almost abruptly from the line of the muzzle. Its ears were of large size—its body compact, supported on stout but clumsy limbs—and its feet armed with claws of moderate dimensions, and blunted at their points. Such were the markings of the bear now before the eyes of Karl; and although he had never seen one of the kind before, he had read of one; and by these peculiarities he was able to recognize the species. It was the Tibet bear (*Ursus Tibetanus*)—more commonly styled by closet-naturalists *Helarctos Tibetanus*—one of the bears that inhabit the high table-lands of Tibet, and is supposed to range through the whole of the Upper Himalayas, since it has been found in Nepaul and elsewhere.

I have said that Karl was badly frightened with this black apparition. This was at the first sight of it, as it came out of the bushes; and, indeed, it is not at all surprising that he was so. There is no one,—not even a bear-hunter himself,—who can encounter a bear upon the bear's own ground without feeling a little trembling of the nerves; but when it is remembered that Karl was quite unarmed—for he had left his gun at the bottom of the cliff—it will not be wondered at, that the appearance of the bear caused him alarm.

His fright, however, was of short duration; and for two reasons. First, he remembered having read that this species of bear is of a harmless disposition; that it is not carnivorous, but feeds only on fruits, and in no instance has it been known to attack man unless when wounded or assailed. Then, of course, it will defend itself, as many animals will do that are otherwise gentle and harmless.

Another reason why he soon got over his fright was, that he chanced to be in such a position that it was not likely the bear would attempt to come near him. He was quite out of its way; and if he only kept silent— which he would be careful to do—the animal might not even look in that direction, but go off again without perceiving him. In hope that such would be the result, Karl sat without stirring, and kept as quiet as a mouse.

But Karl chanced to be building his hopes on a false foundation. The bear had no notion of going off as it had come—it had other designs altogether; and, after shuffling about over the stones—now and then uttering the same asinine snort that had first called attention to it—it marched straight forward to the cliff, just under the spot where Karl was seated. Then, rearing its body erect, and placing its fore-paws against the rock, it looked up into the face of the astonished plant-hunter!

CHAPTER XLIX.

AN AWKWARD DESCENT.

It is probable that the bear at this moment was quite as much astonished as Karl, though perhaps not so badly scared. It must have felt alarm though, for on seeing him it permitted its paws to drop suddenly to the ground, and appeared for a moment undecided as to whether it should turn tail and run back into the thicket. It did actually make a turn or two, growling and looking up; and then, as if it had got over its surprise, and was no longer afraid, it once more approached the cliff, and planted itself to spring upward.

On first perceiving the bear, Karl had been seated upon the ledge, just above the path by which he had climbed up, and it was by this path that the animal was threatening to ascend. On perceiving its intention, Karl sprang to his feet, and set to dancing about on the ledge, uncertain what to do, or whither to flee.

As to opposing the ascent of the bear, he did not think of such a thing. He had no weapons,—not even a knife; and had he attempted to wrestle with it, trusting to his strength alone, he very well knew that the struggle would end either by his being hugged to death

in the arms of the great brute, or pushed off the ledge
and crushed to atoms in the fall. He had no idea,
therefore, of standing on the defence—he thought only
of retreating.

But how was he to retreat? whither was he to run?
It would be of little use going along the ledge, since the
bear could easily follow him; and if the animal meant
to attack him, he might as well keep his ground and
receive the assault where he stood.

Karl was still hesitating what to do, and the bear had
commenced crawling up, when he chanced to remember
the cave. This suggested an idea. Perhaps he might
conceal himself in the cave?

He had no time to consider whether or not this would
be a prudent step. If he hesitated any longer, the great
black brute would lay hold of him to a certainty; and
therefore, without reflecting another moment, he ran off
along the ledge.

On arriving opposite the cave, he turned into it; and,
groping his way for a pace or two, squatted down near
the entrance.

Fortunately for him he had, upon entering, kept well
to one side before he squatted. He had done so, in order to place himself under the darkness. Had he remained in the central part of the "entrance-hall," he
would either have been run over by the bear, or gripped
between its huge paws, before he could have pronounced
those two famous words, "Jack Robinson." As it was,
he had scarcely crouched down, when the bear entered,
still snorting and growling, and rushed past him up the
cave. It made no stop near the entrance, but kept
right on, until, from the noises it continued to make,

Karl could tell that it had gone a good way into the interior of the cavern.

It was now a question with the plant-hunter what course he should follow—whether remain where he was, or pop out again upon the ledge?

Certainly his present situation afforded him no security. Should the bear return to the attack, he could not expect it to pass without perceiving him. He knew that these animals can see in a very obscure light—almost in the midst of darkness; and therefore he would be seen, or if not seen, he would be scented, which was equally as bad.

It was no use, then, remaining inside; and although he might be no safer outside, he determined to go thither. At all events, he would have light around him, and could see his antagonist before being attacked; while the thought of being assailed in the cave, and hugged to death by an unseen enemy in the darkness, had something awful and horrible in it. If he were to be destroyed in this way, neither Caspar nor Ossaroo might ever know what had become of him—his bones might lie in that dark cavern never to be discovered by human eyes: it was a fearful apprehension!

Karl could not bear it; and, rising half erect, he rushed out into the light.

He did not pause by the entrance of the cave, but ran back along the shelf to the point where the path led up. Here he stopped, and for several minutes stood—now looking anxiously back towards the cavern's mouth, and now as anxiously casting his glances down the giddy path that conducted to the bottom of the cliff.

Had Karl known the true disposition of the Tibet bear, or the design of the particular one he had thus encountered, he would not have been so badly frightened. In truth, the bear was as much disinclined to an encounter as he; at a loss, no doubt, to make out the character of its adversary. It was probable that Karl himself was the first human biped the animal had ever set eyes on; and, not knowing the strength of such a strange creature, it was willing enough to give him a wide berth, provided he would reciprocate the civility!

The bear, in fact, was only rushing to its cave; perhaps to join its mate there, or defend its cubs, which it believed to be in danger, and had no idea whatever of molesting the plant-hunter, as it afterwards proved.

But Karl could not know this, and did not know it. He fancied all the while that the bear was in pursuit of him; that, to attack him, it had sprung up to the ledge; and that it had rushed past him into the cave, thinking he had gone far in; that, as soon as it should reach the interior, and find he was no longer there, it would come rushing out again, and then——

It is well known that one danger makes another seem less, and that despair will often lend courage to cowards.

Karl was no coward, although in calm blood the descent of the cliff had cowed him. But now that his blood was up, the danger of the descent appeared less; and, partly inspired by this belief, and partly urged on by the fear of Bruin reissuing from the cave, he determined once more to attempt it.

In an instant he was on his knees, and letting himself over the edge of the rock.

For the first length of himself, he succeeded beyond his expectations, having found the steps below readily enough. He was gaining confidence, and the belief that it would be all right yet, and that, in a few seconds more, he would be at the bottom, where he could soon escape from the bear by taking to a tree, or defend himself with his gun, which was lying, ready loaded, on the ground. All the while, he kept his face upward, except during the moments when it was necessary to glance below, to discover the position of the steps.

No wonder he looked upward, with eyes full of anxiety. Should the bear attack him now, a terrible fate would be his!

Still there were no signs of the animal, and Karl was gradually getting lower and lower in his descent.

He was yet scarce half-way down, and full twenty feet were between his heels and the ground, when he arrived at a point where he could find no resting-place for his feet. He had found one upon a knob of rock; but unfortunately it proved brittle and gave way, leaving him without any thing broad enough to rest even his toe upon. He had already shifted his hold with the hands; and was, therefore, compelled to support the whole weight of his body by the strength of his arms!

This was a terrible situation; and unless he could immediately get a rest for his feet, he must fall to the bottom of the cliff!

He struggled manfully; he spread out his toes as far as he could reach, feeling the rock on both sides.

Its face appeared smooth as glass; there was nothing that offered foothold; he believed that he was lost!

He tried to reach the notches above him ; first with one hand, then with the other. He could just touch, but not grasp them ; he could not go up again ; he believed that he was lost !

His arms were dragged nearly out of joint; his strength was fast going ; he believed that he was lost !

Still he struggled on, with the tenacity by which youth clings to life ; he hung on, though certain that every moment would be his last.

He heard voices from below—shouts of encouragement—cries of " Hold on, Karl ! Hold on ! "

He knew the voices, and who uttered them. They had come too late ; a weak scream was all the answer he could make.

It was the last effort of his strength. Simultaneous with its utterance, his hands relaxed their hold, and he fell backward from the cliff !

CHAPTER L.

A MYSTERIOUS MONSTER.

KARL, poor fellow! was killed, of course; crushed to death upon the rocks; mangled——

Stay—not so fast, reader! Karl was not killed; not even hurt! He was no more damaged by his fall, than if he had only tumbled from a chair, or rolled from a fashionable couch upon the carpet of a drawing-room!

How could this be? you will exclaim. A fall of sheer twenty feet, and upon loose rocks, too! How could he escape being killed, or, at the very least, badly bruised and cut?

But there was neither bruise nor scratch upon his body; and, the moment after he had relinquished his hold, he might have been seen standing by the bottom of the cliff, sound in limb, though sadly out of wind, and with his strength altogether exhausted.

Let us have no mystery about the matter. I shall at once tell you how he escaped.

Caspar and Ossaroo, having expected him to return at an early hour, took it into their heads, from his long absence, that something might be wrong; and, there-fore, sallied forth in search of him. They might not

have found him so readily but for Fritz. The dog had guided them on his trail, so that no time had been lost in scouring the valley. On the contrary, they had come almost direct from the hut to the ravine where he was found.

They had arrived just at the crisis when Karl was making his last attempt to descend from the ledge. They had shouted to him, when first coming within hail; but Karl, intently occupied with the difficulty of the descent, and his anxiety about the bear, had not heard them. It was just at that moment that he lost his foothold, and Caspar and Ossaroo saw him sprawling helplessly against the cliff.

Caspar's quick wit suggested what was best to be done. Both he and Ossaroo ran underneath, and held up their arms to catch Karl as he fell; but Ossaroo chanced to have a large skin-robe around his shoulders, and, at Caspar's prompt suggestion, this was hurriedly spread out, and held between the two, high above their heads. It was while adjusting this, that Karl had heard them crying out to him to "hold on." Just as the robe was hoisted into its place, Karl had fallen plump down into the middle of it; and although his weight brought all three of them together to the ground, yet they scrambled to their feet again without receiving the slightest injury.

"Ha! ha! ha!" laughed Caspar, "just in the nick of time! Ha! ha! ha!"

Of course there followed a good deal of rejoicing and congratulation upon this narrow escape. Narrow it certainly was, for had not Caspar and Ossaroo arrived in the "nick of time," as Caspar expressed it, and acted

13

as promptly as they had, poor Karl would never have lived to thank them.

"Well," said Caspar, "I think I may call this one of my lucky days; and yet I don't know about that, since it has come so near being fatal to both my companions."

"Both?" inquired Karl, with some surprise.

"Indeed, yes, brother," answered Caspar. "Yours is the second life I've had a hand in saving to-day."

"What! has Ossaroo been in danger, too? Ha! he is quite wet—every rag upon his body!" said Karl, approaching the shikarree, and laying hand upon his garments. "Why, so are you, Caspar,—dripping wet, I declare! How is this? You've been in the lake? Have you been in danger of drowning?"

"Why, yes," replied Caspar. "Ossy has." (Caspar frequently used this diminutive for Ossaroo.) "I might say worse than drowning. Our comrade has been near a worse fate—that of being *swallowed up!*"

"Swallowed up!" exclaimed Karl, in astonishment. "Swallowed up! What mean you, brother?"

"I mean just what I have said—that Ossaroo has been in great danger of being swallowed up,—body, bones, and all,—so that we would never have found a trace of him!"

"Oh! Caspar, you must be jesting with me;—there are no whales in the lake to make a Jonah of our poor shikarree; nor sharks neither, nor any sort of fish big enough to bolt a full-grown man. What, then, can you mean?"

"In truth, brother, I am quite serious. We have been very near losing our comrade,—almost as near as he and I have been of losing you; so that, you see, there has been a double chance against your life; for if Ossaroo had not been saved, neither he nor I would have been here in time to lend you a hand, and both of you in that case would have perished. What danger have I been in of losing both? and then what would have been my forlorn fate? Ah! I cannot call it a lucky day, after all. A day of perils—even when one has the good fortune to escape them—is never a pleasant one to be remembered. No—I shudder when I think of the chances of this day!"

"But come, Caspar!" interposed the botanist, "explain yourself! Tell me what has happened to get both of you so saturated with water. Who or what came so near swallowing Ossaroo? Was it fish, flesh, or fowl?

"A fish, I should think," added Karl, in a jocular way, "judging from the element in which the adventure occurred. Certainly from the appearance of both of you it must have been in the water, and under the water too? Most undoubtedly a fish! Come, then, brother! let us hear this *fish story*."

"Certainly a fish had something to do with it," replied Caspar; "but although Ossaroo has proved that there are large fish in the lake, by capturing one nearly as big as himself—I don't believe there are any quite large enough to swallow him—body, limbs, and all—without leaving some trace of him behind; whereas the monster that did threaten to accomplish this feat, would not have left the slightest record by which we could have known what had become of our unfortunate companion."

"A monster!" exclaimed Karl, with increased astonishment and some little terror.

"Well, not exactly that," replied Caspar, smiling at
the puzzled expression on his brother's countenance;
"not exactly a monster, for it is altogether a *natural*
phenomenon; but it is something quite as dangerous as
any monster; and we will do well to avoid it in our
future wanderings about the lake."

"Why, Caspar, you have excited my curiosity to the
highest pitch. Pray, lose no more time, but tell me at
once what kind of terrible adventure is this that has
befallen you."

"That I shall leave Ossy to do, for it was his adventure, not mine. I was not even a witness to it, though,
by good fortune, I was present at the 'wind up,' and
aided in conducting it to a different result than it would
otherwise have had. Poor Ossy! had I not arrived
just in the right time, I wonder where you'd have been
now? Several feet under ground, I dare say. Ha!
ha! ha! It certainly is a very serious matter to laugh
at, brother; but when I first set my eyes upon Ossaroo
—on arriving to relieve him from his dilemma—he appeared in such a forlorn condition, and looked the thing
so perfectly, that for the life of me I could not help
breaking out into a fit of laughter—no more can I now,
when I recall the picture he presented."

"Bother, Caspar!" cried Karl, a little vexed at his
brother's circumlocution, "you quite try one's patience.
Pray, Ossaroo, do you proceed, and relieve me by giving me an account of your late troubles. Never mind
Caspar; let him laugh away. Go on, Ossaroo!"

Ossaroo, thus appealed to, commenced his narration

of the adventure that had occurred to him, and which, as Caspar had justly stated, had very nearly proved fatal; but as the shikarree talked in a very broken and mixed language, that would hardly be intelligible to the reader, I must translate his story for him; and its main incidents will be found in the chapters that follow.

CHAPTER LI.

"BANG."

It so happened that Ossaroo had made for himself a regular fish-net. Not being permitted to poison the lake with wolf's-bane, and having no bamboo to make wicker-work of, he looked around for some other substance wherewith to construct a net; and soon found the very thing itself, in the shape of a plant that grew in abundance throughout the valley, and particularly near the shores of the lake.

This plant was a tall single-stemmed annual, with a few digitate and toothed leaves, and a loose panicle of greenish flowers at its top. There was nothing very remarkable about its appearance, except that its stem was covered with short rigid hairs, and rose undivided to a height of nearly twenty feet. Many plants were growing together, and when first discovered—all three of our adventurers were present at the discovery—Caspar had said that they reminded him of hemp. It was not a bad comparison Caspar had hit upon, for the plant *was hemp*, as Karl immediately made known—the true *Cannabis sativa*, though the variety which grows in India, or rather a drug extracted from it, is called *Cannabis Indica*, or "Indian hemp." It was the tallest hemp either Karl or Caspar had ever seen—some of the stalks actually measuring eighteen feet in length, whereas that of the northern or middle parts of Europe rarely reaches the height of an ordinary man. In Italy, however, and other southern portions of the European Continent, hemp attains a much greater height, rivalling that of India in the length of its stalk and fibre. It was noticed that nearly one half of the plants, although growing side by side, and mingled with the others, were much riper, and, in fact, fast withering to decay. The botanist explained this to his companions, by saying that these were the male plants, and the growing ones the females; for hemp is what is termed by botanists "dioecious"—that is, having male flowers on one plant, and female ones upon another. Karl farther observed that the male plants, after having performed their office—that is, having shed their pollen upon the females—not only cease to grow taller, but soon wither and die ; whereas the females still flourish, and do not arrive at maturity until several weeks afterwards. In consequence of this peculiarity, people who make a business of cultivating hemp pull the male plants at the time they have shed their pollen, and leave the females standing for four or five weeks after.

It is well known that hemp is one of the finest articles in the world for the manufacture of coarse cloth, and every sort of cordage and ropes. The material used for the purpose is the fibrous covering of the stalk, which is separated almost by the same means that are employed in obtaining flax. The hemp, when pulled up, is tied in bundles, and for a time submitted to the action of water. It is then dried and broken, and afterwards "scutched," and rendered still cleaner and finer by a process called " hackling." It makes no difference in the fineness of the fibre whether the stalks be small or large, since the great coarse stems of the Italian and Indian hemp produce a staple equally as fine as the small kinds grown farther north.

The Russians extract an oil from the seeds of hemp, which is used by them in cooking, and by painters in mixing their colors.

Hempseed is also given to poultry—as it is popularly believed that it occasions hens to lay a greater number of eggs. Small birds are exceedingly fond of it; but a singular fact has been recorded in relation to this— that the effect of feeding bullfinches and goldfinches on hempseed alone, has been to change the red and yellow feathers of these birds to a total blackness!

Notwithstanding the many valuable properties of this plant, it has some that are not only deleterious, but dangerous. It contains a narcotic principle of great power; and, strange to say, this principle is far more fully developed in the Indian or Southern hemp than in that grown in middle Europe. Of course this is accounted for by the difference of temperature. Any one remaining for a length of time in the midst of a field of young growing hemp, will feel certain ill effects from it—it will occasion headache and vertigo. In a hot country the effect is still more violent, and a kind of intoxication is produced by it.

From observing this, the Oriental nations have been led to prepare a drug from hemp, which they make use of in the same way as opium, and with almost simi-lar results—for it produces a drowsy ecstatic feeling, always followed by a reaction of wretchedness. This drug is known by the Turks, Persians, and Hindoos, under a variety of names, such as "bang," "haschish," "chinab," "ganga," and others; but under any name it is a bad article to deal in, either for the health of the body or the mind.

But Ossaroo was not deterred by any considerations about its baneful effects; and as soon as he saw the hemp growing in the valley, he recognized the plant with a shout of joy, and proceeded to prepare himself a dose of "bang." This he did by simply powdering some of the dry leaves, which he obtained from the withered male stalks, and then mixing the powder with a little water. An aromatic substance is usually added to give flavor to the mixture, but Ossaroo did not care so much for flavor as strength; and he drank off his "bang" without any adulteration, and was soon in the land of pleasant dreams.

The discovery of the hemp had made Ossaroo unusually happy. He had been suffering for the want of his "betel" for a long while, and the rhubarb tobacco had proved but a poor substitute. But the hemp was the very thing, as it not only afforded him an intoxicating drink, but its dry leaves were also good for smoking; and they are often used for this purpose when mixed with real tobacco. Of course Ossaroo had none of the genuine "weed" wherewith to mix them, else he would not have troubled his head about the rhubarb.

Ossaroo, however, was glad at discovering the hemp for another reason. From its fibres he could make cordage, and with that cordage a net, and with that net he would soon provide their table with a supply of fish.

13 *

He was not long about it. The hemp was soon pulled, tied in bundles, and carried to the hot spring. There it was immersed under the water, and soon sufficiently "steeped;" for it is well known that hot water will bring either flax or hemp to the same state in a few hours that can be obtained by weeks of immersion in water that is cold.

Ossaroo soon prepared a sufficient quantity for his purpose, having separated the fibre by "hand-scutch-ing;" and working continually at the thing, in a few days he succeeded in making a complete mesh-net of several yards in length.

It only remained for him to set it, and see what sort of fish were to be caught out of that solitary mountain lake.

And now for Ossaroo's adventure!

)

CHAPTER LII.

SETTING THE NET.

KARL had not been very long gone when Caspar and Ossaroo both left the hut, but not together. They parted from each other, taking different directions. Caspar had his gun, and went forth to search for game; while Ossaroo proceeded towards the lake, with the intention of capturing fish.

As nothing particular happened to Caspar—not even so much as the starting of a head of game, or the getting a shot at any thing—there is nothing to tell about him; and I shall therefore proceed at once to Ossaroo and his adventure.

The shikarree, on arriving at the lake, soon found a proper place to set his net in. There was a little bay on one side that ran for some twenty or more yards into the land, and ended just at the embouchure of the little rivulet that came from the hot springs.

This bay was narrower at its mouth than elsewhere, where it formed a kind of miniature " straits." The water in the bay was of considerable depth ; but just at its entrance, where the straits were, it was not over three feet, with a white sandy bottom that could be seen shining like silver. Any one standing near this point, in clear weather, could easily observe fishes of several sorts and different sizes passing into the bay and out of it, and disporting themselves over the white sand bed that shone sparkling beneath them. It was an interesting sight to watch them at their innocent gambols, and the boys had more than once gone down to the edge of the straits to observe them.

But Ossaroo had always regarded the sight rather with feelings of chagrin than pleasure; for plainly as these beautiful fish could be seen, not one of them could he capture. Even the shoal-water of the straits, where there was a sort of bar, was too deep to be dammed up in any way, and Ossaroo had tried one or two plans for taking the fish, without effect. He had used his bow, and endeavored to kill them with arrows; but they swam too deep, and, somehow or another, he always missed them. The fact was that Ossaroo was not practised in shooting fish with the arrow; and not understanding any thing about optics or the laws of refraction, he missed his mark by aiming too high.

Had he been an Indian of North or South America, instead of an Indian of the "East Indies," he would have pierced those fishes with an arrow at every twang of his bow.

Instead of that, he only missed them, and was constantly wading in to recover his arrows, but never to bring out any fish. He was, therefore, rather chagrined than pleased to see them so fearlessly and freely playing about over the silvery sand; and this very chagrin had caused him to work with greater diligence while preparing his mesh-net.

The net was now ready, and Ossaroo walked along

chuckling and congratulating himself on the prospect
of speedy revenge—for he had actually become inspired with a revengeful feeling against the poor fish,
because he had not been able to capture and kill them!

The place where Ossaroo intended to set his net was
across the strait that formed the mouth of the aforesaid
bay. He had designed the net for this very place;
and had made it of such length, that when at full
stretch, it would just reach from one side to the other.

The upper edge of the net was attached to a strong
piece of raw hide, for this was more easily attainable
than a rope of hemp; and on the lower edge there was
another strip of hide, to which were fastened the
sinkers. These, with the floats at the top—made out
of a sort of light wood that he had found in the valley
—would keep the meshes fully spread, and hold the net
in a vertical position.

It would thus form a complete gate, shutting up the
little bay, and leaving neither egress nor ingress for
any fish that could not squeeze itself through the
meshes. These last had been made very large; for
Ossaroo did not care for the " small fry."

It was the big fishes he was desirous of capturing—
some of those large fellows who had so often glided
from under his arrows, and put him out of temper by
their saucy sporting.

He would see now if they would so easily escape the
meshes he had so cunningly contrived for them.

Proceeding, therefore, to the straits, he set his net
across the narrowest part, and just by the entrance to
the bay. The thing was easily accomplished. He tied
the raw-hide rope to a sapling on one side, that grew

down by the edge of the water. Then holding the upper edge—so that the net would settle regularly in the water—he waded across, carrying the line along with him, and made it secure on the other side. Of course the sinkers did their work by dragging the lower selvage downward, while the floats kept the upper edge from dipping below the surface of the water.

There was a large tree upon the opposite side—so large that its great branches spread half-way across the little strait—and when the sun was on that side, which it always was after the hour of noon, this tree, covered with thick foliage, quite shadowed the water, rendering it of darkish color, and somewhat obscure. At this hour the fish could not be so easily seen, even against the background of the silvery sand at the bottom.

Now Ossaroo had chosen the hour when the sun was gone behind the tree, for he knew that in a very clear sunshine the fish would perceive the net, and of course put about, and shy off from it. He had, therefore, waited for the afternoon to make his first essay.

Having fastened both ends, and adjusted the whole matter to his liking, he sat down upon the bank; and, summoning all his patience, awaited the result.

CHAPTER LIII.

OSSAROO STUCK FAST.

For more than an hour sat the shikarree watching every ruffle upon the water, and every motion of the floats, but no movement, either of wood or water, seemed to indicate that there were fish in the lake. Once or twice there appeared a little " purl " on the surface, near the line of the floats, and Ossaroo fancied he had made a " take " of it; but, on wading in and examining the net, not a fin could be found, and he had to wade out again with empty hands. These " purls " were occasioned either by very small fish passing through the meshes, or else by large ones who came up, and touching the net with their snout, had taken the alarm and beat a retreat back to the pools whence they had come.

Ossaroo was beginning to grow very impatient with his ill-fortune, and was thinking, too, what a sorry figure he would cut in the eyes of his companions, after returning to the hut. He had calculated on a great triumph to be obtained by means of this net; and now he began to doubt whether it might not turn out a humiliation rather than a triumph.

At this crisis, however, an idea occurred to him

which promised success. It was simply to *drive the fish into the net*, by wading into the water, and making as much noise and commotion as he could. This was certainly a very good plan, and Ossaroo lost no time in putting it into execution. Having procured a long stick, with an armful of large stones, he entered the bay above the point where the net was placed, and then plunging through the water, at the same time beating it with his stick, and flinging his stones into the deepest part, he succeeded in making noise enough to have frightened all the fishes in the lake.

His plan succeeded admirably. In less than five minutes—nay, in less than half that time—the violent shaking of the floats told to the attentive eyes of the shikarree that one or more large fishes were in the net and struggling within its meshes. He now gave up beating the water and ran to make sure of the prey. On approaching the strait, he perceived that a very large fish had been caught. It was near the middle of the net, and Ossaroo, wading out, soon " grabbed " and secured it. The strong creature struggled hard, and endeavored to escape from the grasp of its captor; but the latter put an end to its efforts, by giving it a sharp knock on the head with one of the stones which he still carried.

He next proceeded to release it from the meshes; but these, on account of the desperate struggles which the fish had made, were warped and twisted around its gills and fins, and worked into such a labyrinthine puzzle, that Ossaroo found it no joke to get them clear. He was full ten minutes in accomplishing this feat, but he at length succeeded, and, holding the hugh fish triumphantly in his hands above the surface of the water, he uttered a shout of victory.

He was about to wade out to the bank with his prize, when, to his astonishment, he found that he could not move a step! He tried to lift first one leg and then the other, but without success. Both were held as fast as if screwed in a vice! At first he was only puzzled and astonished, but his astonishment soon changed to dismay, when he found that, exert himself as he might, he could not move a limb! He at once perceived the cause, for there was no mystery about that. He perceived that both his legs were fast in a quicksand, into which, while engaged with the meshes of the net, he had been gradually sinking. The surface of the sand was already above his knees, so that he could not even bend the joints, and there he stood as firmly as if he had been planted!

For some time he struggled to relieve himself, but his struggles were of no avail—he could not drag out one foot or the other. The sand was wedged around his limbs, and held him as firmly as if it had been Roman cement. He could not stir from the spot!

At first, I have said, Ossaroo felt only astonishment, but this feeling soon changed to dismay. It became absolute terror when he perceived that he was *still gradually sinking!*—yes, beyond a doubt, he was going down deeper and deeper. The sand was already up to his thighs, and, as the water was nearly a yard in depth, his chin almost touched the surface. Six inches more, and *he would drown!* Drown, thus standing erect, with part of his head above the surface, and his eyes wide open and gazing upon the light of heaven ! It was an awful situation—a fearful fate that threatened him !   .

It would not be true to say that Ossaroo remained silent during all this terrible trial. He did nothing of the kind; on the contrary, as soon as he became aware of his danger, he set up a continuous screaming, and yelling, and shrill piping, that caused both the woods and rocks to ring around him, to the distance of a mile at least.

Fortunately for the shikarree, Caspar chanced to be within the circumference of that mile, wandering about with his gun. The quick ear of the hunter caught the sounds, and knew that they were signals of distress. Without a moment's delay, therefore, he set off; and, guided by the cries, soon arrived upon the ground.

It was some time, however, before Ossaroo was relieved from his perilous position, for although Caspar could wade in to his side, he was quite unable to drag him out of the sand. In fact, Caspar himself sank so rapidly, whenever he stood still, that he was compelled to keep constantly moving, and changing from one foot to the other. His strength, then, was quite unequal to the task, and both began to be uneasy about the result.

Up to this time Caspar had been laughing heartily at the ludicrous spectacle which Ossaroo presented, with only his head above the water, and his face wearing the most lugubrious of looks; but Caspar's mirth was soon dissipated, when he perceived the real danger in which the shikarree was placed; his laughter was brought abruptly to an end, and an expression of anxiety now clouded his countenance.

But Caspar was just the one for quick thought and action in a case of danger like this, and, almost in an instant, he conceived a plan by which Ossaroo might be saved. Crying to the latter to keep still, he dashed out of the water and loosed the net at both ends. He then drew out the long rope that formed its upper border, cutting away the meshes and floats. This done, he rapidly climbed the great tree, and sprawled out along one of its horizontal limbs that stretched right over the place where the shikarree was fixed. He had taken the rope along with him; and, now throwing one end to Ossaroo, and directing him to fasten it around his body, he passed the other over the branch, and slipped down it into the water.

In a few seconds the rope was made fast upon the body of Ossaroo—just under his armpits—and then both laid hold of the other end, and commenced pulling with all their might.

To their great joy their united strength proved suffi cient for the purpose. It outbalanced the weight and tenacity of the sand; and after a good spell of pulling and tugging, Ossaroo's limbs were drawn upward and once more set free. Then both rushed out to the bank, and the same trees and rocks that so lately echoed the mournful cries of the shikarree, now rang with shouts of joy.

◆

CHAPTER LIV.

A DEMAND FOR BEAR'S GREASE.

THE peril from which he had just escaped, drove all thoughts of fishing out of Ossaroo's head, for that day at least. Moreover, the net was damaged by the rope having been so rudely taken out, and would require repairs before it could be set again; so, taking up the fish that had been caught and the net also, Caspar and the fisherman walked off toward the hut.

On arriving there, they were surprised to find that Karl had not returned, for it was getting late; and fearing that some accident might have happened to him, they lost no time in setting forth in search of him.

As already known they were guided upon his trail by Fritz, and arrived just in time to save Karl's life.

"But tell us, brother," inquired Caspar after a while, "what took you up there anyhow?"

Karl now entered into a detail of *his* afternoon's adventures—telling them at the same time of the hope he had conceived of their being able to scale the precipice with ladders.

When he came to the bear, Caspar was all ears.

"What! a bear?" he exclaimed; "a bear, you say, brother?—Which way did it go?"

"Into the cave—it is still there."

"Still in the cave! Good! we'll have him out—let us go after him at once."

"No, brother, it is better not,—it might be dangerous to attack him in the cave."

"Not a bit of it," replied the daring hunter; "Ossaroo says that these bears are great cowards, and that he would not be afraid to attack one single-handed with his spear. You think so, shikarree?"

"Yes, Sahib, he bear—big coward, me no fear him anywhere."

"You remember, Karl, how the other one ran from us—just like a deer would have done."

"But this one is a different kind," suggested Karl; and Karl proceeded to describe the bear which he had encountered.

Ossaroo, however, knew the animal by the description given, and declared that it was quite as timid a creature as the sloth-bear. He had hunted this kind in the Sylhet Hills—where he had been upon an expedition—and where, he asserted, the Tibet bear was to be found in considerable numbers. It would not be dangerous, therefore, to attack it in the cave, or anywhere else. Such was the opinion of the shikarree.

Karl at length ceased to urge his objections. He began to think that the bear had not been in pursuit of him, after all,—else it would have returned out of the cave on not finding him—most likely the cave was its den, and it was to hide itself there that it had rushed so determinedly past him. This appeared probable enough, since they had been waiting a good while, and Bruin had not yet condescended to show himself upon the ledge.

It was resolved, therefore, that they should all enter the cavern, and kill the bear if possible.

This resolve, however, was not made without considerable deliberation; but two reasons were at length brought forward that not only decided the point in favor of killing the bear, but rendered it a matter of some consequence that they should succeed in this design.

The first reason was that they really wanted the animal, and it was of importance to them that it should be killed.

It was not for its fine skin they wanted it—though that might be of use to them in the cold winter, now near at hand—nor did they want to kill the bear merely for the pleasure and excitement of the thing. No. They had a very different object in view. They wanted the carcass, or rather that portion of it that is termed the "fat." They wanted the "bear's grease."

For what purpose? you will ask. To make their hair grow? Nothing of the sort. The hair of all three, from late neglect, was long enough—quite as long as they could have wished it. Caspar's curls hung over his shoulders, and Ossaroo's snaky black tresses dangled down his back like the tail of a horse. Even Karl's silken locks were long enough to have satisfied the most romantic of refugees. No. They wanted the bear's fat, not for their hair, but for their kitchen. They wanted it to cook with, for one thing, but a still more important use they intended to apply it to,—and that was for making candles! For both of the above purposes they had need of the bear's fat, since the other animals which they were accustomed to hunt and kill were chiefly ruminant animals, with very little fat upon them, and never enough of it to cook their own flesh.

You who live in a land where there is plenty of lard and butter, can hardly understand what it is to be without these essential articles of the *cuisine*. In most civilized countries that valuable pachyderm,—the pig,—supplies the desideratum of lard; and you will scarce appreciate the importance of this article until you have travelled in a country where the hog is not found among the domesticated animals. In such places the smallest morsel of fat is highly prized, for without it, good cooking is a dry and difficult business.

Such considerations as these determined the fate of the bear. The hunters well knew that animals of this kind yield large quantities of the very best fat, which they then stood in want of, and would need still more during the long nights of winter. Perhaps there might be more than one bear in the cave; so much the better; one or more, they must be attacked and killed.

But there was another reason why they had determined to enter the cave; one of far greater consideration than the killing of the bear. It was Caspar who had suggested it.

"Why," asked he, "why might we not get out by this very cave? What if it should prove to run upward, and have an entrance above, or on the other side of the mountain?"

Both Karl and Ossaroo were startled at the suggestion. The idea put all of them into a flurry of excitement.

"I have read of such things," continued Caspar; "of great caverns that extended from one side of a moun-

tain to the other. There is one in America that has
been traced for twelve miles; the Mammoth, I mean !
This might be one of the same kind. You say you
saw far into it, Karl ? Let us explore it then, and see
where it leads to ! "

It was but a slight hope, still it was a hope; and it
could not cost much trouble to give the cave a thorough
exploration. It would be but a small matter compared
with the construction of ladders to scale the cliff; besides, they were now convinced by a farther examination of the precipice that this was not practicable, and
had quite abandoned all thought of it. Should the
cavern prove to be of vast extent, and have another
opening elsewhere than in the valley, they might escape
from their terrible prison, and their troubles would be
at an end.

With such hopes,—that were indeed little better than
fancies,—they consoled themselves for the moment.

It was resolved, then, that on the morrow the cave
was to be entered, For all the assistance they would
have from the light of the sun, they might as well have
begun their exploration at night. But they were not
ready to begin. Torches had to be procured; and a
notched tree by which to ascend the cliff; and to obtain
these required time. They would have them ready by
the morrow.

With this determination, they returned to their hut;
and at once set about making the torches, and preparing the notched tree for their ladder. There were other
little preparations to be made, but most of them were
completed before they thought of retiring to rest.

CHAPTER LV.

BEAR-HUNT BY TORCH-LIGHT.

As soon as it was daylight again, they went to work once more, and finished their preparations for entering the cave, and at a tolerably early hour they took the route for the ravine.

Two of them carried the *improvised* ladder; which was only a slender pine-tree, of about forty feet long, notched by the axe, the notches being at intervals of a foot to eighteen inches apart. At its more slender part, there were no notches required, as the natural branches of the tree, lopped into short stumps, were to be used as footholds, and would serve the purpose better than any notches.

Forty feet of even the slenderest tree when green would be load sufficient for a couple of stout men. This one was not green; for they had been fortunate enough to find one that had fallen long ago, and that was now quite dead and dry. For all that, it "tied" the united strength of Caspar and Ossaroo to carry it along, for it was they who performed this duty. Karl was loaded with the guns, torches, and the great spear of the shikarree. Fritz carried nothing except his tail; and this he bore aloft in a swaggerish manner, as though he

14

knew that something more than common was designed, and that grand game was to be killed that day.

They moved but slowly; but after about two hours' walking, including many stoppages and rests, they arrived within the ravine and under the ledge.

It occupied about another hour to erect the ladder. It was placed nearly opposite the mouth of the cave, instead of by the path; for there appeared a favorable crevice in the rocks, which promised to hold it steady, and keep it from turning round; an important consideration with so rude a ladder. The upper end of the tree was laid into the crevice, and fitted exactly. The lower end was rendered firm by something like a cartload of heavy boulders being built around it. It could neither shift nor turn. It was fast as a shut trap. Nothing now remained but to ascend, light the torches, and enter the cave.

A question, however, arose, whether Bruin might still be inside? It was doubtful enough, and there was no means of knowing. He had ample time to have gone out, since they left the place on the preceding evening, and, very likely, had wandered forth for a nocturnal ramble; but, had he returned? was he now "at home" to receive them? or, was he still abroad, robbing the bushes of their fruit, and the bees of their honey?

No one could tell; there was no sign visible; no hint for visitors. The door was open, and all who came might enter or not, as they pleased.

For a while, our hunters had some hesitation about this matter, and debated the point as to whether it might not be better to lie in ambush, and watch for Bruin going out or returning home. Most certainly the cave was his home. The path leading up had all the appearance of being much used. The rocks were scratched by his claws, and discolored by his feet—his, or those of other animals. Karl had noticed all this, when making his first ascent; therefore, there need be no fear but that the bear would come back in one direction or another.

He might be trapped, and that would save a struggle ; but this mode was not to the liking either of Caspar or Ossaroo, and Fritz apparently voted for a bear-fight.

Ossaroo, especially, declared that there was not the slightest danger in attacking him, armed as they were ; not so much as there would be in an encounter with a sambur stag. He suggested, moreover, that it might be days before they would set eyes upon him ; that he might go to sleep in his den, and lie there for a week without showing himself ; and, therefore, it would never do to wait for him. He must be looked for within the cave, and assailed in his gloomy stronghold. So counselled the Hindoo hunter.

But it needed no argument. Karl alone was for the prudent way of setting a trap, and capturing the animal without risk ; but Karl was as anxious as either of the others to explore the cave. The words of Caspar had made a deep impression upon him ; and, slight as was the hope that Caspar's conjecture might be true, still there was something in it. It *might* be so. Once more, it was like the drowning man catching at the straw.

Without farther hesitation the ladder was set up, as

already described; and, shortly after, all four—for Fritz
is to be counted in this adventure—stood upon the ledge
in front of the cavern's mouth.

Each had now possession of his own weapons : Karl,
his rifle ; Caspar, the double-barrel ; and Ossaroo, his
spear, bow and arrows, hatchet and knife.

There were two torches, each one nearly a yard in
length, with handles that measured nearly another yard.
They were made of splints from the pine-trees, that had
been shaved off while dressing the latter for the bridge.
They were now quite dry, and, tied together in a bun
dle, would burn splendidly. They were no novelty,
these torches. They had made similar ones before, and
tried them ; and, therefore, they could depend upon
them to give them light within the cave.

They entered without lighting the torches, intending
only to use them when it became necessary. Perhaps,
after all, the cave might be of small extent, though Karl
believed that such was not the case. He had noted that
the bear had gone a good way back, as he was able to
judge by his snorts and growling.

This point was soon settled. When they had proceeded many paces from the entrance, and the light of
the sun began to fail them, they could perceive that the
cavern grew wider and higher, and, like a great, black
gateway, yawned far back into the rocks. Apparently,
there was no termination to it !

The tinder which they had prepared was now set on
fire ; and the ends of the torches, touched with pine-tree
resin, were soon ignited, and began to blaze.

All at once the cavern shone with a thousand lights,
which had not been hitherto observed. The sparkling

stalactites projecting downward from the roof, with here and there the drops of clear filtered water, gave back the glare from the torches in a thousand coruscations. It seemed to our young hunters as though they were treading the famed halls of Aladdin's palace.

On they marched along the wide passage, holding their torches on high, and, at intervals, pausing to examine some nook or chamber that opened right or left— still searching for the bear. As yet, they had seen no traces of the animal; though, from the excited baying of Fritz, it was plain to them that either Bruin himself, or some other quadruped, had passed up the cave before them. The dog was evidently upon a hot scent, and lifting it as fast as they could follow him.

A little after, Fritz doubled to one side, and appeared busy with some object by the side of the cave. The hunters were under the impression that the game had been found, and halted, each bringing his piece to the ready.

After a moment, however, Fritz glided out, and again sprang forward on the trail. The torches were carried up to where Fritz had made his temporary pause, and, under their light, a large pile of withered leaves and grass was made visible. It was the snug den of Bruin —still warm where his huge carcass had lain; but the cunning brute was no longer "abed." He had been roused by the noises of his enemies, and had retreated farther into the cavern.

Fritz was again moving forward along the trail, uttering an occasional "growl" as he went. He was by no means a fast dog at taking up a scent, nor yet on the run. These were not his qualities. But he was stanch and sure, and desperate when once he grappled with the game. So sure was he, that, whenever he started off upon a trail, you might rely upon it, with perfect confidence, that the game was before you.

The three hunters thought no longer of looking for the bear anywhere else than before the snout of Fritz; and, therefore, the chase became simplified to keeping the hound in view. The nature of the ground—here covered with blocks of loose stone, there with huge stalagmites—prevented the dog from making rapid progress. The bear had often doubled and halted, no doubt having some difficulty himself in making way in the darkness; and this doubling caused much delay to Fritz; so much, that the torch-bearers could generally keep him in sight.

Now and again, he became lost to view; and then there was a halt, and some moments of indecision, which were ended only by the long howl of the hound echoing through the cavern, and guiding them to his whereabouts.

You will be surprised that they should at any time have lost the chase. You will fancy that, by keeping on, they must overtake Fritz in time, or meet him returning.

Such might have been true, had there been only one passage through this stupendous cavern; but, instead of one, they saw scores of vaulted aisles forking at intervals, and traversing in very different directions. They had long since turned both to the right and the left—more than once turned—without any other guide than the baying of the hound, or the view of his yellow body, as he scrambled along the trail. An immense cavern it was, full of ways, and passages, and halls, and chambers; many of them so like each other, that the hunters could not help thinking they were running in a maze, and going repeatedly over the same ground!

By this time Karl had begun to reflect, and his reflection was, that they were proceeding rashly. Certain ideas were rising in his mind—ideas somewhat undefined—but one among the rest was, that, going as they were, without taking either "bearings or distances," they might get lost!

Before he had time to call his companions to a halt and take some deliberation about the matter, a peculiar noise struck upon their ears—a noise that was easily recognized as being made by the united voices of two angry animals—a dog and a bear.

Beyond a doubt it was Bruin and Fritz—beyond a doubt they were "in grips!"

CHAPTER LVI.

LOST IN THE CAVE.

THE scene of their encounter was at no great distance—about twenty yards off; and, guided by the loud
growling and "worrying," the hunters easily directed
themselves towards the spot. After stumbling over
stalagmites, and now and then hitting their heads
against the projecting points of the stalactites, they arrived upon the ground; and the glare of the torches
was thrown upon two animals—a dog and a bear. They
were near the middle of an immense open hall, or
chamber of the cavern. Both were in fighting attitudes; the bear standing upon the flat top of a rock—
about three feet above the surrounding level—and the
dog assailing his legs, now on one side of the rock, and
now upon the other. The bear was defending himself
with his huge paws; and at intervals flung the forepart
of his body downward, with the design of seizing the
hound in his hug.

Fritz well knew the danger of being embraced in the
fore-arms of a bear, and therefore made his attacks from
behind; springing up at the hind-quarters of Bruin,
and biting him in the hams. To avoid these assaults
upon his rear, the bear kept turning round and round,
as though he was spinning about upon a pivot!

It was altogether a laughable sight to witness the curious contest between the two quadrupeds, and had the hunters been pursuing the bear for mere amusement, they would have permitted the fight to go on for some time without interfering in it. But amusement was just then out of the question. The fat of Bruin was a thing of far more importance; and now that the hunters had become aware of the vast size and endless labyrinths of the cavern, they perceived that it was quite possible in such a place to lose both the bear and his fat. He might have escaped them as easily as if he were in the open woods.

With these ideas, therefore, they were only too anxious to put an end to the struggle, and secure the game.

The bear could not have offered them a better opportunity. His position upon the rock rendered him a conspicuous mark, both for the bullets of the guns and the arrows of Ossaroo. Besides, there was no danger of wounding Fritz, if good aim was taken by the marksmen.

Good aim *was* taken — a couple of loud reports echoed through the cave—one of Ossaroo's arrows whistled, and penetrated the thick shaggy skin—and the next moment the huge black mass rolled down from the rock, and lay back uppermost, kicking his paws about in the last throes of death. Then Fritz leaped upon his upturned breast, seized the white throat between his jaws, and choked and worried at it till the last breath was squeezed out of poor Bruin's body, that the next moment lay quite limp and motionless.

Fritz was now scolded off, and the torches were held

14 *

near, in order that the hunters might examine the game they had killed. A splendid specimen the bear was— one of the biggest and fattest of his kind ; and no doubt would yield them a large amount of the precious " grease."

They had scarcely made this reflection when another of far different character forced itself upon their minds, and compelled them to stand gazing at each other with looks of mute inquiry. Each waited for one of the others to speak ; and although no one had yet said a word, all equally felt that they were in a dilemma.

What dilemma ? you will ask. The game had been secured—what difficulty would there be in dragging it out of the cave, and afterwards taking it home to their hut ?

All this may appear easy enough to you, because you do not yet understand the situation in which the hunters were placed—you do not comprehend why they stood gazing upon each other with troubled looks.

Why they did so was simply this :—while examining the carcass of the bear, they observed that their *torches were burnt out !* Not quite to the ends, it is true ; but so near that they could not be depended on to light them a score of yards. They were already flickering and burning dimly—in a few seconds more they would be quite extinguished ; and what then ?

Ay, what then ? that was the thought that was troubling them—that it was that caused them to stand looking anxiously towards one another.

Even they themselves did not fully comprehend the peril of their situation. They saw that they were going to be left in darkness—the perfect darkness of a dungeon—but it had not yet occurred to them that *they might never again see the light!* That appalling thought had not yet shaped itself in their minds— they only believed that the want of torches would put them to much inconvenience—they would have great trouble, and perhaps difficulty, in finding their way out of the cave, and getting the bear along with them— they might first have to grope their way out, and then get fresh torches, and return for the game ; and all this would take a good deal of time, and give them a large amount of trouble ; but never mind that—the prize they had obtained in the fat of the bear, and his fine hide—which would make a grand winter robe—would repay them for all.

Ha! it was only after their torches had gone quite out, and they were left in total darkness—only after they had groped and groped, and wandered about for hours—now sprawling over loose rocks, now tumbling down into deep clefts—only after they had gone through all this, and still saw no light—no sign by which they could even guess at their whereabouts, that they be- came fully alive to the peril of their situation, and began to experience the awful apprehension already expressed—that *they might never again see the light!*

And such in reality was their fear, when, after hours spent in fruitless wandering, they stood holding each other's hands, crouching and cowering together in the midst of that amorphcus darkness !

CHAPTER LVII.

A RAMBLE IN THE DARK.

THEIR dread was not at all unreasonable, considering the vast extent of the cavern—considering the distance which they knew they had penetrated—considering the various devious and like ways through which
they had passed while in pursuit of the bear—and,
above all, considering the absolute darkness that now
reigned around them. Of course they could see nothing, not even each other; not one of them could have
seen the nose upon his own face, had he been looking
for it.

Place yourself in the midst of complete darkness,
and you will wonder how little progress you can make
in any direction. Indeed, you cannot follow a right
line even were there no impediment in your way.

After you have advanced a few steps, your face will
begin to turn in a new direction, and perhaps keep
turning, until you have gone round the four cardinal
points! You need not be told this; "blind man's buff"
will have imparted to you the idea long ere now. You
will remember that, after having made a turn or two,
you could not tell to which side of the room you were
facing, unless you laid your hand upon the piano, or

some piece of furniture, and recognized it by the touch.

Now just like the blind man in the game, so the tl ree were situated; with the exception that they had no piano—no furniture—no object of any kind—to guide them. They knew not where to turn—they knew not which way to advance—which way to go back.

For many minutes, they stood paralyzed by the confusion. As already stated, they held each other by the hand, and in this way they stood. Each feared to let the others go, lest he might lose them! Of course this was but an idle fear, as their voices would enable them to keep together; but there was something so awe-inspiring in their situation, that they all felt childish and helpless, and they needed the support of one another.

After remaining at rest 'a while, they started off afresh; holding each other by the hands, as they moved. This precaution was more necessary while they were in motion than at rest. They dreaded that one of their number might fall over some high steep or into a deep hole; and while thus clinging together, the danger would be less—that is, if all three did not go over together.

For several hours they wandered about, and, according to their own belief, must have walked many miles; but of course their progress was slow, as they had to feel their way at every step. They grew tired with the effort they had to make, and at intervals sat down to rest themselves; but their feelings would not permit them to pause long; and they would up to their feet again, and scramble on as before.

For many hours—and many miles, say they—they

walked, but saw no ray of light to cheer them—saw nothing, felt nothing that they could recognize. At times they thought they must be far into the mountain —perhaps miles from the entrance of the cavern; at other times they fancied they had gone several times through the same passage; and once or twice they knew they had done so, by recognizing the rocks over which they had passed.

This gave them a hope that in time they might get acquainted with the different turnings and passages,— and that would have been possible enough; but it would have taken a long time, and what were they to subsist upon while acquiring this knowledge? They thought of this, and saw at once the foolishness of the hope they had conceived.

The dog Fritz moved along, sometimes before, sometimes by their side, and sometimes in the rear. He kept silent, seemingly as much frightened as they. They could tell he was there, by hearing at intervals the scratching of his claws upon the rocks, when some boulder lay in the way, and compelled him to scramble over it. What could Fritz do more than they? In such darkness he could not see his nose any more than they? No—but he could make use of that nose to direct himself, which was more than any of his masters could do.

" Ha ! " shouted Caspar, as this idea passed through his mind. " Ha, brother ! Ossaroo ! why might not Fritz guide us ? Why might he not scent his way out of this horrid dungeon ? Surely he must be as tired of it as we are !"

" Let us try what may be done," rejoined Karl, by

his tone showing that he had no great hope in the experiment. " Call him up, Caspar ! He knows you best."

Caspar addressed the dog by name, adding a few coaxing words, and in an instant Fritz was by his side.

" How shall we manage ? Leave him to himself?" inquired Caspar.

" I fear he will stand still, and not attempt to go ahead of us," replied Karl.

" We can try him."

And as Caspar made this suggestion, all stood silent and listening.

They stood a long while to give the dog a fair trial, but he knew not what they wanted, and he remained patiently beside them without manifesting any disposition to leave. The experiment was a failure.

" Now," suggested Karl, " let us urge him forward and follow after—perhaps he will lead us in that way."

Fritz was now commanded to advance, and obeyed the command—for they could hear him start off with a slight whimper; but to their chagrin they found that they could not tell in what direction he had gone. Had he been running on the scent of some animal, his occasional baying would have served to guide them, as it had done while they were chasing the bear. Now, however, the dog ran without noise ; and although they could hear an occasional scrape of his claws, yet it was not sufficiently frequent or continuous to guide them. The experiment again failed, and Fritz was whistled back.

But it was not without result. Like many other failures, it led to reflection and a rearrangement of the machinery. A better plan soon offered itself to the quick wit of Caspar; and Ossaroo had been thinking of something similar when he cried out,—

"Tie string to ee tail!"

"No," replied Caspar, "not to his tail, for then he would not go forward; but let us hold him in a leash with the string round his neck, in a regular way. That will be better, I warrant."

No sooner said than done. Thongs and belts were loosed from powder-horns. and pouches; a leash was constructed and fastened round the neck of the dog, and he was then hunted forward as before.

Caspar handled the straps, and the others followed, guided by Caspar's voice.

In this order they had scrambled along for a hundred yards or more, when the dog began to whimper, and then to bay, as if going upon a trail; and in a moment or two after, he came, all of a sudden, to a stop.

Caspar felt by his strong pulling on the leash, that the dog had sprung forward and seized something. He stooped down and felt before him. Instead of the hard cold rocks, his fingers came in contact with a mass of long shaggy hair.

Alas! their hopes were dispelled. Instead of conducting to the mouth of the cave, Fritz had only brought them back to the carcass of the bear!

CHAPTER LVIII.

CAVERN-LIFE.

THEY were all filled with disappointment, and particularly that the dog, having arrived at the spot where the bear had been killed, would go no farther.   Drive him as they would by commands, or coax him by words of encouragement, he would not part from the carcass. Even when carried off to some distance, and let go, he always drew Caspar back to the same spot.   It was. very vexatious.

So thought they at first ; but after a little reflection, they began to think better of it; and to recognize in this incident something more than chance.   Karl especially thought so, and pointed out to his companions that the hand of Providence had to do with it ; and that that same hand would yet conduct them safely out of the dismal dungeon into which they had so imprudently ventured.

Karl's words had a cheering effect; for he pointed out how fortunate it was for them that they had once more found the carcass.   But for that they should have had nothing to eat, and, as a matter of course, would have soon perished of hunger.

Now, however, that the bear was found, they could

subsist upon his flesh for days ; and during one of these days they might succeed in reaching the entrance. They would take care not to lose the knowledge of the place where the carcass lay ; and whatever excursion they might make from that spot, they should always arrange some clue by which they might return to it.

Fortunately for them there was water in the cavern. In many places it dripped from the rocks in sufficient quantity to give them as much as they wanted for drink ; and not far off they had crossed a little rivulet that ran down the bottom of one of the great galleries. This they knew they could find again ; and, consequently they felt no apprehensions on the score of water.

It was a question, then, how long they would be in finding the entrance, and how long they could live upon the flesh of the bear.

The finding of Bruin's carcass had considerably bettered their prospects ; and as they gathered around it to dinner, they felt more cheerful than they had done since the moment when they had laid it low.

As they ate, it was dark enough around them to have called the meal a supper ; and it was long enough since they had eaten their breakfast—though they could not guess how long—but as they had eaten nothing since breakfast, they styled this first meal upon the bear-meat their dinner.

No dinner or supper was ever cooked like that—*it was not cooked at all!* for they had no fire wherewith to cook it.

They were not squeamish. A very long interval had transpired since they had eaten their slight breakfast. Karl and Caspar had refrained from the uncooked viand until their appetite could resist no longer ; and then the raw flesh of the bear became palatable enough.   It was supper time with Ossaroo.   His stomach had more easily got over its scruples, and he had bolted his dinner long, long ago ; so that when the others sat down to their first meal, Ossaroo was able to join them at his second.

Both Karl and Caspar ate heartily enough,—quite as heartily as if a chandelier with its wax-lights had been sparkling over their heads.   Perhaps the absence of light was a circumstance in their favor.   The huge paws—those " titbits " of the bear's flesh—constituted their dinner ; and hunters will tell you that, boiled, roasted, or *raw*, a bear's paw is not bad eating.

When they had finished their meal, all three groped their way to where they heard the trickling of water.

They found a place where it oozed in a rapid and continuous dripping through the rocks ; and, applying their mouths to this subterranean fountain, they were enabled in a few moments to slake their thirst.

They then returned to where they had dined ; and, being now much wearied with their long-continued exertions, they stretched themselves upon the rocks with the intention of having some sleep.   Though their bed was a hard one, it was not cold ; for in the interior of great caverns it is never cold.   There the temperature is more equable than that of the atmosphere without—being cooler in summer and warmer in winter, so that variety is scarcely known—at all events, the extremes of heat and cold are never felt.   This is the case with the Mammoth Cave of Kentucky, and other large caverns ; and on this account it has been thought that persons suffering from pulmonary complaints might derive benefit by dwelling in caves. There are many such patients who make their home in the Mammoth; and where a commodious hotel enables them to live in comfort, and even luxury! It is possible enough that the mild and equable temperature that exists under ground may enable the victim of consumption to prolong life for a considerable time: but it is doubtful whether any radical cure can be effected in this way; and the unfortunate sufferer, once he emerges from his subterranean dwelling, will be in as much danger from the insidious disease as before.

Little did Karl, Caspar, and Ossaroo, care for the mild atmosphere that surrounded them in the cavern. They would gladly have exchanged it for the hottest country in the torrid zone, or the coldest spot in all the Arctic regions. Biting mosquitos in the former, or biting frost in the latter, would have been more welcome than that mild and gentle climate that surrounded them—that gloomy atmosphere, where sun had never shone, and where snow had never fallen.

Notwithstanding their anxiety of mind, their weariness at length overcame them, and all three fell fast asleep.

CHAPTER LIX.

EXPLORATION OF THE CAVE.

THEY slept a good long while, though, whether it was by night or by day, they had no means of judging. They could only guess at it, by remembering how much time had transpired since they first entered the cave; but to show how little trust can be placed in any conjectures of this sort, they differed from one another in their estimates full twelve hours!

Karl thought they had been wandering about nearly two days and a night; while the others believed the time not so long by twelve hours at least.

Karl adduced a reason for his belief—the ravenous appetite which they had acquired, and which must have taken a long time to grow upon them; moreover, they had slept so long that he thought it must be in the night-time—the natural time of rest, which the nerves would understand without any clock to guide them. Karl admitted that his second reason was somewhat lame, since, having missed one night of sleep, their nerves on the day following would not be very nice about what hour they should feel inclined towards slumber.

It is probable, however, that Karl was right in his

conjecture. They had been long hours wandering to and fro, and had rested many times. The feeling of horrid anxiety under which they had been suffering always impelled them to press on ; and no wonder they had lost all definite recollection of the distance they had gone, or the time thus fruitlessly spent. It had taken them a good while to get the ladder in place; and the first day had been far spent before they were ready to penetrate the cave. It was, therefore, quite probable that their first sleep had been during the second night, after entering their gloomy chamber.

Whether or not they had slept long and soundly enough—though not without troubled dreams—in which they had encountered bears, fierce shaggy yak-bulls, deep dangerous pits into which they were about to fall, and high cliffs they were trying in vain to climb—it was quite natural they should dream of such things.

It was the awaking that was most unnatural. Instead of a bright sunshine to greet their eyes, or the soft blue light of morning, they saw nought—all around was gloom. Instead of the music of birds, or even the cheering sounds of active life, they heard nought. All around was the silence of the tomb !

A tomb it might yet be to them—for a short while, perhaps, a living tomb; but, sooner or later, a tomb for their dead bodies—a sepulchre for their bones !

Such were their reflections on awaking. Their dreams while asleep were even less horrid than the reality to which they awoke !

If the sense of sleep regards not the absence of light, still less is the appetite of hunger affected by it. Once more the bear's paws were drawn upon for a meal, and afforded it without boil or broil, bread or salt.

As soon as they had eaten to their satisfaction, they rose to their feet, and set about the work which Karl had already traced out in his thoughts. Of course, before going about it he had fully communicated his plans to his companions.

They were to make excursions in every direction from the spot where the bear had been killed. There were many galleries leading from the place—they had noticed that while their torches were yet burning. All these they designed to explore, one after another. The explorations were at first to be for short distances, until they had made themselves familiar with the passage extending in some one particular direction. This they would accomplish by *feeling* the rocks on either side, until they became thoroughly acquainted with the pro-tuberances, or other marks that could be used as guides. If none existed, they would make them, by piling up stones at such places, or chipping a piece from the stalactites with the hatchet. Their design, in effect, was to "blaze" the passages, so that they would know them again, just as a woodman marks his way through the pathless forest.

It was altogether an ingenious idea, and one that with time and patience promised success. Indeed, it seemed the only plan that held out a hope beyond mere chance —for amidst so many devious ways, to have proceeded without some plan would have been to trust to chance, and that they had tried already.

They well knew that to carry out their design would require both time and patience; but by this, all three were well drilled in the lessons of patience. The bridge-building had been a school for them. It might not take much time, but it might; and for either result had they made their minds ready.

In all probability, however, they might be long before they should set their eyes upon a ray of the sun's light—before they should see that bright disk of the cavern's mouth, that they had scarce looked at while leaving it behind them.

It was their intention then, first, to take one particular direction, and thoroughly explore that before penetrating into any other. When the first should be traversed, either to its termination, or to such a length as might influence them in believing they were in the wrong way, they would then leave it, and set to exploring some other. Sooner or later, they believed that this would bring them into the passage that would conduct them out of their gigantic prison.

Before setting about the execution of their plan, they once more made trial of Fritz, as upon the day before; but the dog would not part from the spot; and though, encouraged by the voice of Caspar, he would beat about for a certain space—it always ended by his returning to the carcass of the bear.

As soon as they became convinced that Fritz would not guide them, they released him from the string; and then, in real earnest, set about carrying out the design of Karl.

Their mode of proceeding was quite ingenious. They groped about until they found a large passage that led from the chamber or opening in which they were. This gallery they resolved to explore first.

Lest by any mistake they might not find their way back, one always remained at a 'certain point ; while the other two went ahead—stopping at intervals to blaze their way. Of course should the two who acted as pioneers make a wrong turn, so as not to know the route back, the voice of the third would at once guide them.

In this manner they proceeded without much difficulty, though with great slowness. You will fancy they might have gone fast enough, their retreat being thus secured for them. But there were many obstacles to prevent a rapid advance. Each lateral passage they came to,—and there were numbers of these—had to be marked for future examination, and the mark had to be made distinct and recognizable—this operation sometimes requiring a considerable time to effect. They had also to make their blazes at short intervals, so that these might be the more easily found upon their return. Another impediment was found in the clambering over sharp boulders, and getting across clefts that everywhere intercepted their path.

Ay, slowly and with great caution were they compelled to make their advance, and when *night came*— that is, when they had grown wearied and hungry, and wanted food and rest—they calculated they had not proceeded above half-a-mile from their place of departure. Of course no light had cheered them throughout those long working hours ; but for all that they returned to the resting-place with their hearts still buoyed up with hope. To-morrow,—or the morrow after, or still another morrow, what mattered it ?—they felt high confidence that on some morrow they would look once more upon the sun.

15

CHAPTER LX.

PRESERVING THE BEAR'S MEAT.

THERE was one thing, however, about which they were apprehensive, and that was about their larder— how long would it last?   The bear was large, and fat, they could tell by the "feel" of him; and if they drew upon the carcass for moderate rations, it would hold out for many days; but then how was the meat to be preserved?   Lying as it was—still unskinned—it must soon become unfit for food, though not so soon as in the open air; for meat will keep much longer in a cave,— that is, if it be a very deep one, than it will when exposed to the full light of the sun.

This is easily explained.   The principle of decomposition exists in the atmosphere itself, as is well known to every one who deals in the hermetically-sealed air-tight canisters of preserved meats; and if you can but remove the atmosphere entirely from a piece of fish, flesh, or vegetable, it is supposed that it will keep for ever!

In the interior of a cavern, of course there is still an atmosphere, but it is rarer and of a less changeable sort, and, most probably, less active in its powers to cause decay.   Hence it is that within the cave decomposition is slower than without; and, indeed, there are some caverns where, instead of being decomposed, the bodies of men and animals have been found still retaining their proper forms, only shrivelled into smaller size, and dried up like mummies.

Though there was water here and there in the cavern, in all other places it was exceedingly dry. They could tell that the air was so, because the rocks felt dry, and in some places there was dust that was perfectly ready to puff up at the touch. They had noticed this while in pursuit of the bear. Both bear and dog had more than once been found enveloped in a cloud of dust as the hunters came near them with the torches. Indeed, they could tell that the atmosphere of the cavern was dry by simply breathing it in,—it felt dry to the throat.

Under the keen apprehension which they had lest the meat should spoil before they could find the entrance of the cave, their wits were set to work to find some means of preserving it. Salt they had none, and therefore pickling was out of the question. Had they been able to procure the material to make a fire, they could have managed without salt by smoking the meat; but firewood was just then as difficult to be got at as salt. Even without either, had they only been in the open air, with the warm sun shining down upon them, they could have cured that bear-meat so that it would have kept good for months.

Alas! the sun's rays were as inaccessible as either the salt or the fuel.

Preserving the meat by any one of the three different modes of salting, smoking, or jerking, was alike out of their power.

Having already noticed the extreme dryness of the atmosphere, it occurred to them that if the meat were cut into very thin slices or strips, and then hung up, or spread out upon the rocks, it might not spoil at once— at all events, it might keep for a longer period than if suffered to lie as it was in one great mass. This was Ossaroo's suggestion, and a good one it was. At all events, nothing better could be thought of, and after some consideration, they determined to act upon it.

Where were they to procure lights? How was the bear to be skinned without light? How was the flesh to be cut up and spread out?

These were questions that did not present the slightest obstacle—our adventurers scarce gave thought to them. They had by this time almost learnt to work in the darkness; and as for the skinning of the bear, Ossaroo could have performed that operation if it had even been darker,—supposing this to be possible. There was no difficulty about lights; and the shikarree, having been assisted by the others to place the carcass in a proper attitude, set to work with the keen blade of his knife, and, almost as readily as if a dozen candles had been held by him, he stripped off the shaggy hide, and laid it back upon the rocks.

The cutting the flesh into slices and strips would be easily effected, though it would require more time, and should be done with great nicety. If not sliced very thin, the meat would be liable to spoil the sooner.

But the Hindoo hunter was a very adept at this sort of thing, and his skill enabled him to complete the business in such a manner that had his " griskins " been submitted to the light, no one could have told they had been " carved " in the darkness.

The strips, as they were cut by Ossaroo, were passed into the hands of the others, who having already spread out the hide with the hairy side undermost, laid the pieces upon it.

As soon as Ossaroo had stripped the bones pretty clean, it was then time to dispose of the flesh. A question now arose as to whether it would be better to spread the pieces out upon the rock or hang them up upon lines.

Decidedly better to hang them up, thought Ossaroo; and the others agreed with him. They would dry sooner in that way, it was thought; besides, as Caspar suggested, they would be out of the way of Fritz, who, if not looked after, might steal a march upon them, and devour half the meat at a single meal. By all means they should be hung out of his reach.

But how was this to be accomplished? Where were the ropes and lines to be obtained? They had neither poles to serve as uprights, nor ropes to be stretched between them. True, there was a long piece of cord in the possession of Ossaroo, which he had manufactured from the Indian hemp, while making his fish-net; but this would not be enough. It would take many yards of cord to carry such a quantity of meat. What was to be done?

" Cut the hide into strips!" cried Caspar, in answer to the question.

The very thing; and no sooner suggested than carried into effect.

The sliced meat was removed—the raw hide was stretched out, and cut into thongs of about an inch in thickness, and these being knotted together, a rope was soon made that reached from side to side of the great chamber. The ends of this were fastened to the rocks; one was looped around a jutting point, and the opposite was held by being placed upon a little shelf with a heavy stone on top of it; and thus a line, something after the fashion of a clothes-line, was carried across the chamber.

When they had tried its strength, and were convinced that it would serve the purpose intended, they carried the meat slice by slice, and laid it carefully across, until the string was full.

Another line had to be made before all was hung up; and this was made and fastened to the rock, in a similar manner as the first. The remainder of the slices were suspended upon it, and all hands now desisted from their labor. Their day's work was done; for whether it was night or day, they had been busy for a long time, and on the completion of the job were fain to betake themselves once more to rest.

They ate their meal, and lay down intending to sleep only for a few hours, and then to rouse themselves and with renewed energies continue their search after the light of the sun.

CHAPTER LXI.

DREAMS.

KARL in his sleep had a dream, " Let there be light, and there was light ! "

This highly poetic passage of Scripture had been running in his mind during the past hours. He was thinking of chaos before the creation ; and their own situation might well suggest the chaotic age. He was thinking—and reverentially—of the wonderful power of the Creator, who out of such darkness could cause light to shine forth by the simple expression of his will, " Let there be light, and there was light ! "

Karl dreamt that a form had appeared to them,— the form of a beautiful man,—and that from his body a bright light, similar to that of the sun, radiated on all sides. Around his head and face the rays were distributed in the form of a glory, such as Karl had seen upon many old pictures of the Saviour. Looking more attentively at the face, Karl also recognized its resemblance to the same pictures ;—the gentle and benign expression, the noble forehead, and fair curling hair,— all were the same. Karl, who was of a religious turn, believed it was the Saviour he saw in his dream. The cave was no longer in darkness ; it was lit up by the coruscations of light that emanated from the beautiful vision, and Karl could see all around him.

After regarding him for a while, the bright form turned and moved off, beckoning Karl and the others to follow.

They obeyed ; and, after traversing numerous passages and chambers,—some of which they recognized as having passed through while in chase of the bear,—they were guided to the mouth of the cavern, where the strange apparition, meeting the light of the sun, melted into the air and disappeared from their sight !

The delight which Karl felt, at this *denouement* of his dream, caused him to awake with a start, and with a joyful ejaculation upon his lips.   It was suddenly suppressed, and followed by an expression of pain and disappointment.   The happy passage had been only a dream,—a false delusion.   The reality was as dark and gloomy as ever.

The interjections of Karl awoke his companions ; and Karl perceived that Caspar was greatly excited. He could not see him, but he knew by his talk, that such was the case.

"I have been dreaming," said Caspar, "a strange dream."

" Dreaming ! of what ? "

" Oh ! of lights, brother,—of lights," replied Caspar.

Karl was deeply attentive,—almost superstitious. He fancied that Caspar had seen the same vision with himself,—it must have been something more than a dream !

" What lights, Caspar ? "

" Oh ! jolly lights,—lights enough to show us out. Hang me ! if I think I dreamt it after all.   By thunder ! good brother, I believe I was half awake when the idea came into my mind.   Capital idea, isn't it ? "

"What idea?" inquired Karl in surprise, and rather apprehensive that Caspar's dream had deprived him of his senses. "What idea, Caspar?"

"Why, the idea of the *candles*, to be sure."

"The candles! What candles?—Surely, thought Karl, as he asked the question,—"surely my poor brother's intellect is getting deranged,—this horrid darkness is turning his brain."

"Oh! I have not told you my dream,—if it was a dream. I am confused. I am so delighted with the idea. We shall group no more in this hideous darkness,—we shall have light,—plenty of light, I promise you. Odd we did not think of the thing before!"

"But what is it, brother? What was your dream about?—Tell us that."

"Well, now that I am awake, I don't think it was a dream,—at least, not a regular one. I was thinking of the thing before I fell asleep, and I kept on thinking about it when I got to be half asleep; and then I saw my way clearer. You know, brother, I have before told you that when I have any thing upon my mind that puzzles me, I often hit upon the solution of it when I am about half dreaming; and so it has been in this case, I am sure I have got the right way at last."

"Well, Caspar,—the right way to do what? The right way to get out of the cave?"

"I hope so, brother."

"But what do you propose?"

"I propose that we turn tallow-chandlers."

"Tallow-chandlers! Poor boy!" soliloquized Karl; "I thought as much. O merciful Heaven, my dear brother! his reason is gone!"

15 *

Such were Karl's painful surmises, though he kept them to himself.

"Yes, tallow-chandlers," continued Caspar, in the same half-earnest, half-jocular way, "and make us a full set of candles."

"And of what would you make your candles, dear Caspar?" inquired Karl, in a sympathizing tone, and with the design of humoring his brother, rather than excite him by contradiction.

"Of what," echoed Caspar, "what but the fat of this great bear?"

"Ha!" ejaculated Karl, suddenly changing his tone, as he perceived that Caspar's madness had something of method in it, "the fat of the bear, you say?"

"Certainly, Karl. Isn't his stomach as full of tallow as it can stick? and what's to hinder us to make candles out of it that will carry us all over the cave,—and out of it, I fancy, unless it be the greatest maze that Nature has ever made out of rock-work?"

Karl was no longer under the belief that his brother had gone mad. On the contrary, he saw that the latter had conceived a very fine idea; and though it did not yet appear how the thing was to be carried out, Karl fancied that there was something in it. His sweet dream recurred to him, and this he now regarded as ominous of the success of some plan of escape,—perhaps by the very means which Caspar had suggested,— by making candles out of "bear's grease!"

These were pleasant thoughts, but to Karl the pleasantest thought of all was the returning conviction that Caspar *was still in his senses!*

CHAPTER LXII

OSSAROO now joined in the general joy; and the three placed their heads together, to deliberate upon Caspar's suggestion, and to discuss its feasibility in detail.

But neither Karl nor Ossaroo had much need to spend their opinion on the details; for the original " promoter " of the plan had already conceived nearly the whole of them. It was, in fact, these that he had got hold of while half asleep; and which, on first awaking, he believed to have occurred to him in a dream. But there was no dream in the matter. The idea of making candles from the bear's fat had been in his mind before he lay down—he had even thought of it while they were at work in curing the meat.

" Yes," said he, commencing to tell them in detail all that had passed through his mind upon the subject; " I had thought of the candles, while assisting Ossaroo to cut up the bear. I could tell, by the touch, that many pieces of the meat were almost pure fat; and I wondered to myself whether it would not burn and make a light. I know, of course, that there was plenty more in the great stomach of the animal, and that of the real sort of which candles could be made. Would it burn? that was the question that puzzled me. I feared that it would not burn without first being rendered to grease or lard, and a wick put into it,—in fact, I knew it could not; and there arose the difficulty, since we had no fire wherewith to render the fat, and no vessel to render it in, even if we had been provided with fire in plenty."

"Ah! that is too true," assented Karl, rather despairingly.

"Well, so thought I, Karl, and I had wellnigh given up thinking about the matter—of course, I said nothing about it to either of you—as I knew you could not create fuel out of stones any more than I, and there was an end of it."

"Yes—an end of it," unconsciously echoed Karl, in a desponding tone.

"Not yet, brother! not yet!" rejoined Caspar, as he proceeded in his relation. "You see the thing had got into my thoughts, and, after a while, I found myself once more speculating upon it. How were we to make a fire that would melt that fat? That we could strike a light, I knew—we could do that with our tinder or gunpowder; but where were we to get sufficient fuel to make a fire with, and where was the vessel to be obtained, in which to render the lard? At first, I thought only of the fire. If we could once raise fuel for that, the vessel would not be of so much importance—we might contrive to heat a flat, thin stone, and melt some of the fat in that way. If we could not make fine candles, we might dip some wick in the grease, and thus have a kind of taper that would serve almost as well. I knew we had wick—I remembered the long hempen strmg which Ossaroo has got, and I knew that that would serve admirably for the purpose. All that would be easy enough—at least it appeared so—all except the stuff for the fire."

" Very ingenious of you, Caspar ; these things had never entered my mind. Go on, brother !"

" Well—to make a long story short, I have got the fuel."

" Bravo ! good ! good !" exclaimed Karl and Ossaroo in a breath, and in accents of joy. " You have got the fuel ? "

" Yes—I found it, at length ; just as I was bobbing over asleep, the idea crossed my mind ; though I fancied I was only dreaming, and must have afterwards fallen asleep. But I partially awoke shortly after, and took to thinking again ; and then I found the vessel in which we can render our tallow—I think we can."

" Hurrah ! better than all !"

" And now, listen to my plan ; for I have been thinking while I have been talking, and I have it more complete than ever. Maybe you can both add something, but here is what I propose."

" Tell us, Caspar—all right, go on."

" We have with us two guns—Ossaroo has his spear, his hatchet, his bow, and a good quiver of arrows—fortunately his quiver, too, is of thick bamboo, and dry as a chip. First, then, I propose that, with Ossaroo's axe, we break up the stocks of our guns, ramrods, and all— we can soon make others, once we get out—also the shaft of Ossaroo's spear, his bow, arrows, and quiver— never mind, Ossaroo, you can replace them from the forest. This being done, we can make a fire large enough to melt as much fat as will make us no end of dips."

" You are right, brother," interposed Karl; " but how about the vessel to melt it in ? "

" That puzzled me for a while," replied the ingenious Caspar ; " but I got over the difficulty, at length, by thinking of my powder-flask ; you know it is a patent one, and the top screws off.   Well—we can take off the top, empty the powder into one of our pockets, and make use of the bottom part for the lard.   I am sure it will stand the fire, for it is stout copper without a flaw. The only difficulty is, that it is small ; but we can fill it over and over again."

" And you propose to make the string which Ossaroo has got into wicks, and dip them in the hot grease ? "

" Nothing of the sort," replied Caspar, in a triumph-ant tone ; we shall have no dips.   I was contented with them at first, but not any longer.   We shall have can-dles—real mould-candles ! "

" How ?   Mould-candles ?   How ? "

Oh ! that you shall see by-and-by.   Ossaroo would only disclose part of his plans when he went to trap the tiger, and I mean to keep a little of mine to myself, in order to have a *revanche* upon him.   Ha ! ha ! ha ! "

Caspar finished his speech with a laugh.   It was the first time any of them had laughed since they entered that cave—no doubt, the first laugh that ever echoed through its gloomy aisles.

CHAPTER LXIII.

LIGHT IN DARKNESS.

WITHOUT losing farther time, the three set to work to make the fire, Caspar of course taking the direction. The barrels were first taken out of their guns, the locks unscrewed, and then the other iron-work was removed from the stocks. By dint of a little hammering with stones, and cleaving with the hatchet, the butt of each was separated from the heel-piece, and then broken up into small fragments. Even the two ramrods were sacrificed—the heads and screws being carefully preserved. In no reckless humor did they act, for they had now very definite expectations of being able to escape from the cave; and prudence whispered them that the valuable weapons they were thus dismantling might be needed hereafter, as much as ever they had been. Nothing, therefore, was damaged that could not be afterwards replaced—nothing thrown away. Only the wood-work was sacrificed to present necessity. Every article of iron, to the smallest nail or screw, was carefully preserved; and when all were separated from the wood-work, they were placed together and tied into a bundle, so that they might be easily carried along.

Ossaroo's weapon went " to the hammer " next. The

spear-head was knocked off, and the long shaft broken into a dozen pieces. The bow was unstringed and cut into chips, and then the arrows were snapped across, and the quiver split up. All these would be excellent materials, and from their age and dryness would ignite and burn like touch-wood.

An important addition to their stock of fuel was obtained from a source up to this time quite unthought of. They now remembered the two large handles by which they had carried the torches; for they had made them with handles something after the fashion of a stable-broom. These had been dropped at the time the torches went out, and were lying somewhere near the spot. All three set to "grambling," and soon found both of them; and better still, found them with a considerable quantity of the resinous splits of the pine still attached to their ends.

This was a bit of good luck, for the pine-chips thus obtained would be the very thing wherewith to kindle the fire. Already well seasoned, and covered with the resin, that had run over them from the burning torches, they would catch like gunpowder itself.

The whole of the fire-wood was now collected together, and formed a goodly pile. There would be enough for their purpose, even without the handle of Ossaroo's hatchet, which was still left in its socket. It could be drawn out at any time, but very likely would not be required.

Now it was clear to all of them, that their little stock of fuel, if set fire to in the ordinary way, would burn too rapidly, and become exhausted long before their candle-making operations could be completed. This would be a sad dilemma, and would leave them in a worse situation than ever. Means, therefore, must be taken to avoid such a catastrophe, and means were adopted, as follows :—

They first set to work, and constructed a little furnace of only six or eight inches in diameter. This they easily built out of the loose blocks of stone that were lying about. In this furnace they placed a portion of their fire-wood—for it is well known that the furnace is the best plan for economizing fuel. The whole of the heat is thrown upwards, and a vessel placed on top will receive double the heat that it would, if hung over a scattered fire that is open on all sides.

But another important consideration led them to the building of the furnace.

They saw that when the light-wood should be fairly kindled, they could prevent it from blazing too rapidly, by casting upon it pieces of the bear's fat; and in this way not only prolong the burning of the wood, but make a much stronger fire. This idea was a very happy one, and at once secured them against a scarcity of fuel for their purpose. The furnace was made very narrow at the top, and two stones were placed so that the powder-flask,—emptied of its contents of course—should rest between them, and catch the full strength of the upward blaze.

All these things were arranged without light, but when they had proceeded thus far, they worked no longer in the darkness. The chips were placed in the bottom of the furnace—the tinder was ignited by means of flint and steel—its burning edge was placed in contact with the fine resin-covered shavings of pine-wood ;

and in another instant the great vault, that had so late been buried in amorphous gloom, was sparkling like a chamber set with diamonds !

The light enabled all three to do their work with rapidity and sureness.

Ossaroo was seen over the skeleton carcass cutting out the huge masses of tallow, and placing it upon the rocks. Karl was busy in attending to the fire, which, now that it had received several pieces of the fat, burned brightly and steadily—while Caspar stood near occupied with the barrels of his gun.

What was Caspar doing with the gun? Surely it could be of no service now, without either stock or lock ? Ah! you mistake. It was just now that it became of service, and of great service. Only watch Caspar a little, and you will see that he has an object in handling that brace of barrels. Observe!—he has unscrewed both the nipples, and is drawing the end of a string through each of them. The other end of these strings may be seen protruding from the barrels at the muzzle. Those strings are wicks already prepared from the hempen cord of Ossaroo, and you need not now be told what use Caspar intends to make of his beautiful smooth bores, for by this time you will have guessed it.

" Candle-moulds of course ! " I hear you exclaim.

" Candle-moulds of course," I reply; and most excellent moulds they will make, almost as good as if that had been the original design in their construction.

Well, the work went on—the wicks were got into their places—and as soon as the first flask of tallow was rendered into grease, it was poured into one of the barrels. This process was repeated again and again, and several times more, until, to the great delight of all, both barrels were observed to be full to the muzzle.

Of course the barrels were hot, and the grease inside them still in a liquid state. It would be necessary, therefore, to wait patiently until they should cool, and the candles become "frozen" and firm. In order to hasten this result, they carried them to the place where the water dripped from the roof of the cavern; and, resting them in an upright position—so that the drops might fall upon, and trickle along the barrels—they there left them, and returned to the fire.

This was instantly put out—all excepting a slight spark or two to assist in rekindling it. It was a wise precaution, for they knew they would have a long while to wait for the cooling of the candles, and they designed making at least another cast, before attempting to stir from the spot. On examining their stock of fuel, they saw that it would be sufficient to melt the tallow for another pair—they had string enough for wicks—and of the grease the great carcass afforded them an abundance.

You will wonder why the barrel of Karl's gun was not also brought into requisition. That is easily explained. Karl's piece was a rifle, and on account of the grooves inside would not have served at all for such a purpose. Had they attemped to mould a candle in it, the candle could not have been drawn out, and they would only have wasted their labor. This they knew, and therefore did not make the attempt.

During the interval they employed themselves in "flaxing out" the remainder of the hempen cord, and preparing it for wicks. They also enjoyed a meal of the bear's-meat—this time properly cooked—for during the continuance of the little fire, they had taken the opportunity to broil themselves a steak or two ; and after eating this, they felt in much better case to continue their labors.

They waited patiently until the time came round for drawing the candles. It was a good long while, but the time arrived at length, when the barrels became cold as ice, and the tallow inside appeared to be frozen as hard.

The fire was now rekindled—the iron moulds were slightly heated in the blaze; and then the pull was given, slow and steady. A shout of joy hailed the appearance of the long white cylinder as it came softly gliding from the muzzle, until full three feet of a beautiful candle were revealed to the eyes of the delighted trio. The second " draw " succeeded equally well ; and a brace of huge candles, each as big as three " sixes," were now completely moulded and ready to be lit.

A trial was immediately made, when it was found that both burned beautifully.

After a short while, another brace was added ; and they had now at their command light enough to last them for a period of nearly a hundred hours! They could still have moulded more candles—for neither their fat nor their fuel was exhausted—but surely they had enough? Surely in a hundred hours they would look upon a far lovelier light—the light of the glorious sun?

And they did so in far less time—in less than the twentieth part of a hundred hours, they gazed upon the orb of day.

I shall not detail their wanderings backward and

forward, upward and downward, through the vaulted galleries of that stupendous cavern! Suffice it to say, that the bright spot indicating the entrance at length flashed before their eyes like a meteor; and dropping the candles from their fingers they rushed forth, and once more gazed with delighted eyes upon the shining face of heaven!

,

CHAPTER LXIV.

CONCLUSION.

You will imagine that after such a perilous adventure in the great cave, they would never again set foot within its gloomy precincts. Neither would they, had any mode of escaping from their other prison—the valley itself—been offered. But they could think of none, and there still lingered in their mind some slight hopes that one or other of the many passages of the cave might lead through the mountains, or have an opening at the top of the cliffs.

Slight as were the grounds for hope, they could not give them up until they should satisfy themselves by a complete and thorough exploration ; and for more than a week after their adventure, they employed themselves in making huge torches and moulding candles for this purpose.

A large quantity of both were at length prepared, and the exploration commenced.

Day after day they entered the cavern—each day making an excursion that lasted for several hours. Day by day they continued their fruitless search—fruitless, since no outlet could be found.

But it was not till after weeks thus spent—till after

they had traversed every vault of that stupendous cavern, and traced every passage to its termination in the rocks, that they resigned all hope, and gave up in despair.

When the last day's search was ended, and they had emerged from the cave, never to enter it again, all three might have been seen seated upon the rocks near its mouth, in attitudes and with looks that betokened a deep and hopeless despair.

For a long time they sat in silence. The same thought was in the minds of all—the one painful thought, that they were hopelessly cut off from all communication with the world, and would never again look on human faces save their own!

Caspar was the first to break silence.

"Oh!" groaned he, "it is an awful fate—an awful fate—here must we live—here must we die—far away from home—from the world—alone, alone, oh!"

"Not alone, Caspar," replied Karl, making an effort to look cheerful,—"not alone, for God is with us. From this time forth let us strive to forget the world, and make Him our companion. *Let God be our world!*"

THE END.